NOTHING TO FEAR

CORALIE TATE

Happy reading,
Nina !

♡ Coralie Tate

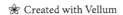

For J, S, and I.

You can never go home again, but the truth is you can never leave home, so it's all right.
—Maya Angelou

Home is where the heart can laugh without shyness.
—Vernon Baker

We meet them at the door-way, on the stair,
Along the passages they come and go,
Impalpable impressions on the air,
A sense of something moving to and fro.

There are more guests at table than the hosts
Invited...

— HENRY WADSWORTH
LONGFELLOW

CHAPTER 1

Sometimes, when the sky was particularly pretty at dawn or dusk, Pearl went out and visited the maple tree under which Willie had finally beaten her to death in 1906.

He'd hanged himself from one of its branches a mere day later, leaving her with mixed feelings about that particular arboreal specimen. The view of the cottage and orchard was lovely from its vantage point, though. Given many decades to reflect upon the matter, she decided that she liked the old maple.

She also liked the women who lived in the cottage now, despite their terrible taste in housing.

And clothing.

In life, Pearl had aspired to elegance. In death, she'd discovered she preferred lively personalities and good humor.

Pearl did not like her great nephew, Douglas. She'd disliked his sullen mien and violent tantrums the one time he came to visit Chaste Tree Cottage as a child, and she found that he had not improved in the slightest when he moved in permanently some thirty years later. He was Willie all over again. Selfish. Weak. Petulant.

And that was before Ida began worming her way into his mind, planting her twisted longings in the poor soil of his underdeveloped character.

Tragic Ida.

Pearl should have sent the children away.

She would send everyone away now. It was high time, and conditions were becoming favorable.

CHAPTER 2

*I*t was a nice door. Solid wood. Probably original to the house. Eliza glanced up to make sure none of the colorful leaded glass from its half window was about to fall on her head. She was going make this sucker close and latch before dark, and she didn't care how much antique oak she had to reduce to sawdust to make it happen. A substantial pile of wood debris and teal paint flakes had already accumulated at her feet on the foyer's black-and-white tiled floor.

The glass seemed to be holding, so she swung the door toward its frame.

It bounced off.

"Shit."

She examined the edge of the door again. The deformity was barely visible, but her fingers sensed the hard vein of a wood knot. She picked up her rasp. Sandpaper wasn't going to cut it.

With the first pass, the rasp shredded the door's front edge, missing the knot completely. "Whoops." Adjusting her angle, she tried again, really putting her weight behind it this time. The tool slid like butter over the knot and Eliza fell forward, planting her hand on a huge splinter.

"Ouch! Mother fu…" She dropped the rasp and stood, making herself look at the chunk of wood piercing the heel of her palm. Another day, another flesh and blood sacrifice. It didn't hurt much—not yet. Pulling it out was going to be another story. She knew from experience.

Living in this house was like dying the death of a thousand cuts.

She grasped the sliver's substantial tip and tugged. Pain lanced through her palm. She looked away, took a deep breath, then tried again. Despite the unseasonable cold of this October evening in Sonoma County, she began to feel queasy and hot.

Finally, the wood slid out, mostly intact. Wiping sweat from her brow, Eliza stepped out onto the porch and considered the splinter. It glinted wetly with her blood in the orangey light of sunset. She should go inside and clean her wound. Find a Band-Aid. But she needed a minute to catch her breath.

Out in the yard, a chill breeze bullied its way through the tangle of tree branches and undergrowth that grew right up to the cottage in places. It smelled like dirt and decay, carrying a whiff of rotting peaches from the old orchard. A limb tapped against window glass on the south side of the house, then dragged slowly across the cottage's weathered siding in a screech that Eliza felt in her gut and bones. She shivered and tugged the zipper of her hoodie up to her chin. "God, this house…" Too bad they really needed to stick it out here for another six months.

Her phone buzzed in her pocket with an incoming message and she thought, *what now?* The sad truth was that she got more calls and texts from the pharmacy regarding her mother's medications than from anyone else. It wasn't the pharmacy though—it was Joey.

Her very hot but mostly absentee upstairs tenant.

Eliza smiled. Joey always texted her when he was coming home for a few days between security assignments. Sometimes he wanted her to check something in his place for him —make sure the fridge was still running, see if rodents had gotten into his cereal. But sometimes it was just to touch base.

She lived for those texts.

Her life might be a bleak existence of managing her mother's mental illness and performing futile acts of maintenance on a terminally neglected Victorian, but somewhere out there, by god, a hot guy was thinking of her.

Before she could click on Joey's message, her phone flashed a notification that she was now connected to the EcoAbode 3 Smart Thermostat. "Lies." She thumbed the window away. Yes, there was a smart thermostat installed in the foyer next to the stairs, but there was nothing else in the house modern enough for it to connect with. No alarm system. No central air. Certainly no solar panels.

Her phone finally disgorged Joey's text: *Coming home tomorrow p.m. for extended stay. Can you turn the heat up in my place?*

Hmm. Joey usually prefaced his requests with a little chitchat—where he'd been, what the weather was like there, funny (though non-NDA violating) anecdotes about the clients he was protecting. Maybe he was having a bad day. He probably wasn't coming home for a long stay by choice— Joey was a nomad to the bone.

Sure, she replied. *You ok?*

A small text bubble appeared. *Yep*. A moment later, he added, *minor concussion—no biggie.*

Eliza's heart gave a hard thump. She didn't know exactly what Joey's work as an executive security specialist entailed, but she worried about him while he was away. Which was stupid, because she had more than enough to worry about between Minnie's mental health and her own threadbare finances.

But she couldn't help it.

How long will you be home? Want me to get you any groceries?
Two weeks. Don't worry about groceries. Thx.

Two weeks! Eliza bit her lip, trying not to be too over-joyed that her crush had a concussion. She loved having Joey around, even though he mostly kept to himself when he was home. His calm and confidence were the perfect antidote to Minnie's chaotic quirkiness and mercurial mood swings. Plus, he really filled out a pair of jeans.

She put her phone back in her pocket, a little surprised to find that she was still holding her bloody splinter. Her hand hardly throbbed anymore at all. "That's the power of…" *erm*, "lust." She flicked the piece of wood into a hydrangea bush beyond the porch railing and considered the door again, still humming the Huey Lewis anthem. She should at least smooth down the part she'd wrecked with the rasp.

She crouched and carefully sanded the splinters away, then fished her utility knife out of her tool bucket and notched the door frame where the knot hit. The door closed and latched when she tested it. *Success.* It looked terrible—a real hack job—but she was beyond caring. She needed to check on her mom. The wind picked up, markedly colder than before. It lifted Eliza's hood and slapped it across her face, causing her to choke on the verse where Huey declared he didn't need money or fame. *Easy for you to say, buddy.* She pushed the fabric and several wild, loose tendrils of hair away from her mouth and eyes. Time to call it a day.

A powerful gust made Eliza stumble as she stood to gather her supplies. Minnie's collection of wind chimes smashed together all around her, discordant. Something clattered violently to her left. "Shit." The aluminum ladder she'd leaned against the porch wall was falling, stripping brittle, decorative scales from the front of the house as it went.

Lunging to catch it, Eliza tripped over her tool bucket and sprawled face-first across the porch floor. She covered the back of her head and neck with her arms an instant before the ladder crashed down on her. Her thick sweatshirt sleeves absorbed most of the impact. Still, the edge of one rung caught her on the temple and another cracked an exposed knuckle. Wind swirled cold along the floor planks, sending grit into her face.

"Ow. *Ow!*" Eliza pushed the ladder away, curling into a fetal position with her throbbing knuckle cradled against her chest.

Abruptly, the wind relented.

She rolled to her back and wiped her eyes on the cuffs of her sleeves. Her chin felt raw. She settled her glasses back on her nose, straightening the frame with a twist. The string of pumpkin lights she'd helped Minnie hang from the porch rafters the previous weekend were in disarray, a noose-like loop of them dangling in front of the door. *Freaky*, she thought, sucking her injured knuckle. The noose spun on itself, dancing in the cold breeze that still swept through the yard and curled around the house.

The door popped open again.

You bastard.

CHAPTER 3

*T*he widow's walk crowning Chaste Tree Cottage came into view as Joey rounded the last curve in the driveway. Limned in hazy moonlight, the brutal wrought iron railing wasn't a cozy or welcoming sight, but at least he knew the decrepit Victorian where he rented a cheap upstairs apartment was still standing.

Small victories.

The pickup's front left tire hit a new rut in the driveway, jolting the cab and nearly wrenching the wheel from Joey's hands. His concussion-related headache throbbed back to life, and by the time he'd rattled and bounced to his usual spot next to Dopey Doug's lemon-yellow Datsun, he felt like throwing up.

He wouldn't, though. He was one hundred percent done with cleaning up messes—his own, or anybody else's.

He set the brake, killed the engine, and studied his surroundings while willing his stomach to settle. The dark could be absolute out here once the sun went down, but tonight the moon was full, casting pools of shadow beneath overgrown trees and scraggly shrubs. Drifts of desiccated leaves lay against the house's foundation. There must have been quite a wind storm while he was away.

The engine stopped ticking and Joey realized he'd almost fallen asleep. *Stupid.* He retrieved his laptop case from the passenger seat and got out. His duffle could stay in the cab until morning.

The air was unexpectedly chilly and damp. When he'd left on assignment two weeks before, they'd been having an endless Indian summer of dry, dusty days and hot California nights. Tonight, the temperature was in the low forties and falling. Mist beaded on his face. Cold licked its way into his collar. He shivered. Definitely time to break out the space heater—and cross his fingers that the house's electrical was up to running it.

Despite the cold, he stood still for a moment, listening. He took a few deep breaths, trying to appreciate the peaceful remoteness of the setting. He'd originally found the cottage while following a detour on the way to a climbing trip in early June. At the time, he'd been thoroughly sick of city life, having just finished a seven-month stint organizing security for a manufacturing executive in Shenzhen. A small apartment in a rural setting sounded idyllic.

He'd filled out an application, put down a deposit, and headed to Shasta feeling like one lucky dude. Housing issue: resolved. In under an hour on his first free weekend stateside, too. He could extend his climbing trip by two days. Maybe three.

Plus, the rent was absurdly cheap.

On move-in day, he'd sat in his truck staring at the house, trying to recover the sense that this was a sweet deal. Maybe he'd been more jet-lagged than he realized when he first visited, because at the time Chaste Tree Cottage had seemed sort of charming.

With his mind clear and his biorhythms recalibrated to

West Coast time, Joey had to revise his assessment: the place was a dump.

Life at the cottage didn't present any silver linings. There were intermittent power issues from the get-go. He found termites wandering along the back of his couch within five minutes of sliding it under the living room window, and the communal washer never smelled right. The floors sloped, the doors didn't latch reliably, and either there'd never been any insulation in the walls or it had all been eaten by rats.

Both scenarios seemed equally plausible.

Joey had spent a lot of time in developing nations, and he wasn't home much anyway, so he managed to ignore the house's problems for a while. He did enjoy the fresh air and quiet, and he liked the building manager and her mother—Eliza and Minnie Philips.

Now, six months later, he was ready to pull the plug. He didn't like being cold, he didn't like having shitty television reception on his days off, and he fucking *hated* the commute.

Joey readjusted his grip on his bag and looked up at the rusted running-fox weathervane atop the cottage's cupola. The poor bastard always lolled toward the northwest, trapped in the trough of a decayed orbit. "By this time next month, you'll be on your own, buddy."

He'd finally done it—found a couple of nice apartments in town and put in applications.

Limping toward the house, he noted that the river, which ran through the property beyond the old orchard, sounded higher than usual. The latest storm must have made it this far north after all.

Before setting foot on the porch steps, Joey opened the flashlight app on his phone and checked them for booby-traps. Or, in Phillips parlance, "DIY décor." Joey had almost lost an eye to something Eliza made out of an old wine bottle over the summer. The real danger was her mother though.

Minnie Phillips liked to crochet, and she had a habit of installing web-like projects in unexpected places—looped between the porch columns, for example—without warning.

Eliza referred to the phenomenon as "crochet bombing."

Joey, who had been trained to deal with actual bombs, had never been closer to death than when he caught his foot in an orange blanket monstrosity coming home in the dark early in September. If he hadn't been carrying his old laptop case at the time, he would have lost a kidney when he crashed through the rotten handrail into a hydrangea bush.

Tonight, the coast appeared to be clear, so he approached the front door, keys in hand.

Unfortunately, keys were not going to get him inside. The damp must have warped the old door enough that it wouldn't latch. Somebody—Eliza, no doubt—had braced something heavy against the inside to keep it shut. Joey's light picked up the mottled turquoise and gold of old bronze and he knew what the object was—a creepy antique andiron that usually hung out in a dark corner under the stairs. The vertical part of the andiron was a rotund cupid whose tiny, vulnerable dick was always about to be savaged by a fanged serpent. Joey instinctively shrank every time he saw it. The little fucker was an abomination and the absolute last thing he wanted to deal with while he was exhausted and hurting, but he guessed that was just too damned bad.

You chose to live here, asshole.

Sighing, he put his shoulder to the door and shoved. It gave a couple of inches, then stuck.

"Fuck."

Joey set down his bag and crouched to see what the problem was, wincing as pain shot through his bruised foot. The andiron was probably caught on one of the floor tiles. He was considering sleeping in his truck when he heard somebody hurrying toward him through the foyer.

"Sorry!" It was Eliza. "I'll get that! Hang on."

The cupid disappeared with a screech and the front door swung open. Eliza gave him a wane smile as she finished dragging the andiron out of the way. She was dressed, as usual, in layers of well-loved, eclectic items—a thin white cotton nightgown that clung intriguingly to her thighs and hips as she moved, a deep green asymmetrical sweater that had been repaired at the cuff with purple yarn, and a soft shawl in shades of turquoise. Her wavy chocolate hair was half up, half falling around her face.

Joey leaned against the doorjamb, his headache receding slightly as he took her in. She was nothing like the highly groomed and coutured people who could afford the services of Griffin Security.

Thank god.

He picked up his laptop case and stepped inside.

"The door keeps swelling. I've sanded it down a bunch of times, but it doesn't stay fixed." Eliza tucked a strand of hair behind one ear, backing out of his path. "It's such a pain in the ass—I'm sorry." She pushed her glasses back up her nose. "I've got a call into a carpenter. In the meantime, maybe I'll light some incense and make a sacrifice." She laughed weakly.

Joey shut the door and replaced the andiron, then he caught Eliza's gaze and, at a loss for how to reassure her, pressed a fingertip to the frown on her lips before she could apologize anymore. "It's fine." The gesture surprised them both. Despite being friendly, they were not on touching terms.

It worked though. Eliza stopped talking and simply stared at him. Her face was pale, and the feeble light of the dusty chandelier above their heads revealed circles under her eyes. Fingerprints smeared the lenses of her glasses. A rebel loop of hair hung oddly over her left ear. She had a scrape on her chin. He should have looked at her and thought: *complicated, steer clear*. Instead, he had to force himself to draw his hand away.

"It's okay, it's an old house. There are going to be issues."

Eliza took a calming breath. "Sorry. It just seems like everything is starting to fall apart all at once."

Joey shrugged. He wanted to put her mind at ease, but he was running on fumes. Besides, he'd tried to be tactful with a lady the day before and ended up concussed. "Go back to bed," he said instead. "Your feet must be freezing."

She looked down at her bare feet as if surprised to discover she wasn't wearing anything on them. She scrunched her toes. "They are, actually." Backing away, she said, "Well, anyway... glad you're home safe."

"Thanks." Joey waited until he heard her deadbolt shoot home, the clunk of it reverberating around the empty foyer. Then he turned off the chandelier, leaving the entry lit only by moonlight and the glow of a smart thermostat somebody had begun installing and then abandoned. The readout on the display was usually counting down to a temperature change that never happened: *72 degrees in 25 minutes!* It could show dozens of random phrases and icons though, and tonight it read: *Connection Unsuccessful*.

"Ain't that the truth," Joey said, tapping the screen as he started up the stairs. He was just getting to the second-floor landing when another door closed in the dark below him.

Doug, he thought. The creepy little fuck had been watching them. How had he missed that?

He really needed some sleep.

CHAPTER 4

*B*ack in her room, Eliza pulled on a pair of nubby warm socks, rearranged her hot water bottles, and added a quilt to her bed—the one her mom had made her in middle school with discount flannel sporting electric guitars and neon daisies. It was hideous but she loved it. And she needed a little extra comfort after that confusing and slightly embarrassing encounter with Joey.

Sure enough, as soon as she burrowed under the covers, her brain started replaying the last five minutes on loop—babbled apologies, her hair repeatedly getting in her mouth, dragging that stupid cherub out of the way with one hand wrapped around his little penis and the other cupping his butt. More apologies. The crushing awareness that she really sucked at building management.

Then, that strange but wonderful moment when Joey had put his finger to her lips.

Was it okay to feel giddy about that? It probably meant nothing to him. He probably had a girl in every port. Or a guy, for all she knew. Or both.

Eliza welcomed the distraction when her gray tabby,

Daisy, jumped on the bed and settled next to her. She scratched behind the cat's ears, then ran a hand down her spine. "That was awkward, Days."

Daisy contorted herself to lick her belly. Eliza thought about how Joey had looked standing in the entry, staring at her with smoldering intensity.

"I mean, he was probably mostly annoyed. He looked exhausted. But I'm choosing to remember it as desire."

Daisy kneaded her claws into the blanket, then pointedly turned her gaze away.

"You're not exactly in a position to judge." Eliza tucked her hands under the covers and wiggled down until only her nose poked out into the cold night air. "Your deepest relationship is with a hair scrunchie."

Daisy stilled, then launched herself off Eliza's stomach and scrambled out of the room.

She was probably going to look for her beloved scrunchie. Eliza froze though, listening. Ever since they'd moved in to the cottage, the cats had been in the habit of suddenly fleeing her bedroom for no apparent reason.

Which was a thing cats did.

But lately it had begun to freak Eliza out. It sometimes felt like there was something happening just beyond her sensory perception—something the cats wanted nothing to do with. She thought back to the sudden, violent gust of wind that had sent her ladder tumbling the day before. That had been weird, too.

The house felt normal tonight though. Cold and damp, but normal. She strained to catch any hint of strangeness, but there was nothing.

After a few minutes, the stuttering rattle of water rushing through the pipes upstairs broke the silence, and along with it, some of Eliza's unease. Joey was here—just feet away, if she could reach through walls.

With that in mind, she tried to relax. She wriggled her toes and flexed her fingers. Breathed in through her nose and out through her mouth. She reasoned with herself, putting forward a very compelling argument as to why she should be able to sleep now: Joey was home and she'd done her duty in making sure he got through the jerry-rigged front door. Her to-do list was compiled for the coming day, and she didn't need to pee. *Come on, Lizzy. Go to sleep. You know you want to.*

Joey finished his shower and presumably went to bed. Daisy came back, along with her brothers, Bo and Luke. Luke smelled like he'd crashed through a rosemary bush somewhere, the scent incongruous but pleasant. The house fell silent again, aside from its usual old house creaks and groans. Outside, the wind picked up, but not in an alarming fashion.

Eliza's mind refused to quiet. Instead, it circled through a litany of all the things she needed to finish before the weekend. The grant application she was writing for a client required a final read-through. She needed to help her mom ship that week's Etsy projects. They were behind on laundry, and she had to organize her mom's pills for the coming week.

Plus, Eliza had promised herself she would finish caulking the downstairs windows before the next storm came through. She'd started earlier in the month and predictably been distracted by a Minnie crisis less than fifteen minutes later. By the time she'd thought about the windows again, three days had passed and it was raining torrents. She'd noticed water pooling on the windowsill above the kitchen sink while drinking her morning coffee. By lunchtime, the goldenrod wallpaper beneath the window had started peeling away like the petal of a malodorous rose. She'd tried stapling the paper back in place, but the wall was too damp and soft to hold the staple.

Unfortunately, the house hadn't dried out appreciably since then, and now they were due for another storm.

A whopper, if the meteorologists were to be believed.

Think about something else. This topic was giving her a small but nagging headache.

Eliza reached over whichever cat was on her pillow and picked up her glasses and notebook from her nightstand. Her favorite pen was in the elastic holder, and a book light she'd had since she was eight was clamped to the back cover. She turned on the little light and flipped to the last panel she'd drawn.

In it, her *almost* totally fictitious hero, Adventure Tenant, was relaxing on a beach with a fruity cocktail after saving another heiress from a series of improbable disasters. Most recently, he'd rescued a hapless Swedish socialite from a volcano erupting in southern France. Before that, he'd pulled a Spanish princess from shark-infested waters after a tentacled sea monster capsized her yacht off the coast of Malta.

It had been hot and dry in Northern California when Eliza worked on those storylines. Tonight, she wasn't in the right frame of mind to write Mediterranean beaches—not with wind whistling around the house and temperatures plummeting.

She flipped to the back of her notebook where she jotted down crazy story ideas for later. At some point, she'd written: Vikings, time travel, vampires, Iceland. *Huh.*

She sketched a horizontal box at the top of a new page and filled in a story title: *Adventure Tenant and the Vampiric Vikings*. Eliza didn't consider herself a particularly talented artist, but the abbreviated style she'd developed over the years worked for her. If she could cobble together some financial breathing room and a better support system for her mom, she'd love to try her hand at publishing a webcomic.

For now though, her drawings were just for her.

Adventure Tenant flowed onto the page in a few quick lines, surveying a bleak landscape of dark rolling hills with his hands on his hips. Eliza added the sheen of moonlight reflecting off snow, then gave Adventure Tenant an anachronistic plaid hunting hat with ear flaps, because he looked cold and she could never bring him to suffer.

The vampire Vikings took more thought, and before long Eliza was fully focused on her project, her mind thousands of miles and hundreds of years away from Chaste Tree Cottage and all of her adult responsibilities.

By the third panel, Adventure Tenant was having a fish fry with a buxom Viking woman, and Eliza was finally sleepy. She turned off her light, set aside her notebook and glasses, and arranged her legs around the cats. It was always a little weird working on the adventures of Adventure Tenant when Joey was in residence upstairs, but desperate times called for desperate measures, and nothing got Eliza out of her own head like sending Joey's fictitious double off to be a hero.

CHAPTER 5

*E*liza woke reasonably rested on Friday morning, but by lunchtime she was dragging. She was addicted to bright morning sunshine waking her up and boosting her mood, but today the sky was opaque with clouds of charcoal and pewter gray and she felt like her mind was wrapped in fog.

Coffee hadn't helped. Maybe lunch would do the trick?

"Nothing to lose by trying." She saved her work, closed her laptop, and dislodged Bo from her shoulder.

She peeked in at her mother on her way to the kitchen. Minnie had her powerful work-light pointed at her lap and was inspecting a pile of knitted stirrup warmers ordered by a gynecologist in Minnesota. The herringbone pattern with a blanket-stitch trim around the cuff was meant to evoke camp blankets. Eliza wondered if the gynecologist offered complementary hot chocolates to her patients. Perhaps strapping woodsmen, too?

"Those are cute, Mom," she said, leaning in the doorway.

Minnie looked up, her smile—thank god—authentic. "I think so. I hope the client likes them."

Some of the tension went out of Eliza's shoulders. If her mother didn't decide to redo any of her projects, they could send everything with the UPS guy when he came by in a couple hours and avoid a late-afternoon trip into town. Eliza could potentially finish caulking the windows and make real food for dinner. Maybe later she would even be able to finish the novel languishing on her bedside table.

Don't get ahead of yourself, Lizzy. So many things might still go wrong.

"Grilled cheese?" she offered. Minnie usually wanted ham and iceberg lettuce on whole wheat for lunch. But maybe with damp creeping in under the doors, Eliza could talk her into something different. "With tomato soup?"

Minnie pursed her lips, considering. Then she nodded. "Sure. That sounds nice, sweetie."

"Give me five minutes." Eliza turned and started down the hallway toward the kitchen.

Her mother's voice followed her. "Those yoga pants are going right up your crack, Eliza Jane!"

"Thanks, Mom," she called over her shoulder. "Thanks for noticing."

"You should dress better, honey."

It was an old argument, comfortably worn-in and faded with age—much like Eliza's wardrobe. It was also a bizarre conversation for them to cling to, considering that the sexual revolution and gender equality were Minnie's bread and butter. Her Etsy shop was literally called Minnie Knits For No Nonsense Women.

That was life, Eliza supposed; your shiny ideals didn't always survive contact with reality. Neither one of them had expected to end up living a threadbare existence together in a falling-down house in the woods.

"I'll dress better when I work in an office," she replied. From the kitchen, she listened for the part about how she would never find a man if she didn't make at least a small effort with her appearance, but Minnie decided to forego that portion of the conversation today.

Just as well, Eliza thought, as she buttered bread and sliced cheese. Her own dissatisfaction with herself and her life was always much harder to ignore when Joey was upstairs. She would be mortified if he heard Minnie hollering about her slovenly appearance and poor romantic prospects.

Eliza put her favorite cast-iron pan on the stove and lit the burner underneath it. The gas ignited unexpectedly fast, with a gut-clenching thump and a sizable ball of fire. She yelped, snatching her already-abused hand away. *Shit.* You couldn't do the simplest thing in this house without risking life or limb.

When the flame had settled down and her hands had mostly stopped shaking, Eliza added a little bit of oil to the pan and swirled it around. Her heart was still racing, and she knew from experience that if she didn't get her body's reaction under control pretty damn fast, she could easily pitch over into a full-blown panic attack.

That was where living in a constant state of high stress got you.

There was no time allotted for panic attacks in Eliza's Friday afternoon, so she bypassed deep breathing and went straight to her most reliable method of self-soothing—plotting out Adventure Tenant's next moves.

She'd left her intrepid hero enjoying a campfire fish dinner and, if Eliza was honest, he was probably about to get lucky. So, what should come after the buxom Viking lady?

Well, Adventure Tenant should come after the Viking lady, if he's a gentleman. She snickered. She cracked herself up sometimes. Eliza would never actually draw Adventure Tenant in the throes of passion—that would be crossing a line. But she liked to believe he had a rollicking sex life.

Unlike some people.

She put the sandwiches in to cook and heated tomato soup in the microwave while she thought more seriously about the upcoming Adventure Tenant panels. She'd like to draw him navigating a river gorge à la *George Washington Crossing the Delaware*. Should he have a crew of Viking oarsmen? Or should she just give him a motorboat? An outboard motor would be easier to draw than a dozen Vikings, and Eliza wasn't afraid of anachronisms.

She put the mugs of soup on a tray and flipped the sandwiches. Despite its heart-pounding start, lunch was looking good. She had a decent grasp on what she was going to draw next time she had insomnia, too.

As she was plating the sandwiches, Eliza heard a chair scrape across the floor up in Joey's apartment. It was hard not to wonder what he was doing, given how much of a fantasy world she was creating based on his travel-heavy and intriguing job as a security professional. If it were Adventure Tenant upstairs, he would be sitting at his table cleaning his gun or translating an ancient coded text.

Joey, on the other hand, might be sitting down to lunch. Or maybe he was filling out forms. Eliza had gone up once to drop off some mail and seen a laptop and folders covering his kitchen table. She hadn't been tempted to incorporate paperwork into Adventure Tenant's missions—the destruction of property forms alone would keep the poor guy at his desk for the rest of his natural life.

She'd given him plenty of other traits in common with Joey, though. He had Joey's stubble and the faint scar along his jawline. He had long legs, a very nice ass, and broad shoulders. In fact, for a guy who generally consisted of less than twenty strokes of a pen, he was *really* hot.

Speaking of which, the pan was starting to smoke. Eliza

had been so busy considering the source of her creative inspiration, she'd forgotten to turn off the burner.

"Creative inspiration, my ass," she admitted to herself. "More like the object of your fantasies, Lizzy."

"Did you say something, sweetie?" Minnie was carrying packages to the front door. That was a good sign.

"Just talking to the sandwiches, Mom."

"Again?"

"Yes, Mother. I have a problem."

"I'll say."

CHAPTER 6

*H*alfway through lunch, Minnie started to pick at her bread crusts, and Eliza knew they were in trouble. "Something bothering you, Mom?"

Sometimes she could head off her mother's worries if they talked about them soon enough.

Minnie didn't answer right away, but she did stop fussing with the crumbs on her plate. "I wish I'd used the same color yarn to edge all the booties. I made them up as matched pairs, but if one gets lost or damaged…"

Eliza pressed on the ratty Band-Aid covering her split knuckle. The tiny throb of pain kept her in the moment—kept her from envisioning her whole afternoon unraveling. "Mom, that's not on you. If something happens after they get delivered, your customer can place a new order. More business for you, right?"

Minnie nodded, though she heaved a sigh of frustration. "Right. You're right, of course." She stirred her soup.

Eliza was sure her mother wasn't done second-guessing herself, but she decided to pretend everything was fine—at least until she'd finished her own lunch. She was going to need her strength. "Why don't you take a walk when you're done eating? Do you have all your packages ready to go?"

Minnie set her jaw and refused to answer. They both knew Eliza was trying to do an end-run around her anxiety. Sometimes the best Minnie could do was keep her mouth shut and let her silence be tacit agreement.

Eliza's appetite vanished as she considered how to best salvage the rest of the day.

After lunch, Minnie tried to pull the package of stirrup booties out of the pile of boxes and envelopes, but Eliza talked her out of redoing the order long enough to bundle her into a coat and send her out the door for a walk in the old orchard. On her bad days, Minnie never went past the stone wall.

Then Eliza put the outgoing mail in her aged Sentra and headed to the post office. The caulking would have to wait.

Normally, she didn't mind the drive to Dos Alamos, but her usual route was closed due to a sinkhole that had nearly swallowed a wine-tour shuttle bus a couple of weeks earlier. The alternate route was an old, single-lane road with blind curves and hairpin turns. She constantly anticipated a head-on collision whenever she drove it.

The old road twisted through the bottom of a gloomy, oak-filled canyon that felt chilly even at the height of summer. Today, with the sky impenetrably overcast, it was like night under the canopy of branches and leaves. Eliza turned on her headlights. Then she turned on the CD player to combat the feeling of abandonment that clung to the area.

Mist hovered above the asphalt where the road dipped into hollows. She hummed along to '90s alt-rock and pretended she was cruising through the Tuscan countryside with Adventure Tenant riding shotgun, until she came to the highway intersection where the forested canyon opened out onto vineyards and fields.

With a sigh of relief, she hung a right and headed into town, feeling a little like she'd been delivered from evil.

~

*M*innie was ensconced on the couch under a pile of blankets, looking at a magazine when Eliza got home. The living room smelled faintly of roses and Eliza wondered if her mom had made some tea. If so, hopefully she'd used the electric kettle instead of the dodgy stovetop. Maybe Eliza needed to figure out how to install a gas cutoff valve for the kitchen.

Like *that* wouldn't be a huge waste of effort and probably a danger in itself.

She nudged her mom's feet over and sat. "Did you have a good walk?"

In most respects, Chaste Tree Cottage was turning out to be a disaster, but the fresh air and proximity to nature did do Minnie a lot of good.

"Mmm-hmm." Her mom lay the magazine on her stomach and smiled tranquilly, obviously having taken a dose of anti-anxiety meds. "There were drops of water gathering on the tips of the leaves. It was pretty."

"I bet. Did you see any critters?"

"Nope." Her mother was blinking slowly. "Just the damp and the trees." She frowned. "A section of the wall is crumbling."

"Really? Where?" Eliza wasn't responsible for maintaining the nineteenth-century stone wall, but the fact that such an enduring feature of the landscape was damaged worried her a little. According to the late Mrs. Effinham, the enclosure had been built by the original homesteader in a years-long fit of grief after his teenaged daughters eloped with disreputable young men who carried them away to the Yukon during the 1880s gold rush. Alfred Stewart had poured blood, sweat, and tears into the thing, and it had been built to last.

Unfortunately, Minnie had fallen deeply asleep, so Eliza would have to wait for the specifics. She had no time to survey the wall herself—she had windows to seal.

In the foyer, the thermostat was flashing a raindrop icon. *Indeed*, Eliza thought, stepping out onto the porch. It wasn't raining yet, but the atmosphere was so thick with moisture that it felt sentient, wrapping itself around her face like a second skin.

Not great weather for caulking, but she didn't have much to lose by trying. So what if it didn't stick? It wasn't like the house had a history of proper maintenance. Eliza couldn't think of a single repair or renovation that had stood the test of time, and plenty of jobs had been left half-done. The back exterior was aubergine and white, while the front was two-tone blue. One wall of the second-floor landing had been covered in orangey faux-wood paneling sometime during the seventies, while the rest still sported faded fifties-era paper depicting spinning wheels, shotguns, and the Liberty Bell. *Yee-haw*.

Then there was the EcoAbode 3 Smart Thermostat, which Doug claimed to have installed sometime prior to Eliza's tenure as building manager. The device had power but nothing to talk to, so it just sat there prognosticating fantasies. Its detachment from reality reminded Eliza of her mom on her worst days. She alternated between wanting to rip it out of the wall and actually being grateful for its company.

Zipping her fleece jacket up to her chin, she carried her supplies around to Doug's side of the house. He'd been complaining about his bedroom window for weeks. The minuscule amount of fresh air seeping in around the frame was probably the healthiest thing in his life, but Eliza was tired of him leaving creepy voicemails full of giggling and heavy breathing on her phone.

As soon as she started working, the bed sheet Doug used as a curtain was drawn aside, and her neighbor's bloated, pockmarked face appeared on the other side of the glass. He'd shaved his beard, she noted, and the freshly exposed skin of his lower face and neck was even more grotesque than the rest of him. While Eliza teetered at the top of her ladder, out in the cold with her hairdryer in one hand and caulk gun in the other, he stared at her. Usually, his eyes were mostly vacant. Today, there was a spark of intent in them that Eliza didn't like at all.

She shivered.

Doug might once have been a semi-productive human being. Who knew? But after losing a couple of fingers in a hunting accident, he'd apparently holed up at the cottage (rent-free, thanks to his great aunt, Mrs. Effinham) and devoted himself to a life of drinking, smoking weed, and watching porn. When he wasn't zoned-out in front of the television, he was angry, aggressive, entitled, whiny, and generally ignorant. He didn't bathe or exercise, and whenever he did leave the house, he came back with large black garbage bags that Eliza was half-convinced contained severed limbs or road kill.

If Doug kept to himself, things would have been okay. But he periodically went through phases where he lurked, watching for Eliza or her mom. He would corner them and subject them to incoherent rants delivered with bad breath, toxic body odor, and spittle.

Eliza would love to evict him. Instead, here she was, out in the cold fixing his window—something Doug could have certainly done himself. Eliza knew he didn't lack for strength in his damaged hand, having been grabbed by him on two occasions.

The sky opened with a roar of thunder when Eliza was only halfway done sealing her own kitchen window. She fought an icy wind to haul her ladder and tool bucket back to the porch. Rain followed her all the way into the foyer. She was soaked and freezing by the time she'd slammed the front door shut behind her and wedged it closed with that butt-ugly andiron. As she trudged, dripping, to her apartment, she glanced at the thermostat. The scrolling message read: *Sunny and 74 in Flagstaff!*

"Ha. Fat lot of good that does me."

~

*A*fter checking on her mother, Eliza changed into dry clothes. Then she went and taped plastic garbage bags over the windows she hadn't sealed. It was tacky and made the house gloomier than usual, but she was willing to sacrifice her remaining illusions of gracious living to be warm and dry.

That done, she debated starting her next grant-writing project—helping a children's non-profit apply for funding to plant a sensory garden. It was the kind of gig she liked, one that made her feel like she was contributing to life outside the cottage. But she was too drained from wrangling Minnie's anxieties and enduring Doug's leering to put her best effort into anything.

"Take the rest of the day off, kid," she told herself. Then she grabbed her book and curled up in the living room to read.

It took a while to get into the story. She'd started and abandoned this novel multiple times over the last month and all but forgotten who the characters were. Eventually though, the plot grabbed her and the magic happened. Eliza's own life receded and she got immersed in a world of treachery, quasi-incestuous affairs, and danger on the high seas.

Minnie slept the rest of the day away, oblivious to everything—the storm, her daughter, specters of poverty and homelessness.

Eliza read until a huge gust of wind shook the house and knocked the power out just before nightfall. Without putting down her book, she retrieved two flashlights and a lantern from the hall closet and kept reading. When daylight failed completely, she lit the lantern and read with her eyes two inches from the page until she had a headache. When she reluctantly set the book aside, it was pitch black outside the lamp's radius and the house was freezing.

"Jesus." Eliza pushed aside the afghan she'd been huddled under, grabbed a flashlight, and stumbled on numb feet to the thermometer on the mantle.

"Fifty-eight. Holy hell." How had she not noticed the cold? She touched the radiator by the couch. It was on, but not putting out enough heat to counteract the chill gripping the house. She cranked it up, tucked her afghan around Minnie, then worked on starting a fire in the fireplace. Rain rattled high up in the flue, and a current of air that smelled like damp brick and moss poured down the chimney shaft, buffeting the initial tenuous flames.

Once the fire was going, Eliza went to see about dinner. The kitchen was freezing, but the garbage bags seemed to be keeping out the rain. Since they'd had a relatively balanced meal for lunch, she grabbed PB&J fixings and took them back to her spot in front of the fire. While she ate a sandwich and seriously regretted not having something to drink, Eliza tried to decide what to do about her mom. It would be easy to leave her asleep on the couch until morning, but mornings were hard when Minnie missed dinner—and the meds that went with it.

On the other hand, waking her was a crapshoot. Minnie might be totally unfazed by the power outage and the cold, or she could panic at the disruption to her routine. Eliza might find herself on the phone in the middle of the night with their psychiatrist. The fact that the doctor billed them at the bottom end of the sliding scale wouldn't cushion that expense very much.

Eliza kneaded her tightening neck muscles. Doubts and fears tried to hijack her brain: *this isn't working, I need help, I can't do this, I'm failing the only family I have.* With effort, she rejected the familiar litany. She had a plan to move them somewhere better, but it hinged on her working, saving, and above all, staying calm. Panic and self-doubt were not on the agenda.

Nevertheless, a final negative thought prevailed: *You're fucked if Minnie has a major psychiatric event.*

Appetite gone, Eliza put the food on the mantle, grabbed her flashlight, and went to crank up the heat in the bedrooms and bathroom.

Minnie's room wasn't too cold, since it shared a wall with the living room fireplace, but the bathroom was miserable. The garbage bag Eliza had taped over the window was flexing and billowing with every gust of wind. Her flashlight beam reflected off trickles of water running down the wall where the duct tape had already failed. She groaned and used a grungy towel from under the sink to absorb some of the water.

Her own bedroom had two exterior walls and was adjacent to the bathroom, so it too was absolutely freezing. She didn't see any window leaks, but the air was clammy with moisture and smelled faintly like unwashed laundry. Had she left something really funky in her hamper? She walked over and gave the basket a sniff, but the odor seemed to be equally dispersed throughout the room.

Shrugging, Eliza set both radiators on max and decided that if it wasn't a whole hell of a lot warmer in a couple of hours, she would sleep in the living room. Betting on the latter, she tucked her flashlight under her arm and pulled the top layers of blankets and quilts off her bed to take with her, yanking to free the material that had fallen between the bed and the wall. Bo and Daisy scrambled away, protesting loudly, and slunk out of the room.

Maneuvering through the bedroom doorway, she noticed a corner of the blankets bumping oddly against her knee. She reached down and found the fabric sopping wet. "Oh, fuck. *Fuck*," she hissed. "This isn't good."

Her brain raced to find a semi-harmless explanation. Maybe it was cat pee. It would take, like, a gallon of cat pee to saturate the blankets, but that could happen, right?

She sniffed her hand. Not pee. Brackish water.

"There isn't even a window there," she complained to the empty hallway. "The freaking wall is leaking? Is that what you're telling me?"

In answer, the garbage bag rippled ominously in the bathroom.

CHAPTER 7

*E*liza was going to have to investigate where the water behind her bed was coming from, but first she took her covers to the living room and draped them over a couple of chairs in front of the fire to dry.

When she turned around, Minnie was blinking fuzzily at her. "What're you doing, sweetie?"

"Drying my blankets. The power's out." Eliza didn't feel a need to mention the leak.

"It's nice and warm in here." Her mom turned on her side and closed her eyes again.

"Yeah, it is. Are you getting hungry? I've got stuff for peanut butter sandwiches."

Minnie was slow to reply. "I'm not hungry. Don't worry about me."

"Okay." Eliza struggled with her conscience. She should insist that her mom eat something, but she could deal with the leak in her bedroom more expediently if Minnie wasn't awake to ask questions.

Plus, she might want some privacy to have a good cry. They needed to stay here at the Cheap-o Chalet for another six months to save enough for the deposit on a better place. Plan B was to pay for a move out of the savings account Eliza had been slowly filling for years so she could afford an MFA program in comics, but she wasn't quite ready to let go of that dream just yet.

Eliza wasn't a big drinker, but a cocktail sounded like a good idea. After all, she should mark Friday night somehow.

The little alcohol they owned was packed away in one of the high kitchen cupboards. Eliza dug through a junk drawer until she found a headlamp contraption that she'd bought for a singles night-hike event in another lifetime. Miraculously, the batteries were still good. She tugged the straps around her head and fiddled with the light until it pointed forward. Then she dragged a chair over and climbed up.

Since she had both hands free, she took her time sorting through the bottles. Many were so old she had no recollection of buying them. Some of the alcohol had turned to sludge. The rum looked okay though, and there was a six-pack of Coke in the pantry for social emergencies. Eliza mixed a rum and Coke in a mason jar and, after a fortifying gulp, headed back to deal with the leak before she changed her mind.

She set her glass on the dresser and dragged her bed toward the center of the room. The top sheet, which had also fallen behind the bed frame, left a trail of water snaking along the floor. The portion of wall she exposed was swollen with moisture above the baseboard.

"That's great. Fantastic." Eliza took another sip of her drink and shivered. The room felt even colder now. At least her wardrobe was at her disposal. She dug through her dresser drawers, adding an orange sweater-vest and a pair of charcoal gray fleece pants to her ensemble. "I'm too sexy for this house, too sexy for this house, *too sexy...*"

Luke, who had wandered in to see what she was doing, took one look at her swollen silhouette and dashed away.

"Thanks, buddy."

After another big sip, Eliza armed herself with a towel from the clothes hamper and approached the puddle spreading at the base of the wall. She corralled water until the fabric was saturated, then stood, wobbling a little from the effects of crouching and drinking. She needed more towels.

The hall closet door was hard to open. "Pain in the ass," she muttered, kicking it shut when she finally had what she needed.

Eliza used three towels to get most of the water off the floor, and a fourth to build a dam around the leaky area. Then she sat on a throw rug with her rum and Coke, and assessed the damage. A three-foot square area of wallboard was visibly soft and bulgy—much like Doug's face. *Yuck.* A wallpaper seam was curling open about twelve inches above the floor. As she watched, a trickle of water started flowing out of it.

"Just stop," she ordered.

It didn't stop.

Eliza sat there until her glass was empty and she couldn't feel her body below the waist. She wanted to tug on the wallpaper and see what was happening underneath, but a tiny, rational part of her mind objected. Yes, the wall was going to have to be torn out at some point, but did she want to live with a gaping hole until a contractor arrived? Even if somebody from Mrs. Effinham's family agreed to emergency repairs, nobody would be coming until Monday at the earliest.

She pulled on a fuzzy pink stocking cap and tapped at her lips, which were now entertainingly numb. Was it a burst pipe or a leak in the roof? Eliza didn't see herself patching the roof.

The cottage was two stories, plus there was a real attic above part of the second floor—the kind you could walk around in. The kind where you could store dead bodies in steamer trunks.

"Happy thoughts," Eliza told herself. Was she out of rum and Coke already?

Adventure Tenant's apartment was right above her bedroom. That was a nice thought.

She tried to calculate which part of his place corresponded to the leak. His bedroom, or maybe his closet. Or, well… maybe somewhere else. Alcohol didn't seem to be improving her spatial reasoning skills.

Luke came in and sniffed her empty glass. When he began licking delicately at the inside, she pulled him into her lap and put the glass out of reach. She pressed her cheek to his fluffy, orange-striped fur and they watched the leak together, Luke's tail flicking in agitation.

The cats often stared at this section of wall, and Eliza wondered if they'd been hearing water dripping. She'd always half suspected they were watching a ghost, but leaking water was more plausible.

Probably.

"It was a dark and stormy night, Luke, and Eliza was freaking herself out," she said, scratching behind his ears. "Let's stop staring at the wall, whaddya say?"

Dumping the cat gently on the floor, she stood and put her glass on a bookshelf out of his reach. She needed to reason rationally.

Fact: the bedroom wall was leaking.

Question: was a burst pipe responsible?

Answer: possible, but unlikely.

Action: look for pipes behind said wall.

Rationale: must know whether to call a plumber, a roofer, or both.

Fact: she didn't want to sound like a dumbass when she solicited help from a contractor and funds from the Effinham family trust.

That was logical. She nodded to herself, the beam of her headlamp bouncing erratically around the room. She would make an exploratory incision where the obvious damage was and go from there. It wasn't like she was going to take an axe to the wall. Eliza snorted. If she owned an axe, it was in the rusty shed out back, and she was *not* going outside in the dark.

She did need gloves and some kind of a tool, however.

The junk drawer in the kitchen yielded a substantial screwdriver and a paper dust mask, which she hung around her neck. She found a single work glove in a box in the pantry. After mixing another drink, she grabbed the right-hand dish glove and a plastic trash bag from under the kitchen sink and took her equipment back to the bedroom.

"I'm looking for pipes," she reminded herself, hefting the screwdriver. "I'm making an exploratory incision. I am not demolishing my bedroom."

Another freakishly strong gust of wind rattled the windows, and a faint screeching sound came from up on the roof. *Probably the widow's walk railing giving up the ghost*, she thought.

"Because that's going to be fun to deal with."

The first cut went smoothly. The flathead screwdriver had a nice, sharp edge, and the water-damaged wall offered little resistance. Eliza scored a neat square and tried to lever it out. Unfortunately, it was attached to a stud.

Not the sexy kind of stud.

"Goddamnit." She tore the tidy square out in pieces and shoved them in the trash bag. Then she widened her search. Despite her best efforts to be careful, the rest of the wallboard came away in huge, soggy chunks covered with dark mold on the back.

Behind her mask, Eliza gagged. This was really bad. Fighting panic, she continued slicing and dicing, hoping to discover that the problem was localized to one small area.

But no—every new piece had more mold than the last.

She crouched and pried at the baseboard. It gave way, releasing a small tidal wave of black sludge that filled the towel dam, crested, and soaked the toes of her adorable panda slippers.

"No!" What the fuck was the matter with the house? Did it have Ebola? Were these fetid house guts?

Eliza threw down the screwdriver, stepped out of her slippers, tossed her gloves on the floor, and backed away. She was *not* crying, but tears might have been rolling down her cheeks.

She bumped into something, yelped, and whirled around. It was just her dresser, but *fuck*, she'd set it rocking and her drink was about to topple off.

"I've got you!" She saved her rum and Coke, but a framed photo of her college friends—from back when she'd had friends—crashed to the floor, the glass shattering.

"I just... I'm going back to the living room," she announced to the scene of wreckage. "I'm going to eat a peanut butter sandwich and sleep in front of the fire where it's warm and dry. If this isn't a bad dream, I'll deal with you tomorrow." Steadied by her plan, she sniffed, pulled a couple pairs of thick wool socks out of her dresser, and grabbed her drawing notebook. Tiptoeing around glass shards and toxic sludge, she left, shutting the bedroom door behind her with extreme prejudice.

CHAPTER 8

*J*oey had awoken Friday morning with a nauseating headache. Normally, he would power through and find something productive to do with his time, despite being on medical leave, but for once he'd thought: *fuck it*. A man was entitled to a day of sloth once a decade or so.

Right?

Plus, the weather was ass-ugly. Gray, damp, cold. He took a couple of painkillers with breakfast, then slept like the dead.

When he woke again at 1600 hours, he had to look at his watch twice to process how long he'd been out. He couldn't remember the last time he'd slept past noon, even considering how often he jumped time zones. He stood, stretched experimentally, and decided his head and foot were a lot better.

Good thing, since he now only had sixty minutes to write his injury report and submit it before the end of the workweek.

He reheated a mug of coffee, set his laptop on the kitchen

counter where the Wi-Fi was strongest but the ambient temperature always lowest, and got to work drafting a description of how he'd been taken out by a fifty-four-year-old woman who probably weighed one hundred and twenty pounds soaking wet.

It was a struggle to maintain a professional tone, since Joey was still pissed—pissed at himself for being caught off guard, pissed at Mr. Morgan for being a schmuck, and yeah, sorta pissed at Mrs. Morgan for taking her rage out on the help.

He found the right form, filled in the data fields, then let the cursor blink in the description box while he gathered his thoughts. "Just the facts," he told himself, and typed: *A verbal altercation erupted between the principal and his spouse in the library at approximately 1850 hours.*

That was the easy part. What followed had to be worded diplomatically, and Joey suspected his mild concussion was adversely affecting the diplomatic region of his brain.

The principal's wife alleged that ~~her~~ a third party had observed the principal ~~playing hide the~~ having sexual relations with the principal's personal assistant in the pool house at approximately 0945 hours Thursday morning.

Joey had already reamed the morning detail for allowing Mrs. Morgan's yoga instructor to wander the grounds unescorted, and had reported the lapse in a separate incident report, so he noted the relevant report number and moved on.

Both clients ~~were shit-faced~~ showed obvious signs of inebriation, but neither appeared to be dangerously intoxicated. At the principal's request, I withdrew. Before I cleared the doorway, the principal's spouse ~~shrieked~~ made a spontaneous sound of outrage. I turned to reassess the situation. At that time, the principal's spouse lunged at the door, ~~slamming my goddamn~~ causing it to forcefully impact my head, torso, and foot.

Joey absently ran his fingers over the lump on his temple and winced. Fucking rich people and their fucking fancy doors. Varnished oak would have made a nice enough statement in his opinion. But no, the Morgans had to have bronze art deco doors that weighed like eight hundred pounds each.

I was briefly stunned by said impact.

Stunned, as well, by the sheer humiliation of having his bell rung by a tiny enraged drunk woman he was supposed to be protecting.

Nevertheless, I signaled for backup and maintained position in the hall outside the library until I was relieved.

He'd then gathered his shredded dignity and limped to the on-site security office where he called his friend Marco for a lift. In the car, Marco had razzed him about it being time to take a desk job. For once, he'd told Marco a desk job sounded pretty damn good.

He wasn't losing his edge. No way. But he could do with a little less client interaction in his life.

He got the report submitted just before 1700 hours. Then he opened a beer, pulled the kitchen chair over, and propped his bruised foot on the counter with an ice pack balanced on top. He would watch some sports news on his laptop, then make dinner. The fridge contained nothing but beer, Gatorade, and a box of baking soda, but there were some cans of chili on the shelf and bread in the freezer.

It wasn't a grandiose plan, but it was easy. Relaxing.

The sports show buffered for a few minutes, then the playback smoothed out. Unfortunately, the first segment was golf coverage. Golf was hella boring, in Joey's opinion, but he didn't want to mess with the laptop. Finally, the hosts switched to college football.

Then the power went out.

"Fuck. Me." Joey set his bottle on the table and stared at the ceiling for a few minutes, hoping it might be a momen-

41

tary outage. The sports show died along with the Wi-Fi, though the laptop screen continued to glow in the dark. Joey's dinner plans were no longer executable without the microwave. When it became apparent that this was no minor disturbance in the force, he lit a camp lantern and stared moodily out the living room window until he realized what he was doing and felt ridiculous.

Reliving the fiasco at the Morgan residence had put him in a shitty mood, and normally Joey would sweat himself into a better frame of mind, but exercise was out for a day or two. He could meditate, but the cottage was frankly not a good place to be opening yourself to the universe. It had bad vibes. Joey wasn't particularly bothered by that—he didn't have a delicate spiritual constitution. But he wasn't inviting the vaguely sour miasma that gathered in certain corners into his chakras.

His mothers had raised him better than that.

Eventually, he double checked his emergency supplies, grabbed a few extra blankets, and went to bed. There was nothing to do, and he wasn't enjoying his own company. Each time he started to doze off, though, something flapped or rattled alarmingly on the roof. It wasn't his problem if the house lost a few shingles or some gingerbread details, since he'd be moving out soon, but Joey couldn't help but think of Eliza and the mess she would have to deal with when the storm passed. It would be decent of the Effinhams to send a service out periodically to maintain the grounds, but they seemed intent on pretending the cottage didn't exist.

Eventually, it wouldn't.

After a while the wind died down, and Joey felt the lassitude of sleep creeping over him. It was still raining steadily, but the noise was soothing. His headache was receding, his foot was in a comfortable position. The absence of pain was blissful.

At first, the voices didn't disturb him.

Just one voice, actually—Eliza's. Joey couldn't make out the words, but he suspected she was talking to her cats.

Were the cats being assholes, though? Because as time went on, her speech cadence became more clipped, and there were noises that sounded like stomping.

The muscles in Joey's face contracted with concern, bringing his headache back to life.

Eliza's footsteps receded for a while, then, just when he began to relax again, she returned with a determined stride. Her voice was loud—loud enough that he caught the odd word: *goddamnit, house, stupid, wall.* Then the biggie: *fuck.*

Joey told himself it was none of his business.

And yet, if Eliza was this pissed off at the house in the middle of the night—and in the middle of a massive storm—maybe some concern was justified.

He sighed and looked at his watch. 2338. *If she's still stomping around and cussing at midnight*, he thought, *I'll go down.*

A minute later, Eliza's kvetching turned to howls. The sounds of a struggle reached Joey's ears and he was halfway out the door before he really considered the nature of the threat. He'd instinctively picked up his Maglite flashlight, but given the tenor of Eliza's earlier complaints, he turned around and grabbed his work gloves and toolbox from the utility locker by his front door.

If there was an intruder, there were plenty of ways Joey could subdue him with his flashlight.

If it was, as he suspected, a home maintenance emergency, he would help patch things up temporarily, so they could all get some sleep.

*H*e hesitated before knocking on Eliza's door. It briefly occurred to him that this looked like the set-up to a porno—power outage, handyman arriving with his "tools" at midnight. Maybe Eliza would answer the door in a satin teddy with a feather boa around her shoulders.

Of course, if she did, Joey would have to seriously worry for her sanity, since the house was freezing. Even the thermostat in the foyer seemed alarmed, flashing a plaintive *"Comfort Settings?"* message at him as he walked by.

Good luck with that, he thought.

Eliza did not answer the door in a teddy or boa. Joey meant to ask if something was wrong. Instead, he heard himself say, "What are you *wearing?*"

Her expression went from annoyed to pissed. "Excuse me?"

Joey tried to mentally backpedal, but Eliza's orange sweater-vest had taken his brain hostage and his mouth was operating on its own. "That is the ugliest sweater I've ever seen. Are you really that cold?" She had a perfectly good, thick sweatshirt on underneath.

"I'm sorry, did you come down here in the middle of the night to insult my clothes?" She wasn't usually so loud. Or belligerent.

On the other hand, he wasn't usually so rude.

"Uh, no. I heard noises. I thought you might need a hand." He lifted his toolbox into the circle of light cast by her lantern.

Eliza's expression softened, although she was still clearly not in a good mood. "Oh. I'm sorry. I guess I woke you up."

He shook his head—cautiously, because the throbbing was back. "Nah, I wasn't sleeping."

The wind had picked up again and a particularly strong gust made it past the poorly closed front door, curling around Joey's exposed neck. Eliza grimaced. "It's freezing. Come in for a minute so we don't let all the heat out."

He followed her to her kitchen, which was, if not comfortable, at least warmer than the foyer. He found he had a hard time dragging his eyes away from her butt, the normal roundness of which was presently enhanced by the thick fleece pants she was wearing. He wanted to pat her, and then he wanted to slide his hands inside those awful pants and see what other interesting layers she might be wearing.

"If you give me a minute, I'll light the stove and make us something hot to drink. Coffee?"

Joey hauled his mind out of Eliza's pants through sheer strength of character. "Uh, thanks."

"Decaf or regular?"

"Whatever you're having is fine." She didn't seem to have noticed Joey's inappropriate fascination with her outfit.

He resolved to stop leering.

There was a *whoosh* and blue flames erupted beneath the kettle. Eliza grabbed two mugs from the drying rack and filled them with granules from a canister on the counter. "Full-strength, then," she said. "I need to sober up."

Joey blinked and cast his gaze around the dark, cold room. "You've been drinking? Tonight?" *By yourself?*

He hoped the last wasn't too strongly implied.

Eliza put a plastic-wrapped plate of supermarket cake on the table, got a knife and two forks from the drawer, and gestured for him to take a seat. "It's a long story. Sit."

Joey wasn't one to pass up either cake or a good story, and his foot was aching from double-timing it down the stairs, so he sat.

She cut two generous slices, brought the mugs of coffee over, and handed him a fork. After she'd taken a few bites of cake and scalded her mouth on coffee, she told him about the leak in her bedroom wall, her efforts to determine its source, and something about liquefied house guts.

"Here, have more coffee," Joey said, sliding Eliza's mug toward her. "It's cooler now."

"Thanks." She took a few halfhearted sips, then stared morosely into the dark brew for a moment.

Not wanting her to lose the thread of the story, Joey prompted, "So, you mentioned house guts?"

"This disgusting sludge came pouring out of the wall, right over the toes of my panda slippers. That's probably when you heard me yell and throw the screwdriver. Sorry."

"No problem." Joey leaned back in his chair, cradling his mug in both hands, and studied Eliza's dejected posture. He supposed sludge coming out of a wall could make a person yell and throw tools. Especially on a night like tonight. "Do you want me to take a look?"

She shrugged. "Sure. I doubt there's anything you can do about it, but…"

He stood and hefted his toolbox. "Can't hurt to look."

Eliza sighed, put down her mug, and buried her face in her hands, sending her glasses askew. "Tell that to my slippers."

~

*J*oey hadn't seen Eliza's bedroom in happier times, but it had probably been a cozy retreat—before the wall disintegrated.

Now, it was a biological hot zone. The smell of mold was overpowering. "I'll help you move your stuff into one of the other rooms in the morning," he told her. "You can't sleep here."

She sighed. "I know. Thanks. I guess I can take over part of the living room until this gets fixed."

There wasn't a chance in hell the Effinham estate would pay for mold abatement, but Joey refrained from saying so. "Let's have a quick look at the wall, then we'll get out of here." Eliza still had a dust mask hanging around her neck. He gave it a tap. "Put this on, okay?"

She complied.

He opened his toolbox, put on a mask of his own, and extracted a large cutting blade. With Eliza's permission—and her screwdriver, since it was already filthy—Joey opened the wall to eye level. There was less mold the further they got from the floor, but the interior of the wall was wet all the way up.

Eliza leaned in and peered at the space illuminated by Joey's flashlight, her soft brown hair tickling his chin. "I guess there's been a small leak here for ages, but this storm made it worse."

He concurred. "Most of the mold is down here where there's some kind of debris." He crouched and poked at some of the sludge on the floor with the screwdriver.

"Is that paper?"

Joey gave the stuff a few more pokes. "Could be. I guess you never know what you'll find in the walls of old houses."

There was a sliding sound and more moldy debris splatted to the floor at their feet. They both jumped back.

"Shit!" Eliza grasped Joey's arm, catching her balance.

Joey was all in favor of having her soft warmth pressed against him, but the ambiance was somewhat lacking, what with deadly mold spores wafting through the air. "Let's close this room for tonight and get out of here. Is there anything you need?"

"So many things." Sighing, Eliza grabbed an empty laundry basket from her closet and filled it with clothes while Joey held the flashlight and lantern aloft.

Back in the kitchen, they washed their hands in freezing

water, then Eliza made more coffee and served herself another slice of cake. Joey briefly considered going back to bed. Instead, he joined her.

"So, where do you think the water is coming from?" she asked. "Could it be a pipe in your kitchen?"

Joey shook his head. "Nope. Maybe something in the front apartment?" His place ran perpendicular to Eliza's, along the back of the old house. The front portion of the second floor was unoccupied.

"They never plumbed the front rooms. It must be the roof." She hesitated, then asked, "Would you come take a look at the ceilings upstairs with me? I want to know what I'm dealing with, but, um, I don't want to go alone."

Maybe Eliza was aware of the house's bad juju, too. It would be impolitic, though, on this dark and stormy night, to discuss it. "Sure, why not?" He couldn't quite remember why getting a good night of sleep had seemed so crucial.

"Really? Now?"

He got to his feet and cleared their dishes. "No time like the present."

CHAPTER 9

"I've always wondered about this space," Joey said, running his hand over the paneled wall at the top of the stairs. He was wearing his own headlamp now.

"You have? Why?" Eliza considered the seventies-era paneling a particularly poor decorating move on somebody's part.

"There must be about six feet of dead space between my kitchen and whatever that room is," he said, gesturing to his left. "Unless there's a deep closet here or something?"

She shook her head. "Nope, no closets in these rooms. That's probably part of why they've never rented them out."

"Huh."

Eliza took a deep breath, then shivered. "So, are you ready to brave the creepy, abandoned part of the house with me?" She'd tried for a certain lightness of tone.

Joey narrowed his eyes at her in concern, doing a fast head-to-toe appraisal. "Why don't I go by myself? You can wait out here. Or in my apartment."

She already knew that she would feel safer with Joey than without him. "No, I'll come. It's my responsibility. But you can lead the way," she offered, dangling the keys in front of her face, "if you want to be chivalrous."

Joey grinned and took the keys. He'd smiled more since they agreed to search for the leak than in the whole time she had known him.

Adventure Tenant, indeed.

Maybe she wasn't too far off in envisioning a wild side to her buttoned-up neighbor. She hadn't realized Joey could be so playful, though. She was going to have to work on some new facial expressions for Adventure Tenant—something besides brooding sternness. Was it too much to hope she might get to personally observe lust or infatuation?

Joey unlocked the door to the front room, shoved it open, and froze. "Whoa."

Eliza's heart jumped into overdrive. Thoughts of lust fled. "What?"

He half turned, leaving space for her to join him in the doorway. She stepped forward and gasped when the beam of her headlamp breached the darkness. Dense, gray-brown curtains of cobwebs hung from every surface and lay heaped in the corners like filthy tulle. The webs undulated gently in the cold air, as if stirred by shallow breathing. There was a quarter inch of dust on the floor.

"Would you believe this room was clean last time I visited?" she asked.

Joey looked understandably skeptical. "When was that?"

She thought back. "Not much more than a month ago. I checked all the windows in the house to see which ones I needed to seal. It was a little dusty in here, but nothing five minutes with a Swiffer couldn't fix."

"Things seem to have escalated quickly. It's probably due to, uh, climactic changes."

Eliza snickered nervously. "It's certainly atmospheric."

In fact, this room was one of the few in the house that

retained some of the original charm and elegance from when it was new, back in eighteen-whatever. The floor was intricate wood parquet that must have been lovely back then, although many of the pieces were damaged or missing now, leaving the surface dull and uneven. The three exterior walls were almost entirely glass, fitted with tall windows that arched gently at the top. It would have been a beautiful day room for children to play in while their minders did mending or crafts.

Tonight, the space felt menacing. Like the residue of a tantrum hung in the air. The wind gusted outside, sending heavy drops of rain bouncing off the panes of glass surrounding them. It sounded like handfuls of gravel being hurled at the house, and a frigid current of air rippled through the cobweb shrouds.

"Shall we?" Eliza was on the verge of chickening out.

Joey smiled and offered her his hand. "Let's do it."

~

Though most of her attention was on ducking under cobwebs and watching where she stepped, Eliza couldn't help but notice that Joey had a really nice hand —strong, big, and warm, with interesting calluses. *This is a hand that can do a lot of things*, she thought, *and do them well.*

Soon—too soon—they found themselves at the threshold of the room they needed to search.

"Mrs. Effinham said they called this the Egyptian room." Eliza's heart wasn't racing exactly, but it seemed to be pounding heavily in her chest. She sidled a little further into Joey's personal space.

"Did they now?" He looped an arm around her waist. Her heart tripped over its own feet, then settled into a happier rhythm.

"I know. It doesn't conjure up the coziest image. There are no mummies, though—I promise."

"I'm holding you to that." Joey bent to study the antique rim-lock mechanism on the door. The porcelain knob was cracked and chipped, a green and gold motif barely discernible through the damage. "Do we need a key?"

"No. It wasn't locked last time I came up."

He turned the knob. It spun uselessly in its socket. "Huh." He let go of her and crouched to have a better look, repositioned the knob, and tried again. Finally, the latch pulled back and the door swung open. "That needs to be fixed," he noted absently. Glancing at Eliza, he added, "I mean, it's not a priority, obviously."

She laughed. "The roof should probably come first."

Joey pushed the door further ajar and stepped in. Eliza stayed close on his heels. She remembered this room as being unremarkable. The walls were covered in faded blue wallpaper and dingy white wainscoting. On the far wall, white paneling that almost matched the wainscoting extended all the way to the ceiling. An incongruously vivid Laura Ashley wallpaper border of red hibiscus flowers ran around the top of the other three walls, sagging like bunting where it had come loose.

The only Egyptian touch was the cobwebs, which definitely gave it a tomb-like vibe. If anything, they were thicker here than in the solarium, hanging in cords that spun lazily on themselves when disturbed.

"Maybe the airflow through here is different," Joey said, poking at a strand with his flashlight. "It's weird, the way it's hanging in ropes."

"Uh-huh. The airflow." Eliza thought about how the wind had made a noose of their pumpkin lights the evening she'd found out Joey was coming home. A draft curled through the room from the open door and a cord of web lifted, catching at her neck. She turned, startled, and the rest fell across her face. "Get it off!" she yelped, swiping at her mouth.

"Let me see." Joey tucked his flashlight under his arm, deflected her hands, and carefully wiped the web from her cheeks and chin. His fingers were warm and dry—decidedly masculine against Eliza's skin. She suppressed a shiver of wanting.

"Thanks," she said when he leaned back to evaluate his work. *Thanks for giving me sexy jitters on top of the panic jitters.*

"Did I get it all?"

Um. "You got most of it." Joey's gaze followed her finger as she rubbed at her lips. She was on the verge of making a crack about him liking to watch women touch themselves when a floorboard creaked underfoot and the door swung shut, latching with a clunk.

"Oh. Oh, crap."

Joey took her hand and squeezed. "Don't worry. It'll open again. It's just a question of getting the knob in the right place."

Eliza couldn't repress the small tremor that moved through her body. Her heart was pounding again. "Let's find the leak and get out of here."

"You got it." Joey turned and placed her fingers at the small of his back. "Hang on to me. We'll stay together, okay?"

She nodded and sank her fingers into the warm fabric of his sweatshirt, her throat tight with gratitude.

The room itself was small—probably only nine by twelve feet. Even batting cobwebs out of the way, it took very little time to examine the far wall from one end to the other. They found no sign of water damage, although the air smelled like a bouquet left in a vase too long. A little floral, a lot swampy.

Eliza huffed in exasperation. "I don't get it."

Joey tilted his head, calculating. "There's got to be dead

space between this wall and my kitchen. I'd say we're a good three feet from the leak here."

Dead space. That phrase again. Eliza shivered. Why couldn't this just be easy? The cobweb on her neck seemed to throb against her skin. She still sensed feathery touches across her lips. "You know what?" Her voice shook. "We should come back in the morning. When it's lighter."

Joey turned and studied her face. "Sure. We'll tackle this when we've had some sleep and we can see better." He took her hand and led her back to the door. "Don't panic if the knob doesn't catch right away. I've got this, okay?"

"Uh-huh." Eliza's neck was chilled where it was exposed to the air, the skin tight. Her lips were tingling—not in a good way.

The knob spun uselessly again. Joey smiled reassuringly and repositioned it. Still, the latch didn't catch.

"Joey…"

"Don't worry. If I can't open it with the knob, I'll find another way."

The tight feeling settled around Eliza's collarbones, becoming more substantial. "I think I'm having a panic attack." Her voice sounded far away and tinny to her own ears.

Part of her couldn't concede that this was something her body was doing to itself. It felt like an act of malice. Like the room was smothering her. The words *get out* ran like a mantra through her brain.

Joey stood, put his hands on her shoulders, and pressed down firmly. "*Eliza.* You're fine, honey. I'm right here. Take a deep breath."

She gulped, then managed a couple of gasping breaths that were visible in the cold air when she exhaled. He leaned closer and she caught his scent, warm and vibrantly alive in contrast to the abandonment of the room. She rested her forehead against his chest and focused on his heartbeat until the panic receded.

Apparently, Real Life Joey was an even better tonic against stress than Adventure Tenant.

When he seemed satisfied that she was back in control, Joey steadied her on her feet and handed her his nice, heavy flashlight. "Point the beam at this hinge here," he instructed.

Eliza clutched at the solid metal tube like her life depended on it. "You're going to take the whole door off?"

"Maybe."

She couldn't help wondering how the house would feel about being dismantled. Especially when Joey pulled out a utility knife and started scraping paint away from the hinge to find the top of the pin. Softened by humidity, it accumulated in little globs on the blade, then fell to the floor like sloughed skin.

Was she imagining the scent of an unwashed body? Nausea twisted Eliza's stomach. Apparently the panic hadn't gone far.

Unable to get at the pin, Joey began unscrewing the bottom hinge, handing her the screws as he removed them: one, two, three. The metal stung her palm. *Residual heat from the friction*, she told herself.

A minute passed with no more screws forthcoming. "Problem?"

Joey was staring at the hinge, which hadn't moved one iota. He scrubbed a hand over the top of his head—the first sign that he wasn't entirely relaxed about the situation. "The hinge is painted onto the door. I can pry it off, but it'll damage the wood. Let me look at the lock again."

Eliza was on the verge of telling Joey to do whatever he wanted as long as they got out, pronto. The screws throbbed in her clenched hand, biting into the flesh of her palm.

She told herself to calm down and kept her mouth shut.

Joey studied the knob mechanism for another minute, then stood and ran his fingers around the outside of the door.

"Press against this corner here with your foot."

"Uh, what?"

He pointed at the lower right corner of the door. "Press there with your foot. Firmly."

Eliza slid under his arm, fitting her back to Joey's front. His warmth was an oasis of comfort. "Like this?" She planted her right heel and pressed the toe of her shoe against the door as hard as she could.

"Let's see." Joey placed his hands toward the top of the door and pushed upward.

Eliza felt something shift.

"Try the knob now."

She dropped the screws into her pocket and grasped the knob. The porcelain was *cold*. Far colder than it ought to be. She let go, shaking her hand as if the cold were something she could fling away.

"Eliza?"

"Just a sec." She pulled her sleeve over her hand and grabbed the knob again, wrenching it clockwise. The mechanism ground and creaked in protest, but she felt it catch. Finally, the door surrendered, popping open.

Eliza lunged, throwing herself through the gap, and beat a frantic retreat.

Joey was right behind her.

CHAPTER 10

*J*oey woke at 0800 the next morning when the power came back on and his bedside lamp sprang to life, shining right in his face. It was like starting the day with an interrogation. *Good morning, sunshine. Tell us who sent you.*

He swung his feet out of bed and self-assessed. His smashed foot was still sore, but the swelling was better. He flexed his toes and ankle experimentally. Bolting down the stairs the night before hadn't set him back much. Apart from the ding to his ego, anyway. He and Eliza had fled the Egyptian room like kids playing Bloody Mary at a slumber party.

"Sheesh. What a badass." Joey rubbed his hands over his face and combed his fingers through his hair, working carefully around the lump at his temple. If he believed in man cards, he would be forced to surrender his right about now. He'd staged a number of tactical retreats over the years and had never come so close to shrieking while he hauled ass.

The thing was, Joey had thought he was accustomed to the cottage's brand of bad juju, which he might describe as latent melancholy with just a whiff of bitterness. Nothing that couldn't be exorcized, so to speak, by turning on some classic rock or NFL coverage.

The atmosphere they'd encountered last night was something else entirely. More of a presence than an echo. Walking into the Egyptian room had felt like pushing through a veil, and not just because of the dust and cobwebs. There'd been an inexplicable temperature drop. Then a clutching, longing desperation had throbbed to life around them as soon as Joey touched Eliza's cheek to wipe away the web. He'd been seized by want—his own familiar sexual response, laced with a thread of frustration and petulant darkness that was definitely not familiar.

Joey had instinctively tamped down on the alien desire; it was his job, after all, to quickly identify wrongness and keep it far, far away from his principal. The intrusive feeling had evaporated instantaneously, like a stitch resolving itself in his chest, and then it was just him, Eliza, and a whole lot of hot chemistry in a cold, creepy room.

Not romantic, but not wrong either.

Definitely not wrong, he thought.

Inconvenient? Yes. Ill-timed? Affirmative. But very nice.

In another time, another place…

"Get it together," Joey told himself, standing with a groan. He stretched, scratched his belly, and adjusted his pants around an ambivalent erection. His dick wanted Eliza but found the circumstances troubling.

Smart dick.

~

*A*fter a fast and unfortunately tepid shower, Joey got a pot of coffee brewing. He might be on medical leave, but he wasn't on vacation. He wasn't going to spend another day napping or moping, and he wasn't going to let this burgeoning infatuation for Eliza eat up his time either. He would help her move her stuff when she was ready, but he would not sit around making action plans for repairing the house or finding new accommodations for the Philips ladies.

No sirree.

While the coffee percolated, he zipped a fleece vest over his army hoodie and wandered over to the living room window to survey the storm damage. A piece of blue siding lay tangled in a rose bush that had once covered an arbor, but was now an amorphous mound of thorny canes and fragile petals. Otherwise, it was hard to say what part of the devastation was from the storm and what was the result of decades of neglect. Tall weeds growing between bloated hedges lay beaten down, tangled and soggy from the rain. Frost lingered in the shadows. The trees surrounding the yard—noticeably more bare than the day before—seemed to lean precariously toward each other, and toward the cottage; except for that sturdy maple out by the stone wall that stood tall and clung tenaciously to its leaves, whatever the season.

Joey considered the lesser vegetation again. Maybe he should spend half a day with a chainsaw and a weed-whacker clearing things back while he was home.

Maybe you should remember it's not your problem.

The coffeemaker burbled to a stop in the kitchen. He poured himself a mug, sipped, and tried to focus on important things: career advancement, middle age, retirement savings, the rising cost of elder care.

Predictably, every train of thought circled back to Eliza.

If he transitioned to management, he would get a salary bump and a nine-to-five schedule. Which would make it a hell of a lot easier to have a family.

Eliza, Minnie, and the cats sprang to mind. They would make a nice family.

"God. You're pathetic. At least think about sex," Joey told himself.

No problemo, his libido replied.

He'd always found Eliza cute and personable. He respected her sense of responsibility and found her pragmatism and offbeat humor refreshing. And that was the extent of his feelings, right?

Apparently not.

A little drama, a little peril, and suddenly he had protective and proprietary urges brewing. Real caveman shit. He wanted to drag Eliza against his body and sink his fingers into her hair. He wanted to leave bite marks on her neck and slide his hands into her pants. He wanted to flex his muscles. Plan and execute a clean extraction. Throw himself into shelter-making activities. Hole up somewhere warm and safe and fuck like bunnies.

Remember, you respect her sense of responsibility, Joey told himself.

Then he adjusted his pants again, told his inner caveman to pipe down, and made a bowl of oatmeal. He had a plan, and it involved spreadsheet analysis—not seducing his building manager through acts of domestic heroism.

Well, except for helping move Eliza's furniture. And having another go at finding the leak in the roof.

He sliced a banana into his bowl, topped the whole thing with a handful of granola, and sat at his kitchen table for a working breakfast. Unsurprisingly, the internet connection was slow. Eliza never seemed to have connectivity issues, but upstairs was a different story.

Instead of messing with the router, Joey set up a hotspot with his satellite phone and logged on to the company website to access the files he needed for phase one of his life upgrade—writing a feasibility report re: opening a new division of Griffin Security.

Joey had written plenty of reports, but his experience was all with the client side of things: security assessments, daily activity logs, wrap-up reports. This was his first foray into the world of upper management.

Since leaving the military and joining Griffin Security, he'd been a live-in-the-moment guy, working hard and playing harder. He'd taken assignments in parts of the world most people had never heard of, and tried every adrenaline-charged outdoor activity ever invented. He spent a few weeks stateside with his moms every year, but otherwise he was constantly on the move.

He and Marco had hiked Machu Picchu, heli-skiied in Switzerland, and climbed sea-cliff faces in Corsica. Joey had backpacked through southeast Asia with his best friend Jake while on a year-long assignment in Jakarta, and he'd talked Meg and Gordon into paragliding off the coast of Mozambique with him while they were all working in Africa.

Good times.

But all Joey's friends had eventually opted out of that lifestyle in favor of, well, adulthood.

Marco had three kids now, and a nine-to-five gig working client retention for Griffin. Meg and Gordon had gotten married, divorced, and remarried to other people. Jake was living in Australia with his husband, Henry. They had a hydroponic cucumber farm, three dogs, and a small herd of goats. They most emphatically did not travel anymore.

Marco attributed Joey's recent life dissatisfaction to a nesting urge. "You're looking to settle down, man. It's normal. What's not normal is how long you've been living like an entitled frat boy."

That comment had stung. Joey had been raised on a civil servant's salary, and gotten his degree while working full-time after leaving the army. His only experience with frat boys was providing security for their parents, which sometimes involved diplomatically dragging one back to a hotel by his ear.

And Joey wasn't looking to *nest*. Marco was projecting. Clearly.

He just didn't want to live in a crappy apartment in the middle of nowhere anymore, and he wanted to learn more about the business side of running the security company. He wasn't giving up being adventurous; he was choosing a different kind of adventure.

The problem was, Brian Griffin was unconvinced that after ten years of thriving on a nomadic lifestyle, Joey was ready to commit to a zip code and a long-term management job.

Fair enough, since he hardly believed it himself some days.

Getting concussed by a client wielding an art deco door had been a tipping point, though. Back at the office, Joey had dropkicked his duffle into the employee lounge—uncharacteristically angry—and snarled, "Fuck this shit. I'm done!" to what he thought was an empty room. Unfortunately, his boss happened to be raiding the employee fridge for creamer. Brian had raised an eyebrow and asked Joey if that was so.

He'd assured him it was.

Eventually, they reached a compromise—Griffin gave Joey two weeks to research and write a proposal for the business expansion while he healed and got an attitude adjustment. "If you can stay out of the field that long," Brian had said, "we'll talk."

Joey could stay out of the field for two weeks. Easy. He would do his research, write the proposal, help Eliza with her mysterious leak, and other than that... *nada*.

In fact, bad juju aside, he was looking forward to staying in one place and relaxing for a while.

Really.

~

*S*craping noises from downstairs pulled Joey out of his research sometime later. He checked the time on his laptop. Almost 1000 hours. He saved his notes and headed down, ignoring the pocket of cold, damp air at the base of the stairs. He also refused to read anything into the message on the thermostat: *Monitoring attic. Alert. Monitoring attic.*

Minnie answered the door wearing either a blanket with sleeves, or a very freeform sweater. There was no doubt that she'd made it herself, since it contained the same orange yarn as the porch décor monstrosity that had almost killed Joey over the summer.

"Oh, Mr. Cooper. Is something wrong?"

Minnie Philips was warm and kind. She was also perpetually anxious and had one foot firmly anchored in an alternate plane of existence. As such, Joey elected not to discuss wet rot and black mold with her. "No, no problem, Mrs. Philips. I just came down to help Eliza move some things."

She smiled uncertainly, hesitating. Then, something clicked for her. She relaxed and invited him in. "I'll be working in my room. You kids let me know if you need a snack."

Who does she think I am? Joey wondered.

The Philips's apartment smelled like somebody had opened a coffee kiosk in a crypt. Joey found Eliza in her bedroom inspecting the back of her dresser, a steaming mug cradled in her hands. She wore fingerless gloves with a pattern of glittery black ravens worked around the wrists. She'd ditched the cushy fleece pants, but the cuffed flannel-lined jeans she was wearing this morning were equally alluring on her softly rounded frame.

"Starting without me?" he asked from the doorway.

Eliza turned and tucked a chocolate-brown lock of hair behind her ear, then rubbed her brow as if trying to erase a headache. "I wanted to see if there was mold on my stuff before we dragged it into the living room."

Joey stepped closer, wanting her in his personal space again. "What's the verdict?"

"Everything looks okay except for my bed frame—there's a little fuzz on that corner."

He crouched and studied the damage. "We can treat it with bleach. It'll be fine."

She nodded. "I got lucky." Then she laughed, pink spreading beneath the freckles on her cheeks. "I mean, the house is self-destructing around us, but at least our stuff is fine. For now."

Famous last words, Joey thought. Out loud he said, "So, all of this is going to the living room?"

Eliza had already removed her bedding and clothing, and was presumably washing everything—he'd heard the machines going in the communal laundry room. Without her colorful fabrics, the room was bare and shabby. The air seemed particularly clammy where the bed had been.

That couldn't be healthy.

He glanced at Eliza. Her eyes were a little red and she had a sniffle. Maybe she was just cold and tired. But maybe those were symptoms of black mold exposure.

Not for the first time, Joey thought that the only way to fix the cottage might be to burn it down.

~

*I*t didn't take long to make a sleeping area between the living room fireplace and one of the bay windows. Eliza's bed and nightstand fit snugly together in the corner. Her dresser had to go across the room behind the couch, but she didn't mind.

"I'd say this is actually an improvement, in some ways," she said, folding a flannel quilt and tossing it across the foot of her bed. "I have natural light and a reliable heat source. What more could a girl ask for?"

"Well…" Joey glanced at Minnie, who was sitting on the couch tearing apart a knitting project and sighing compulsively. *A girl could use some privacy from her mother*, he thought.

Eliza followed his gaze. "I mean, a door would be nice, obviously."

Minnie snorted, set her pile of yarn aside, and got to her feet, sniffing dramatically. "I know when I'm not wanted. I'll be in my room, kids."

Joey, despite his extensive professional training at interpreting human behavior, couldn't get a read on Eliza's mom a lot of the time. She was everything all at once—anxious, brittle, warm, funny, fragile, apologetic. Eliza was smirking now though, so he relaxed. Minnie was obviously stressed by them moving furniture around—and taking it out on her knitting—but her sense of humor was intact.

They did a quick round of vacuuming and dusting once she left. The living room was the only truly nice space in this whole rotting shithole. The fireplace still had its original carved-marble mantle and surround—top quality workmanship, even if the miniature neoclassical columns worked into the sides were a bit much. The walls were covered in carved paneling crowned with elaborate molding. While somebody, in their infinite wisdom, had installed acoustic foam over most of the ceilings in the cottage, the living room still had its original pressed-tin tiles. It was a warm, elegant room that gave you a sense of what the house must have been like in its heyday. It even smelled like better times—rose, lavender, pipe tobacco, leather-bound books. As if the memory of a cozy evening clung to the space.

When Joey mentioned the pleasant scents to Eliza, she hesitated, then nodded. "I know what you mean. But it doesn't smell like that in here all the time. It kind of comes and goes. I had this vague theory that heat brought the scents out, but after last night I'm not so sure."

Joey inhaled deeply, scanning the room. The aroma did seem to have become more pronounced, and nothing in the space was an obvious source. "Okay. That's interesting."

"Isn't it just?" Eliza replied dryly.

"I'll take pleasant inexplicable odors over slamming doors and cold spots any day."

"You and me both."

~

When they were done cleaning, Joey hauled a heaping basket of clean linens back from the laundry room. He was watching Eliza make her bed—and indulging in idle thoughts about joining her in it—when Minnie appeared carrying a tray loaded with teacups, saucers, and a plate of graham crackers. "Yoo-hoo!"

The sight of graham crackers brought Joey's adult-rated fantasies to an abrupt end.

"You've been working so hard," Minnie said, setting her offerings out on a small claw-footed side table whose spindly legs were wrapped in knobby teal yarn. "I brought you snacks."

The look Eliza shot Joey was both pleading and directive:

Please, for the love of all that's holy, sit and have tea with my mother.

Bemused, Joey decided that a gentleman didn't turn down tea and graham crackers. "I'd love a snack."

While Minnie finished arranging the food and drink, he took the empty tray and stashed it next to the couch, then moved three mismatched chairs around the table. He hadn't had graham crackers in thirty years, but they were tasty. Chamomile tea wasn't his thing, but since his delicate cup was approximately the size of a thimble, he managed to choke down his portion.

Unsure of what he might contribute to tea party conversation, he made himself comfortable and listened while Eliza navigated a conversation with her mother about a rush order for custom dog sweaters a customer wanted in time for Halloween. Apparently, the pattern had to be converted, the desired yarn was in short supply, and Minnie was conflicted about the ethics of making dogs wear sweaters in the first place. Somehow, Eliza managed to engage on the topic and ask relevant questions while simultaneously mitigating her mom's concerns.

Somebody should hire her as a tactical negotiator, Joey thought. She was brilliant.

When Minnie started to look tired, Eliza encouraged her to go rest. "We'll clean this up, Mom," she said, gathering the teacups and tiny plates back onto the tray.

Minnie excused herself and Joey carried the tray back to the kitchen where he and Eliza washed the tea set and put it away. "Mom loves getting this stuff out," she told him. "Thanks for being a good sport about it."

"Not a problem." Joey closed the cupboard door and stretched, working some kinks out of his neck. When he glanced at Eliza, she was staring at the bruise on his left temple.

Seeing she'd been caught, she blushed. "Sorry. I was wondering what happened. You don't have to tell me, though."

Joey hated to ruin the mystique he cultivated with the ladies, but Eliza didn't need anyone else in her life feeding her distorted realities. Minnie's behavior was charmingly daffy, but dealing with her skewed perception all the time was probably doing a number on Eliza's own mental health. "Somebody slammed a door on my head."

She cringed. "Why? And *who?*"

"My client." He reached over and tucked a strand of hair behind Eliza's ear, hoping to erase the sympathetic pain on her face. "She was, uh, upset."

Eliza blinked. "What did you do?"

Joey found himself laughing about the incident for the first time. "She caught her husband cheating. I was collateral damage."

Eliza moved closer to examine his face, a hand on his cheek. After a moment, she shook her head and sighed. "If you're going to get hurt, Joey, you need to come up with better stories about it."

He put a hand on her hip, making sure he had her attention. "I wouldn't lie to you, Eliza." He'd grown very used to only telling people what they needed to know. Obfuscating was a tool he deployed often in his work as a security professional, in the name of discretion. He realized that he didn't want to keep things from Eliza, though.

She stilled, eyes locked on his. "I was kidding."

"I'm not."

"Okay."

Joey let go and stepped back. Did he have a gift for killing the mood, or what?

"Do you still want to look for the leak?" he asked. "I can go by myself if you want to work on your laundry."

Eliza folded her arms across her chest and studied him for a moment before turning her gaze to the ceiling. "Thanks, but I'm going with you. We're a team, right?"

Joey grinned, relieved. "Absolutely."

Eliza blushed and, after a tiny hesitation, touched his arm. "Let me just finish a few things here first."

CHAPTER 11

*J*oey went back to his place to have a real-food lunch and get some more work done while Eliza did her thing.

To his relief, he was finding the research Griffin had assigned him interesting. He would have felt like a huge asshole if it had turned out that he really was only cut out for field work. Some of the stuff he'd learned in the business classes he'd taken during college started coming back to him, and he could finally see the applicability of his degree.

Better late than never, right?

He worked until almost 1600 hours, when he decided he'd better check on Eliza. It had sounded like she was going to come up as soon as she'd finished putting her laundry away, but maybe he'd misunderstood?

She answered the door looking harassed. "Sorry. I'm sorry. It took a long time to get my mom to eat lunch. We can go now."

Sensing that she didn't want to relive her afternoon, Joey didn't press for details. Instead, he picked a piece of lint out of her hair and cupped her face in his hands for a moment before smoothing some wayward layers back toward her frizzing updo.

Eliza blushed at his touch, some life coming back into her expression. Joey wanted to wrap her in his arms until all her stress evaporated, but now was not the moment. Eliza wouldn't really be able to relax until they found the source of the leak. He gestured at the staircase. "Shall we?"

They both paused in front of the thermostat, which was flashing *INPUT CODE!*

Eliza shook her head. "Let me check my cereal box."

"You talk to it too, huh?"

"It's better company than some people around here." They both glanced at Doug's door.

Eliza led the way upstairs, brandishing a large, fluorescent-pink feather duster. They stopped at Joey's apartment so she could raid his toolbox (not a euphemism, unfortunately), choosing a claw bar, Joey's biggest flathead screwdriver, and a small mallet. Eliza slid the claw bar and screwdriver into the front pocket of her sweatshirt, but kept the mallet in hand.

She seemed calmer once she was armed.

The sky was dark and it was raining again—hard, icy drops that were only a couple of degrees shy of hail. They donned their respective headlamps and opened the door to the solarium. Eliza's back was rigid with tension under the loose hoodie she wore.

Joey squeezed her shoulder, then stepped in ahead of her and shoved a rubber wedge under the door to keep it open.

"Oh, you're a genius."

He grinned at her over his shoulder. "I have my moments."

Eliza cleared a path into the middle of the gloomy room

with her feather duster. "It's not so bad during the day, huh?" Her tone of voice suggested she wasn't looking for a dissenting opinion.

Joey shrugged. "Nothing to worry about." Although it smelled weird —a little medicinal—and there was a certain viscosity to the air that didn't seem attributable to humidity or dust. Also, a lot of the cobwebs they'd cleared the night before seemed to have grown back.

Eliza hunched into her sweatshirt, pulling the hood higher around her neck. He put a hand at her waist and nudged her toward the Egyptian room. "C'mon. We're losing daylight."

She laughed. "I've always wanted to hear somebody say that."

"Losing daylight?"

"Uh-huh. It sounds so... I don't know. Adventurous."

Joey snorted. "I'll keep that in mind." If she was turned on by tough-guy clichés, bedroom talk would be a lot of fun.

It was significantly darker and colder in the Egyptian room than in the solarium. The air tasted like despair. Joey wanted to laugh at himself for thinking so, but, well... maybe later.

They turned on their headlamps and Eliza tugged on the strings of her hood until her mouth was covered. Joey shoved two wedges under this door to be on the safe side and followed her as she cleared a path through the cobwebs to the far wall. In here, too, the cobweb ropes seemed to have multiplied.

"I still don't see any leaks, but does this part of the wall look bubbled to you?" She was poking tentatively at a section of paneling that did, indeed, bulge a little.

Joey crouched and pressed on the wall with his gloved hands. The wood flexed under his palms, brittle and puckered as if it had gone through a few wet/dry cycles. "There's definitely some damage here."

"There's a seam in the paneling," Eliza said, tapping at a small gap with her crowbar. "Maybe we should peel it back and see what's underneath." She hesitated, then added, "Do you think the Effinhams will mind?"

Joey thought the beneficiaries of Mrs. Effinham's estate would have the house demolished as soon as it got out of probate, but it would be cruel to say so. Unlike him, Eliza and her mom weren't prepared to fly the coop, and Eliza was clearly invested in her maintenance role.

"That's just how you deal with leaks. Gotta get inside the wall to see what's happening."

"Right. Okay." Eliza glanced back at the door to the solarium, then slid the claw bar under the panel. It had been mounted with both nails and glue. She worked patiently, trying to keep the panel intact. Joey thought it was a waste of effort, but he didn't say so. There were days when a person couldn't stomach gratuitous destruction.

After a few minutes, she stopped to peer closely at a spot about four feet above the floor.

"There's something metal here. It looks like a hinge."

"What?" Joey bent to see, his head right next to Eliza's. An odor of mildewy wood dust clung to the paneling, but Eliza smelled amazing. Sweet and bright, like strawberries and citrus. Joey manfully resisted burying his face in her hair. He really had to get her alone somewhere comfortable and safe one of these days so he could deploy his tough-guy bedroom talk.

"Do you see it?" she prompted.

"Uh." *Time and place*, Joey reminded himself. "Yeah, that's a hinge. Weird." He stepped back to look at the wall again. The floor made a tortured creak under his boot and they both spun to look at the door behind them. It slipped a couple of inches before the wedges caught and held.

Eliza raised the claw bar. Joey adjusted his grip on his Maglite. There was something a little too sentient about that door.

"It'll hold, right?" Eliza asked.

"Definitely." This damn house was already testing the limits of Joey's inclination to not lie to her.

Eliza gave him some potent side-eye and pulled the mallet out of her pocket, giving it an experimental swing. Clearly, she was prepared to make her own doorway if necessary.

He fully supported that plan of action.

But first, they should do the job they came for. "Why don't I take a whack at the panel? I may be able to get better leverage on it."

She pursed her lips. "We're going to have to take it off in pieces, aren't we?"

"Probably."

Eliza gave a jerky nod, eyes fixed on the solarium door. "Go for it."

"Yeah?"

"Yeah."

Joey traded her his heavy flashlight for the claw bar and took over the campaign of destruction.

The paneling came off in small pieces at first. He kicked them into a pile and kept chipping away. When the crowbar slid into a deep pocket, he pulled experimentally to see if he could tear off the rest intact. It looked like it would hold together. He tugged, bracing one foot on the wall. With a shriek, the paneling tore away and a piece the size and shape of a coffin lid clattered to the floor between him and Eliza. A cloud of dust billowed up, scattering over their feet like ashes.

Eliza was white-knuckling the flashlight, her breaths shallow. She hadn't taken her eyes off the door to the solarium.

Joey took his glove off and reached for her arm. "Are you okay? Do you want to leave?"

She shook her head, gaze darting between the exit and the piece of wood on the floor. "I'm fine. Not yet."

"Okay."

He turned back to the wall where another door was now exposed. It was narrow and tall, like maybe it had been stolen from a broom closet. Squiggly glue tracks laced with splinters covered it from top to bottom, and the wood was riddled with nail holes. Whoever'd placed the paneling had wanted to make sure it stayed put.

"No knob though," he said, thinking out loud.

Eliza glanced over her shoulder, eyes widening when she saw the door. "*No way.* There's really a hidden room?"

Between the dust they'd stirred up and Eliza's infectious tension, the atmosphere had grown stifling. And there was a scent in the air, like rotting flowers, that was getting stronger by the minute. Still, Joey was stoked. He'd never discovered a secret room before. Part of him wanted to put the claw bar and mallet to good use and force his way in immediately.

Eliza looked like she'd had enough excitement for one day, though.

"Maybe we should figure out how the door works in the morning," he suggested. "We're supposed to have a break in the rain tomorrow. The light will be better."

Eliza adjusted her grip on the Maglite, her breath whooshing in relief. "Sounds good. I should check on my mom. She might be wondering about the noise."

They left the doors propped open and went back to Joey's apartment to put his tools away. Eliza thanked him for his help and said she'd see him in the morning. She hesitated at the top of the stairs, though.

Joey was leaning in his apartment doorway, prepared to watch and listen until she was home, safe and sound. "What's wrong?"

She shoved her hands in the pockets of her jeans and turned back, biting her lower lip in indecision. "Can we shut the door to the solarium? I feel weird leaving it open."

Truthfully, Joey did, too. His apartment felt unchanged to him, but there were definitely bad vibes stirred up in the solarium and the Egyptian room. Why invite them to spread? "No problem."

He walked back and bent to retrieve the doorstop.

It wouldn't budge.

He put his shoulder to the solarium door and shoved, giving the wedge a kick at the same time. Nothing. *Weird, weird, weird*, he thought, repeating the action. Abruptly, there was a drop in air pressure and the door flew inward, freeing the wedge and sending Joey to his hands and knees. A moment later, it flew back at his face. Joey threw himself backward, narrowly avoiding being smashed by a door for the second time in one week. The door met its frame with a resounding smack. There was a split second of silence, then the lock audibly engaged. With no help from Joey whatsoever.

"Holy…" Heart pounding, he got to his feet. "There must, uh, be a gust of wind coming from somewhere," he said. *Right. Absolutely.*

Grabbing the rubber wedge, he backed across the landing to where Eliza waited, frozen, looking like she was about to barf. Clearly, the "gust of wind" explanation didn't resonate with her.

Joey tucked the wedge in a pocket and took her freezing, shaking hands in his, pulling her close. "Hey, we're okay."

Eliza squeezed his hands. In a thin voice, she asked, "Do you want to stay downstairs tonight?"

Sadly, this wasn't a come-on. She was terrified.

Joey had inconvenienced himself for the peace of mind of hundreds of people he liked a whole lot less than Eliza, so it was easy to agree. "I'd be glad to. Thanks."

CHAPTER 12

While Joey was upstairs packing an overnight bag, Eliza checked on Minnie, who was dozing in the recliner in her room, then braved her bathroom for a quick shower. The water was freezing. The garbage bag over the window rippled and flexed continually.

But surely she was safe in her own apartment, right?

She lathered, scrubbed, and rinsed frantically, then dashed to the living room, dripping wet, with her towel clutched around her while suds were still going down the shower drain.

She hadn't felt safe.

In the living room, she stoked the fire and bundled herself into yet another ensemble of yoga pants, several layers of shirts, and a sweatshirt.

And socks. "Can't forget the socks," she said, pulling on a thick pair while her hair dried in front of the fire. She was still trembling. The slam of the solarium door and the snick of its lock still vibrated in her bones. Her hands were bloodless and cold. She clutched the colorful wool of her mom-made socks like they were a magical security blanket for her feet. They were orange, with a purple likeness of Gloria Steinem on the calves.

She did feel a little better, gazing upon Gloria's silhouette.

There was a knock at the door and she jumped, heart racing, breath catching. "It has to be Joey." She twisted her hair up into a damp bun and went to let in her slumber-party buddy.

Joey had changed into worn jeans, a soft sweater, and a fleece vest. Despite some residual tension creases around his eyes, he looked sexy, calm, and fantastically reassuring. As well as extremely touchable. Eliza usually wanted to draw things that caught her attention. Tonight, she wanted to drag Joey to her bed and spend the rest of the evening exploring the contrast between the softness of his clothes and the hardness of his muscles.

It would be a huge bonus that, the closer he was, the safer she felt.

Unfortunately, there was her mother to consider. She stowed that fantasy and showed him where to put his things instead.

"Is the couch going to be okay for you?" It was too short, but inviting him to take her bed would likely lead to a very awkward conversation. *You can have my bed, but I won't be in it because you are so hot, but my mother might walk in at any moment, and also this house is freaking me out and I don't think even your level of hotness could inspire me to come so long as we're in it.*

"I'll give it a shot."

"What?"

"The couch." Joey gestured at the green velvet monstrosity she and her mom had been dragging around for almost two decades because it was so damn comfortable. "Otherwise, I have a camping mattress." He dangled a bag the size of a water bottle between them.

Eliza grabbed the bag, grateful for a conversational redirect. Could he tell she'd been mentally ravishing him? Probably. Nobody had ever accused her of being inscrutable. She turned the dense package around in her hands, willing herself to stop blushing. "This is a mattress?"

"Yep. Self-inflating, too." Joey's tone was dry, his expression smug.

He definitely knew.

"What will they think of next?" She added the mattress to his pile of stuff, which included a duffle, a sleeping bag, and his laptop case. "You're very prepared. Is there anything I can get you?"

He smiled and sat on the couch in a man sprawl, gaze circling the room. She'd noticed that he scanned his environment continually—doors, windows, occupants—just like she checked her mirrors while driving. Ingrained instinct.

"Your internet password would be handy, since I have some work to do."

~

*O*nce he was online, Joey seemed to have no trouble focusing on his project. Eliza tried to follow suit. She needed to give her brain something normal and productive to do.

Not grant writing, though. The idea of a sensory garden was sort of terrifying at the moment, "sensory" being altogether too close to "sentient."

She opened an apartment hunting website and repeated a search she'd done dozens of times over the last few months. As usual, her parameters generated zero results and the website suggested she try again. She closed the page instead. They just couldn't afford anything better than the cottage yet.

From behind her laptop screen, she watched Joey work. His degree of focus was intimidating. And sexy. Very sexy. She should try not to lust after him while he was her guest, but his competence and fluid grace were incredibly distracting. Not to mention that five o'clock shadow. Those hands.

Before Joey could catch her staring, she opened the tabs to her favorite webcomics and made herself focus on the latest updates. Then she spent a few minutes contemplating the blank homepage of the free website she'd signed up for a year back and never touched. She tried to envision Adventure Tenant panels filling the screen. She chose a background color—a deep burgundy that would complement a lot of his wardrobe if she ever colorized her drawings—and logged out. She needed to resolve some of her feelings about Joey before she shared Adventure Tenant with the world. And she should decide about the MFA program, too.

For years she'd been sure that, if circumstances permitted, the thing she most wanted to do was go back to school and get a masters in comics. Now though, school sounded confining. Like another pseudo-life, when what she needed was to live for real.

She set her laptop on the table next to her and stood, stretching.

"Everything okay?" Joey asked.

"Yep." *Just courting an existential crisis.*

He nodded and got back to work.

Eliza retrieved her drawing notebook from her nightstand. Her pen was missing—probably thanks to Bo. She opened a new pack of brush-tips and took her materials back to her seat near the fire.

She couldn't draw Adventure Tenant with Joey sitting right there, but she had another character she liked visiting when she was in an off mood—Easy.

Easy was a full-bodied woman with curly hair who

81

marched around cityscapes and famous historical places with a huge pair of shears in her right hand. She didn't talk. She didn't interact with almost anyone at all. She just walked her pissed-off walk, and every couple of panels she would stop and cut something out of the background with her shears, roll it up like a poster, tuck it under her arm, and march on.

On one level, Easy was clearly an expression of Eliza's own desperation to have a more interesting life. But she often surprised her, too—wanting things that Eliza herself never even thought about.

Tonight, Easy stomped down an idealized street in Victorian London. Maybe a movie set, maybe just fiction. She was, as usual, completely unfazed by the stares of the people around her. She cut out a gas street lamp, a watchman with a huge ring of keys at his waist, a horse-drawn cab, and part of a garden wall with a door in it and a vine growing over the top. She stomped past a bakery and cut out the entire window display of buns and cakes, then abruptly disappeared off-screen. Eliza drew a panel with the baker scratching his head in front of his wrecked shop, then capped her pen. Easy was such a weirdo.

Eliza felt better, though.

Setting her notebook and pen aside, she checked on her mother, who was still asleep.

Since Joey was still working, Eliza got her phone out and checked six versions of her horoscope while she warmed her butt in front of the fire. It was a mixed forecast for Scorpios, but one said explicitly that she should pay attention if her cautious inner voice told her to walk away from something mysterious. "Huh."

"What?"

"Uh, nothing."

Joey closed his laptop and turned his full attention on her. *Wowza.* Not drawing a desk-jockey version of Adventure

Tenant was a huge oversight on her part. At some point he'd slipped on a pair of reading glasses. They brought out the hint of salt-and-pepper at his temples and in the scruff on his chin, and magnified the intensity and intelligence of his gaze. Sometimes, Eliza realized, you wanted a man who looked like he could defend you from a bear with his fists. Sometimes you wanted a guy who could whip off his glasses and tell you he'd found a new deduction that would save you thousands on your income taxes.

Damn if Joey wasn't both, wrapped up in a hot, hot package.

"What on Earth are you thinking about over there?"

Eliza felt herself blush. What kind of expression was she wearing? Had she been drooling?

"Er, horoscopes."

"That must be some horoscope." Joey set aside his laptop. "Are you going to meet a hot guy? Inherit a fortune? Oh! Maybe you're going to marry a sexy billionaire."

Eliza's cheeks were flaming. *Asshole*. Had she just been crediting him with a powerful intellect? "It told me not to explore haunted rooms."

Joey blinked. "You're kidding. Right?"

"Well, it said to listen to my inner voice if it cautions me against exploring something mysterious."

He frowned. Maybe he thought she was fabricating a reason not to explore the hidden room together.

"I'll show you." Eliza sat next to him and pointed at the horoscope in question.

Joey leaned in to see the screen. He smelled fantastic. "Huh."

"Weird, right? It's like they know me."

Joey rubbed a hand over his stubble. "Okay, find mine."

"You want me to ask you what your sign is?"

He grinned. "It looks like you're going to have to."

Eliza sighed, but of course she was dying to know Joey's sign—and what their relationship prognosis might be. "Fine. What's your sign, bay-bee?" she drawled.

"Are you a pick-up artist? You do that so well."

"Just tell me your sign, buster."

Joey sat back and stretched his neck to either side, all insouciance. "Cancer."

Eliza clicked on the cancer icon and they read his fate with their shoulders pressed together: *While you've been taking a playful approach to life recently, today you are craving more intimacy and attachment.*

She felt Joey shift uncomfortably on the couch beside her. "Direct hit, huh? Time to settle down with your own billionaire?"

He cleared his throat. "Billionaires are mostly assholes, trust me. I have been thinking about making some changes, though."

Oh. Eliza's heart sank. He was probably leaving.

Joey picked up a pen and started weaving it through his fingers. "I'm working on getting out of the field. Taking a management position at my company."

"You said you were a security professional, but I don't know what that means. What do you do?"

He shrugged. "I keep people safe for money."

"So, you're a bodyguard?"

"Basically. Sometimes I gather intel or organize assets. But mostly I'm clearing rooms and scanning crowds. Watching video feeds. Standing by a door."

Eliza looked at the bruise on Joey's temple. "I've heard about you and doors."

He laughed. "Mostly it's boring as hell. But then I get a few days or a week off, and I can do anything I want. The job's over."

Turning to lean against the armrest, Eliza drew her knees

up to her chest and considered the man in front of her. "That's sounds great." Really great, in fact. Responsibilities that ended? Groovy. "Why stop?"

Joey pulled her feet into his lap. "I'm tired of... being invisible to the people I'm around the most. If you're good at your job, the clients forget you're there. I want to have a life where people don't forget about me."

Eliza's eyes filled. Her heart ached at the idea of wonderful, kind, compassionate Joey feeling invisible. "I don't forget about you."

Talk about an understatement.

Outside, the wind howled, lashing the house with rain.

Joey smiled at her. "I don't forget about you, either."

Eliza gulped. This felt big. Scary big. Should she tell him more? About how the thought of him got her through her worst days?

Maybe she should just crawl into his lap and kiss him.

The lights went out, plunging the room into darkness. Joey sighed, set her feet back on the couch, and got up to turn on the lanterns.

Oh well.

"Lizzy?" Minnie called from her bedroom. "Are you there?"

Crap. Eliza turned on her phone's flashlight app and got to her feet. "I'm coming, Mom."

～

*W*hen Eliza went to help Minnie light the kerosene lantern in her room, she found her mother's hands alarmingly cold. The new storm front had brought a relentless, freezing wind that was forcing its way into the cottage through every poorly sealed door and window. Eliza had been so enthralled by spending time with

Joey in front of the fire, she hadn't noticed how cold the house had gotten. Again.

God, what a shitty daughter she was.

She cranked Minnie's radiator up as high as it would go and convinced her to come out to the living room for dinner.

They ate cheese sandwiches on the couch, while Joey used empty tin cans and the oven rack to heat a pot of soup over the fire. Minnie was unusually content. "This is like camping," she said, picking stray crumbs from her lap. "Do you remember the trip we took to the redwoods when you were little?"

Eliza rarely remembered the things her mother wanted to talk about, but in this case she recalled being snuggled between her parents in a too-thin sleeping bag while rain sheeted off the tent. She'd been cold but thrilled by the novelty of sleeping outdoors. It was the last family trip before her dad got sick.

"It rained."

Minnie nodded, smiling sweetly. "But we were prepared. We were cold, but we didn't get wet. Except for your shoes. You left them outside."

Eliza grinned. "I remember that, too. Dad carried me to the car in the morning after I poured the water out of them."

A smile lingered on Minnie's face while she watched Joey tend the food, probably mostly due to her fond recollection of that camping trip. But maybe her mother was also happy to have company. Eliza didn't like to admit it, but she got tired of it being just the two of them all the time.

Maybe her mom chafed at the insularity, too.

It wasn't about having a *man* in the house, though. It was just the enlivening effect of opening their little circle of codependency to another human being.

"It's lovely to have a man in the house," Minnie whispered.

Eliza sighed. Okay, it was lovely to have a man in the house—this particular man, anyway.

She went with Minnie at bedtime to make sure her room was warm enough, and to switch out the kerosene lantern for a battery-powered one. She might find herself on the cusp of kissing Joey again, and she didn't want any interruptions this time.

Her mom was unusually cheerful, humming snippets of Beatles' hits while she pulled on wool socks and a flannel nightgown. Maybe they would have an uneventful night. Eliza's whole body got loose and warm at the thought of having hours of intimate time with Joey. Discovering how he kissed and what his hands felt like on her body when she wasn't wearing so many layers.

Stepping back into the hallway, she shined her flashlight toward her own bedroom door, just to make sure it was closed. The beam reflected ominously off the hall floor.

"Aw, shit."

Joey emerged from the bathroom, toothbrush in hand. "What's wrong?"

Wordlessly, Eliza stepped back so he could see the puddle of water on the floor. Then she ran the beam up to the ceiling where a new area of water damage had appeared halfway between her bedroom and Minnie's.

"That's not good."

Eliza groaned. "Joey," she whispered, "I can't move my mom out of her room. We have to stop that leak."

Joey had changed into plaid pajama pants and a fleece pullover. He did not look like a man who was anxious to tackle a home maintenance issue. Nevertheless, he pointed his own flashlight at the ceiling and studied the way the drips were tracing an uncannily straight line to Minnie's room. "Give me a sec to put my jeans back on."

CHAPTER 13

They stopped by Joey's apartment for tools and he grabbed his rain jacket. A puddle was beginning to spread across the second-floor landing between his place and the vacant rooms, making it feel a little like the great outdoors inside the cottage. The staircase might be a majestic waterfall by morning.

Eliza stopped between the puddle and the solarium door. "Would it be crazy if we went through the wall here instead of tearing open the hidden door?" She rapped experimentally on the corridor paneling, which flexed beneath her knuckles.

Joey gave the idea due consideration. If they breached the wall in the right place, it would be the most expedient way to get to the leak. But he wasn't sure he wanted a gaping hole in the wall right outside his apartment. Who knew what they might find in the hidden room?

Plus, they didn't need to release mold spores into the common areas.

"We'd better not."

Eliza sighed, not overly surprised. "Never mind. Let's do this. I'm wearing my Gloria Steinem socks. It will be fine."

Joey snorted. In his line of work, you inspired confidence in yourself and others with excellent research, meticulous planning, and having the right tools and personnel for the job. But maybe Gloria Steinem socks were the silver bullet in this case. "You're in charge of the light. I'm in charge of demolition." He handed her a bucket and a tarp to tuck under her arm. "And you can carry these."

"Onward." Eliza sketched a salute, flashlight to headlamp. She'd opted for redundancy in light sources, which was probably a good call.

Joey overdid the rubber doorstops. That was just common sense at this point. It was colder in the solarium than in the hallway, and colder still in the Egyptian room—like they were spiraling towards a crypt. When Eliza set the bucket and tarp next to the hidden door, her breath was visible in the beam of his headlamp. Each exhalation seemed to meet a barrier of cold hostility, dissipating in wisps and curls a couple of inches from her face. Joey himself felt like he was trying to breathe at altitude—like there wasn't enough oxygen.

The bad juju was really stirred up tonight.

He gauged a point of entry in a soft section of wall next to the door, told Eliza where to stand so she'd be out of the way of flying debris, and raised the mallet.

She gasped.

He turned. "What's wrong?"

Eliza glanced around the room, shining her dual beams into the corners. "It's just, I'm kind of afraid you're going to piss off the house and it will retaliate."

Joey let the mallet fall to his side. "Do you not want me to do this?"

She closed her eyes and took a deep breath. The flashlight trembled in her hand, but she held her ground. "I'm being crazy. Don't listen to me—just do it."

"You're not being crazy," he reassured her. But, not wanting to give Eliza time to conjure further doubts, he slammed the mallet into the wall.

It easily pierced it, releasing a dank, fetid odor that made Joey recoil. The smell wasn't as bad as a decaying body, but it was deeply unpleasant. He turned his head to the side and coughed.

Behind him, Eliza gagged.

"Are you okay? Do you need to leave?"

Eliza had pulled her sweatshirt cuff from her jacket sleeve and was using it to cover her mouth and nose. But she shook her head. "No. Keep going. It feels, I don't know… better in here. Like you lanced a wound."

Joey grimaced at that image, but he couldn't disagree. The atmosphere in the room felt less hostile now—as if maybe the house were resigned to this secret being revealed.

Or maybe it's regrouping. He hoped not.

"Okay. I'm on it."

It took him about five minutes to open a section big enough for them to walk through. The wall, it turned out, was not the product of quality workmanship.

"Come on," Joey said, kicking debris to the side. "Let's see what we've got here."

Eliza handed him the flashlight and he wrapped an arm around her waist so they could both lean in and see what was on the other side of the wall.

"Well…" Eliza began.

Joey hadn't actually thought much about what might be in the secret room—he'd kind of been focused on figuring out how the door might work. But he wouldn't have guessed this. Whatever this was.

As he'd imagined, the room was about six by nine feet. The only clear space was a narrow path leading from the door to a leather club chair that was cracked and peeling, and a spindly side table. Every other square inch of the room was stacked with magazines, books, calendars, posters, advertising flyers... paper ephemera of all kinds.

Which was all sopping wet and rotting, because somebody had installed an old sash window in the ceiling as a skylight, way back before vinyl flashing and building codes were a thing, and it was leaking around its entire perimeter.

"Oh, god," Eliza gasped.

"I know—what was this guy thinking? It looks like he plugged the gaps with rags." For the first time in his life, Joey made a tutting sound.

There was a pause. Then Eliza asked, "What are you talking about?"

"That lazy-assed attempt at a skylight. What are you talking about?"

"This," Eliza gestured at the piles in front of them. "All I can see are pin-up magazines. This is somebody's wank room or something. Ugh!"

Joey shone his light lower. Sure enough, the top layer was all scantily clad females frolicking and inviting the viewer to come hither. The images weren't very risqué by modern standards, but the sheer volume of material, and the fact that it was stockpiled in a secret room furnished with nothing but a chair and a smoking table, supported Eliza's theory. This was a vintage, er, man cave.

"This is one hell of a collection."

Eliza turned and stared at him in disbelief.

"One hell of a tasteless and offensive collection," he amended. "And definitely a health hazard. Can you imagine what all this wet, moldy paper weighs?"

"I guess we're going to find out, since we'll have to move a lot of it to get to the skylight."

～

*J*oey had everything they needed—trash bags, plastic gloves, masks—in his apartment. They were back in minutes, equipped for dirty, back-breaking work. "Test the floor before you put your full weight anywhere," he said.

"You got it."

Eliza worked feverishly, filling bags at a pace Joey found hard to match. He figured she was as motivated by the prospect of getting rid of the smut as she was by dealing with the skylight.

As if sensing his thoughts, she turned to him after she'd dragged a third heavy bag into the Egyptian room. "It's not because I object to this stuff on principle," she said, wiping her nose on the back of her sleeve. "I mean, a lot of it is just pattern books and advertisements and stuff." She held up an ancient *McCall's*, gritty with wet debris. The look that particular season had involved huge plumed hats, furs, and skimpy nighties. "It's the fact that somebody sort of entombed himself in here with them. And then left them to rot." Eliza tossed the magazine in a bag and cleared her throat. "Sorry. That got a little dramatic."

"No problem." Joey swung a bag through the doorway, then pulled off a glove to push his hair off his forehead. He was sweating, despite the cold. "Although, personally, I'm more disturbed by his remodeling strategies."

Eliza snorted and went back in for another load.

They got into a rhythm, shifting hundreds of pounds of *Police Gazette* magazines whose covers featured women in their unmentionables for some reason, stacks of girly postcards fused together by the damp, albums full of cigarette cards, and the occasional ruined letter. Beneath those, they found more general interest magazines—*The Saturday*

Evening Post, Harper's, Vogue, Cosmopolitan, Ladies' Home Journal...

It all went into trash bags.

Somewhere, a historian was weeping and didn't know why.

Finally, they were directly beneath the skylight. Joey had brought a stepladder. He checked that the floor was solid, then climbed up.

It looked like something—maybe a tree branch—had punched a hole in the roof. Instead of patching the hole, their not-so-handyman had hacked away at the opening until it was roughly square, then nailed an old window into the spot. *Genius.* Gaps around the window had been plugged with plaster-saturated rags and newspaper, half of which were now gone. It was a wonder this whole section of the house wasn't in the basement.

"I'm going to pull the window out," he told Eliza, "then tack down the tarp outside."

She looked horrified. "Outside? Please tell me you're not going out on the roof."

"Nah. I can do it from here. I might go out and fine tune things later."

"Okay. Tell me how to help."

"Stand by with the tarp. And be ready to call 911 if I drop this on my head."

"Funny."

Considering how much rain was pouring in around the window, it was surprisingly difficult to pry out. Securing the tarp was a complete shitshow. Eliza stood below him, providing an extra pair of hands. After twenty minutes of cussing and contorting himself, Joey finally succeeded in diverting most of the rain.

Eliza slid buckets into place while he dried his face and hair with a towel. "Will it hold?"

She was pale with exhaustion, so although Joey had some misgivings about the tarp resisting strong winds, he didn't share them. "It'll get us through the night. I'll check the buckets in the morning."

Eliza pulled off her gloves. "I'll come with you."

"Sure. If you're awake."

She laughed. "I have to get up anyway—make sure my mom is off to a good start."

"Do you ever get a break? Don't you have family that can help out?"

Eliza smiled tiredly. "Nope. It's just me and my mom."

"How long?"

"How long has she been this way?"

He nodded.

"She had her, uh, major breakdown eight years ago. She was in an institution for about six months. When she was ready to go home, I got rid of my apartment and moved in with her. So, since then." She shrugged.

Joey was stunned. Eliza watched over her mom as vigilantly as any security professional. Only she was doing it alone, twenty-four/seven. He would have lost his mind by now.

He sure as shit wouldn't still have a sense of humor.

"You are one badass woman," he told her, pushing her glasses back up her nose and smoothing her hair. He wanted to kiss her, but they were both exhausted, filthy, and chilled to the bone.

Eliza leaned into his touch and closed her eyes. After a moment, she abruptly roused herself and stepped away with a wane smile. "Sorry, but I need to go to bed."

CHAPTER 14

*S*unday dawned clear and cold. Or, at least, Eliza assumed it had. It was certainly sunny and freezing when she woke at ten.

"Oh, shit." She never slept this late—it didn't pay to let Minnie start her day in her own head. She vaulted out of bed, tripped over a magazine rack she didn't have to worry about in her bedroom, and fumbled into her robe and slippers. How could she be so clumsy and disoriented after six full hours of sleep?

The couch was vacant and Joey's stuff was folded neatly on a side table. Her heart stopped pounding quite so hard. If he was still here and hadn't woken her, Minnie was probably fine. She headed for the kitchen, then stopped short when she heard murmured voices coming from her mother's room. *Huh?*

Joey was comfortably sprawled in Minnie's green Naugahyde recliner—the one that was usually stacked high with craft materials, and woe be unto anyone who touched them. He had his laptop out and was absentmindedly scrolling and clicking while he carried on a conversation with Minnie, who was knitting next to the window.

Minnie started giggling under her breath at something Joey said, and Eliza felt her jaw drop. When was the last time her mother had giggled?

She walked in and perched on the corner of the bed. There was a breakfast tray near the footboard, nestled in amongst bags of yarn and fabric. She lifted the lid on a small saucepan. "Hot chocolate?"

Joey set his computer aside and reached for the pan. "Yeah, but it's cold. I'll go warm it up."

Eliza looked around. "No power still?"

He shook his head. "No, but I can light a burner on the stove."

Minnie stopped knitting and glanced over. "He made toast on the stovetop with that camping thingy. It was surprisingly normal."

Eliza rose to follow Joey to the kitchen. "I would take some surprisingly normal toast."

~

*T*he kitchen was dark and freezing. "You don't have to be here," Joey told her. "I'll bring it to you."

"I'm fine. I want to see you use the camp toaster." Also, she wanted to ask him about her mom's morning and find out if he'd checked the buckets.

Possibly, she also wanted to bask in the sight of a handsome, competent, gainfully-employed man making her a primitive breakfast over an open flame. She had so few pleasures in her life at the moment. A tiny voice in her head warned that she was in danger of never having a purely erotic fantasy again if she kept fawning over Joey performing domestic miracles.

She was surprisingly fine with that.

They talked while he worked at the stove. He added more milk and cocoa to the pan and set it on low. In the meantime, he had four pieces of bread toasting on another burner. The camp toaster was something Eliza and her mom had found at the back of one of the cupboards when they moved in. Eliza had thought it was a bizarre cheese grater until Pinterest set her straight.

"What are the chances I'd burn myself using that thing?" she asked, watching as Joey turned the slices of bread around with a fork. She envisioned the contraption tipping over and herself trying to catch it with bare hands.

He grinned at her over his shoulder. "It'll get you eventually. This device was not invented with safety in mind."

She propped her chin in her hands, elbows resting on the tabletop. "You seem to be doing okay."

"This isn't my first rodeo with one of these things—I've cooked in camping conditions all over the world."

Eliza sighed. "That is so sexy."

Oh, crap.

Joey turned to look at her, a piece of toast dangling at the end of his fork. "Did you just say camp cooking is sexy?"

Eliza's cheeks were flaming. *Stupid mouth.* "Apparently, I did."

He pondered that for a moment. "Can you tell me what, specifically, is sexy about it? Because I'd like to be able to reproduce that effect."

She smiled and shrugged. "I guess it's the fact that not only will you cook for me, you're capable of doing it in primitive conditions. I'm not sure other women would be affected in the same way—it's been a very long time since anyone has made me breakfast."

"I don't care about other women," Joey said, and Eliza felt suddenly warmer.

He poured the hot chocolate into a mug and handed it to her. "Listen, the toast is going to be stone cold in seconds once it comes off the grill, so be ready to move fast when I tell you to, okay? I'll butter it and we'll rendezvous in your mom's room."

Just like that, he turns off his emotions and focuses on the job, Eliza thought. *Hot.* Too bad they were rushing to her mom's room. That was just tragic.

~

*J*oey worked on his laptop while Eliza ate her breakfast and enjoyed the shit out of not being the sole responsible party in the room.

According to Joey, Minnie had been up since dawn, knitting like a fiend. She'd eaten the food he'd put together and asked him if he'd ever been to Nepal. Coincidentally, Joey *had* been to Nepal, and they'd had a lengthy conversation about Nepalese cuisine.

Eliza was both delighted and troubled by her mother's rapport with Joey. It was great to see them enjoying each other's company, but it seemed to confirm she'd made the wrong choice in moving them to the cottage.

At the time, Minnie's mental health had been stable and they'd both been frustrated with living in a small, dark apartment where the two of them vied daily for workspace at the kitchen table.

Eliza had searched rental listings every day for months, looking for a bigger place with better light that they could afford. It had to be within a half-hour's drive of Minnie's doctor and psychiatrist—that was non-negotiable.

Chaste Tree Cottage came up in every online search, but Eliza ignored it. She was not taking her mother to live in the middle of nowhere.

That would be ridiculous.

Yet, the old Victorian gradually wormed its way into her consciousness. Somehow she saved it to her "favorites" list by accident. Afterwards, every time she clicked on another more reasonable property, the site offered a helpful side-by-side comparison with Chaste Tree Cottage. Somehow, the cottage always came out ahead—greater square footage, affordable rent, three acres of undeveloped woodland criss-crossed by walking paths, river access.

Eliza started dreaming about living there. In her dreams, it was always sunny and her mother was always happy. On one occasion, her dream cats kept climbing into the washing machine, narrowly avoiding death by spin-cycle. The dream washer was a new, front-loading machine though, and the cats didn't die, so she convinced herself it was a good omen.

New appliances were a huge selling point.

She'd first visited on a gorgeous spring day, eighteen months prior, when all the trees in the abandoned orchard behind the cottage were in bloom. The sky was cloudless, the house fairly glowed with grace and good cheer, and Doug was absent—probably in rehab, but maybe his uncle Ray had simply arranged for him to take a day trip.

In any case, she'd been smitten, and a week later she was putting the utilities in her name.

Minnie threw herself into creating items for her Etsy shop during the first few months they were there. She took long walks around the property and came back radiant. Her appetite was excellent and she took care with her appearance.

Eliza found herself giddy with relief, and she got a hell of a lot of grant writing done. She bolstered her MFA savings and began researching programs. She'd been toying with the idea of starting a webcomic for a few years, but her attempts to draw something that wasn't crazily self-indulgent always bored her after a few panels. Realistically, she was probably lacking inspiration because of her cloistered lifestyle. But she told herself that what she was missing was formal training.

Things had deteriorated over the last summer. As the weather grew warmer, Minnie's anxiety came creeping back. Her psychiatrist adjusted her medication, but she never quite recovered the equilibrium she'd enjoyed when they first moved to the cottage.

More worrisome, there were occasionally days when she was apathetic, and Eliza had to remind her to eat. Was it just the anxiety? A little depression?

Or was it something worse?

Because they'd been through much, much worse.

Eliza set the rest of her toast on her plate and wiped the crumbs off her fingers, careful not to get any on the blankets. Maybe it was the isolation. Maybe Minnie would stop backsliding if she had a social life.

All the more reason to pull the plug on this rural-living experiment.

~

*E*liza excused herself to get dressed after she'd eaten. When she came out of the bathroom, Minnie was still working in her room, but Joey was gone.

Rather than ask her mother where he was and risk upsetting her, Eliza went back to the living room and pulled out a pen, a pad of paper, and her plastic filing box. Based on the state of the secret room alone, it was clear that she needed to get her little family the hell out of here. Running away screaming was the most appealing strategy, but for Minnie's sake she needed to ignore the creepy shit and approach this logically.

Pushing her filled drawing notebooks to the back of the

box, she dug out a folder containing the advertisement for the resident manager position at the cottage and her contract. If she was going to bail on her apartment and her job, she'd better make sure she left with her reputation intact. Dos Alamos was a small pond, and the Effinhams were big fish.

Rereading the job description, she marveled at both the Effinhams' cheek and her own gullibility: *advance your career opportunities... looking for entrepreneurial spirit... join our team... knowledge of state fair-housing laws expected... exceptional ability to resolve unique problems.*

"What a sucker. What the hell was I thinking?" At the time, she'd found the ambitious language kind of charming. Now it seemed purely delusional, and she already had more than enough delusional thinking in her life, thank you very much.

Bo wandered over and jumped in her lap. Eliza reorganized her materials to accommodate him and moved on to her contract, which was clearly a boilerplate document somebody had copied from the internet. Some of the responsibilities were applicable—collect rent, show apartments to potential renters, pay utilities, maintain resident files, address maintenance issues.

Other duties were pure fantasy. Maintain waiting list? Supervise on-site staff? Provide event support for community activities? Maintain suggestion box?

Ha.

There was no staff, apart from herself. Joey would definitely not be interested in taking part in community activities with Doug, and Doug didn't need a special box for suggestions—he just harassed her on the phone and in person when he wanted something.

Still, she'd done a competent job on most counts. The house was falling down around them, but not for lack of effort on her part. There were only so many maintenance expenses you could pay out of the rent money when the rent was that far below market.

She made sure the financial files were up to date, then went through the tenant records. Joey's file consisted of a pay stub, a copy of his deposit check, his rental application, and his lease. Four pieces of paper.

Eliza had three folders for Doug. The first held his lease and a note from the late Mrs. Effinham indicating that Doug, being family, didn't have to provide proof of employment, references, a deposit check, or an application. "And he definitely didn't undergo a background check," Eliza muttered, putting the file back.

The second folder was about an inch thick and contained documentation of every professional interaction Eliza had ever had with Doug—mostly her responses to maintenance requests and repeated efforts to collect at least a portion of the nominal rent he was supposed to pay. The file didn't paint a pretty picture of either the cottage or Doug, but everything was in order.

File number three was a log of the most egregious incidences of harassment Doug had perpetrated against Eliza and her mother since they'd moved in. None were serious enough alone to warrant reporting, but if Doug ever crossed the line, she wanted to have documentation of his prior behavior. She wasn't entirely sure where that line was, but she figured she'd know it when she saw it.

She moved the harassment folder into her personal section and put a check next to the "files" entry on her task list.

The maintenance issues still nagged, though.

Eliza scratched and petted Bo until black-and-white fur blanketed her thighs, the paperwork, and large swaths of couch cushion. She would call a couple of contractors to walk through the house and bid on the most critical repairs, submit their bids to the estate, and leave the rest in their hands.

One way or another, she was going to get her mom and the cats out of here. It was probably time to bite the bullet and dip into her MFA savings. So far she hadn't touched that money because there wasn't enough to pay for a long-term lifestyle upgrade. With everything that was happening, a short-term solution sounded just fine.

CHAPTER 15

Once Eliza had eaten, Joey headed to town for supplies—more cans of soup, maybe some chili. Stuff they could heat in a pot for a nutritious, one-dish meal. At least one more storm was supposed to blow in before the end of the week, and the Philips ladies' emergency rations were minimal, consisting primarily of low-sodium diced tomatoes, garbanzo beans, and pears in syrup.

Instead of turning toward Dos Alamos when he got to the highway, Joey sat and drummed his fingers on the steering wheel, letting the truck's engine idle. After days of being cooped up in the cottage, he wanted to go somewhere where there was a little hustle and bustle. Dos Alamos would be dead on this cold, dark day. He turned south and put a call through to Marco.

"Hey, what's up?" It sounded like Marco was also driving.

"Where are you?"

"Running errands for my little brother." Marco's brother, Tomás, was sort of a suburban recluse. Joey had only met him once, in passing, at a family birthday party. He seemed normal enough, if quiet—had a degree in mathematics and worked from home editing academic articles. Marco drove to Novato a few times a month to check in and take care of stuff Tomás wouldn't do for himself—oil changes, appliance repair, conversations with the neighbors.

"Do you have time to meet for lunch?" Joey asked. He felt guilty as fuck for going out to a restaurant while Eliza and her mom ate like refugees back at the cottage, but he needed a burger. Possibly a steak. Something manly and robust.

~

They met at a family-style Mexican place in a strip mall. Neither of them said much until they'd ordered, collected their beers, and demolished two baskets of chips and salsa.

Finally, Marco leaned back and asked, "How are things at the cottage?"

Joey snorted. "Suboptimal."

"I'd never have guessed. What now?"

"Flood. Pestilence." Joey took a long pull off his beer. "Famine, if I don't get to Costco today." He briefed Marco on the power outages, the leak, and their search for its origin. He didn't mention the self-closing and locking doors.

Marco shook his head. "Who cares where the water is coming from? You need to pack your shit and move out. Black mold is nothing to fuck around with."

Joey shifted in his seat. "I'm working on it."

"But?" Their food arrived. Marco doctored his with salt and a worrisome quantity of the house hot sauce.

Joey savored the first bite of his carnitas taco. It would have tasted better if he didn't know that Eliza was probably eating a peanut butter sandwich standing up while figuring out which catastrophe to deal with next. "I haven't told Eliza I'm looking for a new place. It's shitty timing, moving out when the cottage is giving her so much trouble. And I don't like the idea of her living there alone."

"She has her mom."

Joey grunted. "Minnie's great. Really. But she's a liability more than an asset."

"She seems like a nice lady." Marco scooped beans and sour cream onto a chip and managed to look thoughtful while he chewed.

"She's a very nice lady." Joey took a long pull on his beer. "But she's a very nice lady with significant mental health problems."

"Like what?"

"Anxiety, for sure. But there's something else. She's off in her own little world a lot of the time. And the way Eliza watches her…"

"Yeah?"

Joey pushed his plastic basket away. "She's scared. Things must have been really bad at some point."

His friend frowned and picked at the label on his beer bottle. Maybe he was thinking about the many scared women they'd protected over the years. Most clients were easy to hand off to the next detail. Others, not so much.

"You think Minnie's dangerous?"

"No." Joey made himself pause and do an objective assessment. "I doubt she's a threat to others. But she might be a danger to herself."

The guy behind the counter put out a last call for the spiced coffee steeping in a clay pot on the counter. Marco raised his hand and went to collect two steaming to-go cups and a steel pitcher of cream. The guy objected when Marco pulled out his wallet, saying the dregs were strong enough to give them heart attacks—that seemed to be the gist of the conversation, anyway. Marco said something about testicles (possibly), put a bill in the tip jar, and brought the potentially fatal coffee back to the table.

His expression turned speculative as he loaded Joey's coffee with cream and slid it to him. "How's the report coming? You itching to get back in the field yet?"

"No. I like the research. It's interesting." Joey took a sip and felt his heart rate jump immediately.

"So you wouldn't be interested in taking a new assignment?"

Joey had to suppress his conditioned response to the words *new assignment*. His mind and heart were on the same page: no more fieldwork. But he'd involuntarily pinned on the location of his gear bag, ready to go wheels-up at a moment's notice. "Nope."

Marco must have sensed a minute hesitation. "That guy in Alabama is running for congress again. He asked for you specifically. There's a nice bonus on the table."

Joey remembered the guy in Alabama very well, and the memory was enough to kill his conditioning dead. "No fucking way. That guy deserves to get popped."

"You could use the bonus money as a loan to get the Philips ladies into a better place. Walk away with an easy conscience."

Under no circumstances was he walking away. "I said no."

Marco smirked. "Got it. You have till Monday to change your mind."

~

*J*oey was still agitated when he passed the Dos Alamos city limit sign. The caffeine was messing with him, but more unsettling was the realization that he'd meant what he told Marco—he had no intention of walking away from Eliza.

He didn't know what that meant for his plans. Somehow, he'd never considered the specifics of them being together. Living together. When he'd had idle thoughts about doing the family thing, he'd envisioned a nice ranch-style house somewhere with a big yard and nice neighbors. But the places he'd applied for in town were all lofts—kind of on the industrial side. Open floor plans, high ceilings, and not a mother-in-law unit in sight.

At the local Costco, Joey went straight to the grocery section and filled his cart with disaster essentials: cans of beef chili, boxed mac 'n cheese, trail mix, peanut butter cookies, and instant coffee. He added some shelf-stable bricks of vegetable soup and a two-pack of cereal, in case Eliza and her mom had healthier preferences. In the bakery section he tossed French bread, cornbread, and brownies in the cart. He swung by the bulk beverage aisle for a couple cases of water and a box of individual servings of milk. He was almost to the registers when he turned around and went back for cat litter, cat food, and a pair of work gloves for Eliza.

Standing in line behind an elderly couple bickering about cholesterol levels, Joey probed his feelings about turning down the new field assignment. What if it had been for a client he liked? Would that have made a difference? How would he have felt, returning the report files to Brian Griffin and abandoning that project?

Shitty. That's how he'd feel.

The line moved forward and Joey put his smaller items on the conveyor belt. The couple in front of him was paying with a combination of gift cards and small denomination bills. Mostly ones. They were buying Metamucil, Ensure, bananas, drumsticks, and a shit ton of assorted chocolates. Plus, three tiny fancy dresses for granddaughters or maybe great-granddaughters.

Oddly, Joey had no trouble picturing being old with Eliza.

(Well, older, anyway. Did anyone ever picture themselves being as old as the couple at the register?) He just couldn't get a handle on how they would get from here to there. How did they date and get through the major life changes they both had on the horizon? Would Eliza even be willing to try? Compromise would be inevitable, and there weren't too many areas in Eliza's life where she could compromise. She and her mom were already living too close to the edge.

Joey paid, got some cash back to bolster his emergency stash, and picked up a pizza to take back to the cottage. It wasn't carnitas tacos, but it made him feel marginally less guilty about sneaking off for a restaurant lunch while Eliza battled black mold and structural damage out in the hinterlands.

~

*D*riving through Dos Alamos proper, Joey detoured to have another look at the apartment he was most interested in—an industrial conversion on the top floor of an old dried-fruit packing plant from the late nineteenth century. It was more space than he needed, and the second floor was slated to have a business of some sort go in before long, so it might be noisy during the day. But it had lots of light and room to breathe. Most importantly, it was good, solid construction, recently retrofitted. New electrical. New plumbing...

What would he do if the guy sent him a lease to sign?

Joey idled across the street for a couple of minutes, gazing at the brick façade where you could still make out hints of fancy lettering. Something "& Co." He checked his phone for messages. Nothing. No news was probably good news where Eliza was concerned. Did he want to hear from the property management company? Realistically, none of them could stay at the cottage much longer, so somebody ought to have decent housing lined up.

The drive back was tedious, since the main route was still closed. Slowing for every twist and turn made it feel like a freaking expedition to get back to Eliza and her mom. God forbid they have a medical emergency before the good road opened again—you literally couldn't make a fast trip to town to save your life.

Maybe it was because Joey had spent the better part of the day out in civilization eating tacos and shopping at Costco, but he was keenly aware of the trees closing in around him, blocking the light. In summer, this was a popular scenic drive. Now it was like driving through a tunnel of gnarled, clawed hands.

He gave the pizza box a shake and lifted the lid so its heady perfume filled the interior of his truck. How bad could things get when you had pizza within reach?

CHAPTER 16

*T*he sun was already low in the sky when Joey got back. The solarium windows glowed throbbing pink with the light of sunset. He grabbed the pizza and the flat of chili—unloading the rest could wait till after dinner.

His breath ghosted in front of him as he crossed the yard. He would be surprised if it didn't freeze during the night. He tried the light switch in the foyer. Nothing. The battery backup on the thermostat was working though, because the display was scrolling a message about the kids' room being unoccupied.

As if anyone would live in the cottage with kids. You'd have to be crazy to bring kids into this house.

Joey was unlocking Eliza's door when Doug stepped out of his apartment. *I must really be off my game.* He'd almost forgotten about Doug over the last few days, and he didn't forget about people he didn't trust. Especially when they lived within feet of his residence.

He turned to find the other man staring at him.

"Can I help you?"

Doug shrugged. "My apartment's cold."

111

"Join the club, buddy. Eliza has a call in to somebody to look at the boiler tomorrow." Joey wasn't one hundred percent sure that was the case, but Doug didn't need to know that.

The guy's gaze fixed on the food. "Whatcha got there?"

"Supplies." In the interest of getting Doug to go back inside his apartment, he asked, "Do you have food for tonight?"

He could spare some chili.

Doug shrugged again. "Doritos. Cereal."

"Jesus." Joey pierced the plastic overwrap and pulled out a can. "Take this. It'll go great with the chips."

Doug looked doubtfully at the chili, then eyed the pizza like he was considering murdering Joey for it.

"Hey." Joey channeled his mom's cop voice. "You have a nice evening, now, okay? Stay safe."

Doug momentarily shifted his attention to Joey's chin, then took the chili, went back into his place and slammed the door.

Psycho.

~

*H*e dropped off the food in the kitchen and looked for Eliza. The only one home was Minnie, who was listening to a Walkman. *Talk about a blast from the past.* She was keeping time with her foot while she stared out the window, looking content, so he didn't bother her with questions about where her daughter was.

He couldn't imagine why Eliza would have gone back upstairs by herself, but that was the next logical place to look.

When he stepped into the solarium, he called out so she would know he was there.

A startled squeak came from the Egyptian room. "Joey?"

"Yeah, it's me," he said, heading her way. It felt normal in the solarium now—no inexplicable temperature fluctuations or hostile vibes. Just dust and the same proliferation of cobwebs.

He whistled in appreciation when he saw what Eliza had accomplished. "Wow. All I did today was buy food."

Most of the magazine collection had been bagged and dragged into the Egyptian room. All the wall debris was cleaned up, including the big piece of paneling, which she must have cut into pieces. The buckets had been emptied and replaced under the skylight. Eliza looked exhausted, and her hair clung to her cheeks in sweaty tendrils, but she surveyed her work with satisfaction. "I have to get contractors out here to bid on repairs, so I'm clearing space for them to look around."

"Do you think the estate will cough up the money?" Maybe it was time to stage a gentle intervention with Eliza vis-à-vis the cottage's likely future. Or lack thereof.

She shook her head. "No, but I still have to go through the motions, you know?" She bit her lip, then said, "I decided... I really have to get my mom out of here. Find a new place for us to live."

She looked like she was worried about letting Joey down by saying that.

He closed the distance between them and, after a moment's consideration, pushed the bandana she was wearing back a little so he could kiss the top of her head. Most of the rest of her was coated in mold dust. "That's a really good idea."

"You don't think I'm... I don't know, being flaky?"

Joey snorted. "I've never met anyone less flaky in my life. Come on." He put an arm around her shoulders and she relaxed against him, looking around the space. The sun had set, the last rosy glow quickly disappearing from the sky. Eliza had hung two lanterns from nails in the secret room and set a third on the floor in the Egyptian room, but without any daylight coming in, it would be too dark to work.

Plus, a restless, irritated energy seemed to be creeping into the space as the light fled. Outside, the wind picked up, sending something sliding down the roof above their heads with a skittering, scraping sound, like rodent claws.

Under his arm, Eliza shivered.

"I've got pizza waiting downstairs," he said, rubbing her arm briskly. "Why don't you call it a day?"

Eliza groaned. "Yes, please. That's the best invitation I've had in forever."

While she took off her gloves and wiped her face and hands with a wet wipe, Joey went to get the lanterns. He was reaching for the second one when the floor just beyond the club chair gave way beneath his right foot. Both lanterns clattered to the ground as he flung his arms out for balance.

Behind him, Eliza screamed.

"It's okay," he called back over his shoulder. His right leg had disappeared to mid-thigh, but the wood under his left foot seemed to be holding.

Eliza approached carefully, stopping before she got to the most damaged part of the floor. "How can I help?" She crouched and held the third lantern aloft so they could both see what was happening.

Moving as little as possible, Joey tried to extract his leg from the floor. He couldn't get the necessary leverage without shifting his mass over the rotted boards. His left foot was screaming under the pressure of bearing too much weight—a miserable reminder he was supposedly on medical leave. "Do you have a board or a ladder around here? Something we can lay across the floor?"

Eliza looked around the room, as if hoping there might be something there she'd missed. "I think there are some boards in the shed."

He sat back on his haunches, trying to find a better position, and shook his head. "I don't want you out there in the dark. Can you think of anything else?"

"What about the ironing board in the laundry room?"

"That might work." The lanterns Joey had dropped were broken. "Take that one with you," he said, tilting his head at the kerosene lamp in Eliza's hand.

She looked torn. "I don't have a flashlight or anything to leave you. You'll be in the dark while I'm gone."

Joey gave her what he hoped was a reassuring smile. "I'll be fine." His body was telling him this was not a position he could maintain for long, but, yeah, he'd be fine.

"Okay. I'll hurry. Don't move," she added with a weak grin.

Joey listened to her footsteps fade away. The dark was more complete than he'd expected. Belatedly, he remembered that his phone was in his hip pocket. It had a flashlight feature, but he would have to shift his weight to just one hand and his bum foot to reach it. He wasn't sure he wanted to do that. He could handle the dark.

He adjusted the position of his hands, regretting leaving his gloves in the truck. The floor seemed unnaturally cold. The part of his leg that had disappeared through the floor was disconcertingly numb. A rush of drops fell from the skylight into one of the buckets, startling him and making him jerk back against his trapped leg.

Keep it together. Your brain's playing tricks.

A frigid gust of air moved between Joey's legs and he cringed, his dick shrinking into his body. *Bad touch. Bad juju.*

He was not comfortable with this.

CHAPTER 17

*E*liza rushed down the stairs, visions of Joey being eaten alive by the house making her heart pound. Hadn't she read a book like that once? What if she got back upstairs and the only sign Joey had ever existed was his cell phone lying abandoned on the floor? She was so focused on imagining horrifying supernatural threats that she didn't see Doug until he blocked her path in front of the laundry room.

"Hey," he slurred. He'd obviously been drinking, although his breath also reeked of chili. "Where're ya goin'?"

Eliza eyed him, trying to decide if she would be better off ignoring him or placating him with a response. Drunk Doug was usually easy enough to redirect, and she didn't have time for him to get belligerent—not with Joey disappearing into the floor upstairs.

"To the laundry room."

He leered and chuckled. "Oh, yeah? What's in the laundry room, baby?"

Ugh. "An ironing board."

She tried to move around him, but he pivoted and backed her into the side of the staircase. "Don't leave. I know you want me." He was breathing heavily. Aroused? Or just unaccustomed to this much activity?

"Get away from me. I'm serious, Doug. I don't have time for your bullshit."

He grinned and grabbed her arm, giving it a bruising squeeze. His face was inches from hers. "*Bullshit?* That's not a nice word for a lady to say. Ladies should say *yeah, baby, give it to me, uh-huh…*"

Doug's thrusting belly brushed against Eliza's hip and she finally snapped, kneeing him in the balls as hard as she could.

The crotch of his sweatpants, stretched tightly between his thighs, kept the full force of her knee from reaching its target. Nevertheless, he yelped and fell back on his ass at her feet. Eliza brought her arms up and adjusted her stance, ready to fend him off if he came at her again. Her heart was racing, the thudding of her pulse almost violent enough to make her nauseous. Or maybe that was the adrenaline.

Doug didn't make any attempt to get up.

"Don't you ever," *gasp*, "come near me," *gasp*, "again." Fighting a panic attack, or an asthma attack—whatever this was—Eliza stepped shakily over his right leg. "You hear me?"

Doug just stared at her blankly. He probably wouldn't remember anything about this confrontation in the morning, unless his bruised testicles jogged his memory.

She got the ironing board from behind the laundry room door and headed back toward the stairs. Doug was trying to roll to his side, so she used the ironing board to nudge him flat on his back again. Just to be on the safe side.

In the foyer, the thermostat, by rare coincidence, was flashing the words, *Power Restore.*

Eliza laughed, hysteria tinging her voice. *That's right, fucker. I'm in charge.*

*J*oey didn't say "thank god you're here" when she got back, but he exhaled like he'd been holding his breath the entire time Eliza was gone. His skin looked clammy in the flickering lantern light, and his body shook with the effort of keeping his weight away from the rotted portion of the floor.

She approached cautiously, ironing board at the ready. "You want me to slide this in front of you, right?"

He nodded. "In front of my leg. If that doesn't work, I'll try with it on the left side of my body."

She slid the ironing board into place and scooted back a couple feet. Joey really looked spooked. Maybe a distraction was in order. "So, I probably just lost my job."

Joey continued working out the placement of his hands on the board and tugging experimentally at his leg, but he glanced her way. "What? Why?"

"I kicked Doug in the nuts. You know he's related to the Effinham family, right? Otherwise, he wouldn't be here."

Joey stopped looking freaked out, so points to her for that.

"What did he do? *What did that piece of shit do?*" The tendons in Joey's neck popped into even greater relief and he tore his leg out of the floor, sending the ironing board skidding away in a cloud of splinters. Suddenly, he was looming protectively over her.

It was a nice view. She needed him not to murder Doug, though.

She got to her feet and stepped into Joey's personal space. "I'm fine."

He was breathing hard. His eyes were hard. Eliza wondered what else was hard. Once again, she realized she'd missed the mark with Adventure Tenant. Her fictional version of Joey was clever and fearless, but always jovial and suave. This Joey radiated a primitive brutality that made her gut clench and her skin prickle. But definitely not in a bad way.

After a moment, he tilted his head to scent along her neck, then pressed his cheek to hers.

They were barely touching, yet it was the single most erotic experience of her life. By far.

Finally, he relaxed minutely. "You're fine. Although," he turned away to sneeze, "I think you've reached your limit for exposure to mold dust."

Eliza laughed. "I definitely have." She cupped his face in her hands, studying him. He was fine, too. "Are you ready to get out of here?" A chill current of air had begun wrapping itself around them, and since the moment Joey had touched her, a giddy excitement had been building in the room.

"Let's go."

~

They found Doug passed out on the floor where Eliza had left him, his hands slackly covering his crotch. "Piece of shit," Joey reiterated. He nudged Eliza toward her apartment. "Go lock yourself in. I'm going to haul his sorry ass back into his place."

Joey still looked homicidal, and Eliza considered warning him not to do anything rash. But ultimately, she trusted him to be smart. "Okay."

Leaving the lantern on the newel post at the bottom of the stairs, she went inside and closed the door, watching through the peephole as Joey stared distastefully at Doug for a moment before grabbing him under the armpits and dragging him into his front hall.

Joey reappeared less than a minute later without

reddened knuckles or blood on his hands, which was for the best. Obviously.

Eliza opened the door for him and he stepped in, lantern in hand, looking intense and remote. Then he made eye contact with her and his expression shifted to intense and very, *very* present.

She liked that a lot better.

Then he spoke. "You can't keep living here, Eliza."

"I beg your pardon?" She shut and locked the door, grabbed Joey's wrist, and lifted the lantern closer to his face.

He sighed. "It's not safe for you to stay here. Even if you get the sheriff to bring Doug up on charges, odds are he'll be back here the next day. I'm going back to work soon. You and your mom will be alone out here with him."

"Do you think I don't know that?" She let go of Joey's arm and pulled the bandana out of her hair in annoyance, tossing it toward the coatrack. "We can't just leave, though."

Joey opened his mouth to protest, but she spoke over him.

"Look, I'm supposed to give three-months notice if I'm going to move out. I may need a good reference from the Effinhams, so I'm going to stay until I can come to an agreement with them."

Joey set the lantern on the mail table and leaned against the wall, arms folded. "Any other objections?"

"Yes!" She folded her arms, too. "Minnie and I don't have the kind of savings and credit we'd need to move on short notice. It'll take a miracle to find a new place we can afford as it is, and I can't take my mom somewhere temporary and put her through two moves, Joey. I just can't."

He was shaking his head. "Look, you have grounds for terminating your contract early."

Eliza forced herself to take a deep breath. "You're upset…"

"Damn right, I'm upset! You're not?"

"Of course I am! Although," she felt compelled to add, "I did enjoy kicking Doug in the balls."

Joey cracked a smile.

Her annoyance faded. "I'm being pragmatic, Joey. I'll call a lawyer and get strongly worded letters sent to Doug and the Effinham estate if they're not reasonable, but I can't just grab my mother and run."

He straightened and began to pace, cussing under his breath. He was adorable, all worked up on her behalf. "Okay, let's compromise…"

"Joey, I don't need to compromise with you about this—it's my life."

He rubbed at a spot in the middle of his forehead. She was no doubt giving him a migraine. She felt bad about that—he was just trying to do his thing. Protect her. She wasn't like his clients, though. She didn't have limitless resources to throw at this problem.

He came to a stop in front of her and straightened her glasses, which were catywampus again. "Look, we're friends, right?"

Where was he going with this? For a moment, she'd been sure she had the upper hand. "Yes," she agreed warily.

"And as your friend, I'm entitled to worry about you, wouldn't you say?"

She searched his face, looking for some kind of clue. His expression was carefully blank. "Sure. You can worry about me."

"And, as your friend, I'm probably allowed to make suggestions when you find yourself in a difficult situation."

Eliza shrugged. "You can make suggestions. I don't have to take them."

Joey's posture relaxed, like he knew he was going to get his way. She should have been exasperated, but instead she was intrigued. She'd seen a lot of iterations of her hot neighbor over the last few days. Which Joey was this?

He sidled further into her personal space and stroked her cheek gently with a fingertip. Maybe he was going with a Lothario approach. Her lady bits gave an anticipatory throb.

"Do you respect me, Eliza?"

"What?" Okay, maybe not Lothario.

"Do you respect me? It's a straightforward question."

She didn't know Joey very well, in truth, but when she consulted her gut, the answer was right there. "Yes, I respect you. You're a decent guy."

He smiled wryly at the faint praise. "So, even though you've never seen me at work, hopefully you'll believe me when I tell you I'm very, very good at what I do." He swiped his thumb over her lower lip. "Can you believe me, Eliza?"

The man had a point. Maybe she shouldn't be too hasty about spurning the advice of the resident bodyguard.

Executive security professional.

Whatever.

"I believe you." Her voice quavered. She felt vaguely embarrassed. Or maybe that was arousal. Either way, heat rushed to her face.

Joey seemed transfixed by the color staining her cheeks, his gaze shifting from one cheek to the other. It didn't stop him from carrying on in a measured tone. "Doug has been harassing you since the beginning, hasn't he?"

Eliza dropped her gaze and hooked her index fingers through Joey's belt loops. "Yeah. I've documented it all, but nothing on its own was worth reporting."

"That's good—the documentation, I mean." Joey settled his hands at her hips. "But that's for later. Right now, you need to recognize that Doug's behavior is escalating. Since we don't know what triggered the escalation, whatever strategy you had for dealing with him before is no longer valid. You can't assume he's going to be where you expect him to be, or do what you expect him to do."

Eliza swallowed hard. She'd been thinking along exactly those lines—she could handle another few weeks of living across the hall from Doug, because she knew how to deal with him.

She could see the flaw in that logic.

Joey wasn't done annihilating her remaining sense of security, though. "You can't count on the lighting in this building. You're isolated out here. The doors only lock when they feel like it." He cleared his throat. "Literally. Doug knows your mom is vulnerable. If you think he won't hurt her to get to you, you're wrong."

Eliza shivered and wrapped her arms tight around herself. The wave of empowerment she'd been riding evaporated, leaving her hollow with fear instead. "You're being kind of a bastard, Joey."

"Sorry, honey." He lifted a hand to gently smooth her hair back. "I'm scared for you. I look at you and your mom living out here at the cottage, and I see nothing but threats and safety issues. Everything about this place is a disaster waiting to happen."

Despite being sort of pissed at him, Eliza leaned in to rest her forehead on Joey's chest. He was warm and alive, and although she didn't appreciate having her nose rubbed in her poor choice of living arrangements, she was glad he was there.

"That was some tough love, Joey." She wrapped her arms around his waist and pressed her cheek to his chest, listening to the thump of his heart under her ear. This, at least, worked —the way they fit together, the heat between them. "I need a minute."

"We have all night," he said, holding her with one hand at her nape and the other around her waist.

123

She snickered and Joey froze, then pulled her even closer and murmured in her ear, "Whatever could you be thinking, Ms. Philips?"

"I'm thinking it's a real shame I live with my mother and sleep in the living room."

CHAPTER 18

*J*oey held Eliza in the dark entryway for what seemed like a long time. It wasn't awkward. On the contrary, he'd never been this content in his entire adult life. Eliza fit against him like a piece of a puzzle he hadn't known was missing, and she smelled fantastic—despite having spent a couple of hours bagging moldy pornography and fighting off the local sexual assailant.

The longer they stood there though, the more his attraction to her became physically apparent. He adjusted his pants and shifted his hold on Eliza, so his boner wasn't pressed against her. "Sorry. It's confused."

She sighed and wriggled out of his arms. "Oh, I don't know. I think it's on the right track. But my mother is sleeping fifteen feet away and I need to start dinner."

The mention of Eliza's mother dampened his ardor considerably. He checked the door lock again and picked up the lantern. "Let's go see if the pizza is still edible."

The kitchen felt about ten degrees colder than when he'd dropped off the food earlier. The black plastic over the window was flexing rhythmically like a lung.

This was no place to enact a domestic fantasy.

"You grab the pizza and a can of chili," he told Eliza, "and I'll bring the rest of the groceries to the living room. We can decide what we want to eat where it's warm."

Eliza had her arms wrapped tightly around her body, her hands tucked into her armpits. She was staring at the covered window, transfixed. After a moment, she reached for the pizza box without averting her gaze. "Good plan."

The living room, having been unoccupied for hours, was only marginally warmer than the kitchen. Fortunately, the ambiance was far less sinister, and the fire came back to life fairly quickly. They took turns in the bathroom, changing their clothes and cleaning up at the sink. Then they ate cold pizza while heating chili and bread on the grill.

Minnie ate a decent amount of food when she joined them, but was markedly less relaxed than she'd been that morning. Joey was half surprised by her change in demeanor, half not. Sure, it was a dramatic reversal, but the house had grown so oppressively cold and inhospitable over the course of the day, anybody would be affected.

Doug's behavior had certainly deteriorated.

Minnie's quiet anxiety must have fit a pattern Eliza recognized. She went on alert, becoming watchful, suspicious, and focused.

It occurred to Joey that he shouldn't have come down on her so hard about Doug. Eliza was deft at gauging people's moods and anticipating their likely actions. She had to be, to keep up with Minnie. Given time to reflect on the situation, she would have correctly evaluated the threat Doug posed. The only question was would she have figured it out fast enough?

When they'd finished eating, he gathered the dirty dishes and took them to the kitchen. When he got back from washing up, Minnie was knitting and Eliza was sitting on the

126

couch staring at the fire. She was angled to keep her mother in her line of sight.

Joey had retrieved one of the headlamps from the coatrack by the front door. He sat at a small table with the lanterns he'd dropped upstairs and his multitool. If the problem was loose wires, he could fix them.

It wasn't long before the battery-operated lamp was functional. He took it to where Eliza's mom was sitting and set it to illuminate her work. Minnie smiled at him in thanks, which he took to be a sign she was hanging in there. She spoke as he was sitting down to work on the solar lantern. "I had the strangest dream earlier. When I was sleeping in my chair."

Eliza's gaze snapped to her mom. "What kind of dream?"

Joey wondered if Minnie suffered from recurring nightmares.

"I was locked in my room, but my room was all stone."

Eliza's forehead creased. "Well, it's pretty cold in the house, mom. We should make a couple of hot water bottles for your bed tonight."

Minnie pursed her lips. "I wasn't just locked in. Somebody was holding the door shut. Every time I tried to wake up, I fell deeper asleep."

A chill ran down Joey's spine. As far as he could figure, his leg had gone through the second-story floor into a dead space between Eliza's bathroom and hall closet, less than a meter from Minnie's bedroom door. The way the cold had wrapped around him while he was trapped there had felt... maybe not malicious, but definitely intentional.

Grasping.

He remained uneasy, even after the conversation turned to other things and was surprised when, an hour later, Minnie announced she was going to bed without a hint of apprehension. He caught Eliza's gaze. She bit her lip, then shrugged and went to pour the water they'd been heating near the fire into rubber hot water bottles.

When Minnie was tucked in for the night, Eliza came and perched on arm of the couch next to where he was working on the solar lantern. "No luck?"

Joey set down his screwdriver and rolled his shoulders. "Nope. This one's toast."

Eliza sighed. It was a sigh that encompassed so much more than a broken lamp. Even the warm glow from the fire couldn't soften the lines of fatigue and worry etched in her face.

Joey pulled her into his lap and gently rubbed her back until she relaxed with a groan and tucked her face against the side of his neck.

"I'm so scared," she whispered. Her breath warmed Joey's skin as her words injected cold into his bones. "This house... I feel like I'm going crazy. And Doug."

Joey pressed his cheek to her hair and focused on the warm weight of her body. "I don't know what's going on with the house, but you're not crazy. It's giving me the creeps, too."

Eliza shuddered and he held her tighter. "The thing is, the house doesn't worry me when we're together. So," he nibbled the shell of her ear, "we should probably spend as much time together as possible." She shivered and he ran a finger down her side until she squealed and twisted in his lap, the sound shattering and over-bright in the tenebrous old room.

"You're a nut, Joey."

"Shh. Not many people know that about me."

She toyed with his collar, then spread her hand over his heart. "I like you anyway."

He swallowed hard. "Thanks." He could count on one hand the number of people in the world who knew him well enough to say that and have it mean anything. He slid his hand under Eliza's ass and squeezed. "I like a lot of things about you, too, Ms. Phillips."

She wriggled and laughed. "My gentle nature, my tractability, my unerring good sense…"

"Hey," he interrupted. "I hope you're not being down on yourself. You have excellent sense."

"Right. That's how I ended up living in a decaying haunted house with a sociopath across the hall."

"Just because the situation has deteriorated, doesn't mean it was a bad choice initially. Nobody can see the future. I shouldn't have come down so hard on you, earlier."

Eliza raised her eyebrows in genuine surprise. "You were right, though. I was thinking I could handle Doug for another few weeks, but that was the old Doug who just harassed me to fix stuff and stared at me while I worked. I wasn't taking into account, um, recent developments."

Joey gritted his teeth. He'd love to inflict some *developments* on Doug.

He forced himself to relax. "You would have assessed the situation correctly, given time to reflect. And we have a few days before I have to go back to work. I'll help you make a plan." He hesitated. "I mean, if you want my input." He was hurtling headlong into having significant feelings for Eliza—feelings of fondness, lust, and protectiveness—but he shouldn't assume she welcomed his involvement.

She shifted to look him in the eyes. "Of course I do. Definitely."

～

*B*efore they got ready for bed, Joey told Eliza he was going to grab a few things from his apartment and check the weather. "Lock the door behind me, okay?"

"Sure. Hold on, though." She went to the table in the hallway and dug a copy of her apartment key out of a drawer. "Take this."

It meant a lot, her giving him a key when she'd just been attacked. He leaned in and kissed her gently. "I'll be back soon."

Upstairs, he threw the remaining food from his kitchen into a shopping bag and put a few more items of clothing in a duffle. What he really wanted was his gun. In all likelihood, his presence would be enough to deter Doug from having another go at Eliza, but he wasn't taking any chances. He holstered it at his lower back under his hoodie and considered the other items in his gear locker.

Body armor, extra ballistic plates... nope and nope. First aid kit, yes. He tossed that into the duffle, then added a pink, keychain-sized canister of pepper spray he'd gotten as a freebie with his new body armor, duct tape, a six-pack of disposable restraints, a thermal imager he'd confiscated from a guy in Florida, and a Ziploc bag of wireless window alarms.

That should do it.

Actually, it was overkill, but he felt better.

He zipped the bag shut and headed downstairs. Still uneasy from his earlier encounter with the house, he checked the thermostat to see if it had anything to say for itself. The display read: *Select your Background Color.* Joey snorted, shaking his head. What had he thought it was going to say? *Run for the hills?*

When he opened Eliza's door and set the duffle inside, she came out of the living room with a lantern to make sure it was him. "Leave this here," he told her. "I'll deal with it when I get back."

"Okay." She shifted uncomfortably, arms crossed tight over her chest. "You're going to, uh, check the weather?"

He hesitated. *Shit.* The lying thing again. He really had to kick this habit of placating people with easy half-truths. "I'm going to have a quick look around Doug's apartment."

"Oh." Some of the tension went out of her body, and Joey thought he'd made the right call, not lying to her.

"I'll be right back," he promised.

~

*H*e'd left Doug's place unlocked when he dropped him off. His first priority had been getting Eliza settled and making sure she and Minnie were safe and comfortable for the evening, but he'd always intended to go back and do a search.

Forewarned was forearmed, and all that.

He hit the LED night vision setting on his tactical flashlight, pulled on gloves, and stepped inside.

Doug hadn't moved from where he'd left him, although he had curled up a little against the cold. Joey had made sure the radiator was on before leaving him passed out on the floor, but it wasn't comfortable in the apartment by any means. The floor in particular radiated a chill that eddied in small drafts around Joey's ankles.

A touch at his pant leg startled him and he stifled a gasp. He looked down and found one of Eliza's cats—Luke, he thought—studying Doug with equal disdain. After a moment, the cat glanced at Joey and slunk back out of the apartment, belly low to the floor. "Smart cat," Joey murmured.

He stepped quietly around Doug and began a thorough search of the premises.

The apartment smelled pervasively of marijuana, which was not surprising, given the sheer quantity of pot Joey found in plain sight in every room. He left it alone. Ditto the baggies of pills. Maybe they could get Doug charged with intent to sell. Failing that, maybe the pharmaceuticals would keep him mellow.

Doug's porn collection was massive, which wasn't a surprise, either—although the fact it was all on VHS tapes was a little shocking. Had Doug really never learned to exploit the internet? Joey perused the titles and decided it was good news the creep had eclectic taste in smut. He would have been seriously worried if Doug had a type and Eliza fit the profile.

He saved the bedroom for last, figuring whatever was in there was likely to be the most disturbing.

He wasn't disappointed—although the exact expression of Doug's disturbance was not something he would have guessed in a million years. Blow-up dolls, sure. Toy dolls? Not so much.

Doug's bedroom was sparsely furnished with only a queen-sized bed, a moisture-swollen, white particle-board cabinet serving as a night table, and a kitchen chair with dingy laundry draped all over it. The rest of the space was occupied by piles of soft plastic dolls. Hundreds of them. They'd been heaped together carelessly, legs and arms akimbo, skirts flipped up or pulled out of shape across their small cloth and plastic bodies. Thick blankets of cobwebs covered them. A row of decapitated doll heads sat along the top of Doug's headboard, their foreheads sliced open horizontally to give them a gaping mouth above the eyebrows. Those were dust-free.

Joey shook his head. "You are one sick puppy, Doug."

Without touching the dolls, he searched the room. If Doug was going to notice anything having been disturbed, it would be his collection.

Joey was almost relieved when he found a small handgun and a hunting knife stashed in the night table. At least he knew what to do about those—he confiscated them.

CHAPTER 19

*E*liza felt so safe with Joey in the apartment that it came as a terrible shock when he left and she was immediately gripped by cold dread.

Minnie was sleeping quietly, thanks to her evening pills. The only noises were the crackling fire and the wind rattling around the house. Eliza sat with her legal pad in her lap and a lantern at her elbow, trying to take notes. Make a plan. But all she could do was listen, almost paralyzed, for trouble. A delayed reaction, she rationalized. Completely normal, given everything that had happened.

When the front door opened after a small eternity, she startled, her heart going into overdrive. It had to be Joey, but her fingers wrapped involuntarily around the poker she'd taken from the fireplace.

She relaxed a fraction when he called out quietly, "It's me."

True relief didn't come until he stepped into the living room with his duffle in hand.

She studied his face. "Is everything okay?"

Joey nodded, a single dip of his chin. He was tense, the

tendons in his neck standing out. "I'm going to put some food in the kitchen, then I'll be back. Do you want anything?"

"No." *Just you.*

When Joey returned from the kitchen, he brought his duffle over and crouched at Eliza's feet. He'd been limping earlier in the evening. Now he was wincing at the light, and Eliza wondered just how beat-up he was. She felt shitty for not asking if he was okay before they embarked on their demolition odyssey. He seemed so invincible, she'd forgotten he was on medical leave.

"I found this in my stuff upstairs." Joey opened his hand to reveal a pink, cylindrical object. "It's for you. It's pepper spray. You depress this button and the stream comes out here," he said, pointing.

"Um, thanks?"

He smiled tiredly. "It's supposed to go on a key chain, but we'll attach it to a hair elastic or something, so you can wear it on your wrist when you're outside the apartment." He set it on the table next to her chair.

She found herself reaching out and cupping his face, briefly caressing the stubble on his chin. "You give me the nicest things." The words were flip, but judging by the intensity of Joey's gaze, he'd heard what she really wanted to say. *Thank you for being here.*

He took her hand in his and kissed her palm. "Is your mom a heavy sleeper?"

Despite the sexual chemistry that was undeniably heating up between them, Eliza was caught off guard. "Are you...? Wait. Are you asking for sex reasons?"

Joey laughed quietly, some of the tension seeming to leave his body. "That wasn't my intent. This time," he added with a twinkle in his eye. "I have wireless window alarms to show you. On the quietest setting, they shouldn't wake your mom unless she's a light sleeper."

In spite of everything, Eliza smiled. "Darling, you shouldn't have."

"Never say I don't know how to treat a lady right."

~

*J*oey had *a lot* of alarms in his bag—plus zip-ties, expandable metal rods, mini cameras, and yards of cable and wires. He seemed to be wearing something very gun-like at his waist, and he'd set a wicked looking knife on the coffee table along with the rest of his equipment.

"It looks like you're ready for the zombie apocalypse," Eliza observed, trying to lighten the mood.

He glanced up from an inventorying and organizational process that was clearly as familiar to him as brushing his teeth. "Apocalypse? No. I could handle a local uprising."

"That's good."

It was, wasn't it? They *were* sort of on their own, cut off from civilization. This was all getting a little too real for her, though.

Joey demonstrated how the alarms worked with the sound on low, then started installing them. Eliza followed him around with his supply of double-sided sticky foam shims and a pair of scissors, helping compensate for all the irregularities in the old window frames. They worked fast, only opening the windows for a few seconds at a time. It was raining again, freezing drops that sliced across Eliza's skin.

Joey was in a strange, grim mood. He frowned while he worked, pausing periodically to stretch his neck and roll his shoulders. His jaw worked like he was consciously refraining from grinding his teeth. Eliza wanted to believe he was struggling with the effort of not ravishing her sexy bod, but there was no way he could see it under all the layers of wool and polyester blend she was wearing.

When the last alarm was set, they moved the marble-topped sideboard in the hall to block the front door and got ready for bed. When Joey went to unpack his sleeping bag, Eliza patted the mattress beside her and said, "Why don't you sleep with me tonight?"

Joey froze, one eyebrow raised.

"I'm not changing my mind about sex, with my mother in the next room," she clarified, "but you would be more comfortable over here. With me."

Wouldn't he?

Tendrils of doubt began to ease their way into Eliza's chest. Then Joey broke into a cat-got-the-canary grin and tossed his sleeping bag back on the couch.

"Damn straight."

$\approx$

*W*hen Joey slid under the covers, a cold draft of air accompanied him. Then Eliza was struck by the reality of what a large, muscular man he was, and she got very warm, very fast. Should she ask if she could hold him?

Before she could decide, Joey flipped her on her side and spooned up behind her in a deft move that suggested he had plenty of experience putting people exactly where he wanted them. She went with it, settling back and wrapping his top arm more comfortably around her waist.

Rain rattled in the chimney flue. Tree limbs scraped across the side of the house and tapped at the windows. Joey might have been thinking about sex, but there were too many layers of clothing between her backside and his groin to be sure. She was definitely thinking about sex, fighting the urge to arch back against him.

She swallowed hard. "Are you, um, comfortable?" Her voice came out breathy with lust, which was a first for her. Her loins were probably going to quiver next.

Joey sounded deeply satisfied. Maybe a little sleepy. Like a lion, or something. "Mm-hmm."

Her loins didn't quiver—they throbbed with heat and want, clamoring for the kind of attention they hadn't experienced in years. She held her breath, mind warring with body. She wanted him.

She was also not having sex in the living room while her mother was sleeping feet away.

Plus, the scent of roses and pipe tobacco had been lingering in the air since they'd stoked the fire last. The atmosphere didn't feel hostile, but there really shouldn't have been any atmosphere at all.

Change of topic, Lizzie. "You seemed upset when you came back. Was the, uh, weather really bad?"

Joey groaned and rolled away. "Doug. God. Such a freak."

Eliza turned and found him staring at the ceiling. "Specifics?"

He sighed and rubbed his hands over his face. "He has a really large collection. Of dolls. Like, piles of dolls on his bedroom floor."

"He… what? Dolls? Like, inflatable dolls?"

"Nope. Toy dolls. For kids." Joey's tone was grim.

"That's unexpected. I mean, porn…"

"Oh, he has lots of porn. It's just, he has about as many dolls as X-rated VHS tapes."

"Dolls." She tried to process that. "*VHS.*"

Outside, the wind gusted and sleet pinged off the window at Eliza's back. The room got colder around them, but the bed was an oasis of warmth. "Well, at least he didn't have any guns or anything."

Joey sighed.

"Wait, he does have guns?" Eliza was wide-awake again.

"Did. He *did* have one gun and a knife. I took them away."

She slumped in relief. "Oh, thank god. Where are they now?"

"Locked in my truck. I'll figure out what to do with them tomorrow."

∼

*T*he downside to sharing her bed with Joey was that Eliza didn't get to sleep in. It was barely daylight when she felt the mattress shift as he got up. She turned on her side to watch him stoke the fire. It was awfully nice to watch somebody else take care of things from the comfort of her warm bed.

When he left the room, she felt a bit bereft. Fortunately, he reappeared after a moment with Eliza's coffee paraphernalia and their electric kettle, which he plugged in and turned on.

Wait, they had power again? She sat up. The cats tumbled off of her legs. "Is the electricity back on?"

Joey looked over. "Yeah. Sorry I woke you." He reached and turned on a lamp.

"No, that's okay. There are so many things I want to do while the power is on!" She slid her feet out from under the covers. Then pulled them right back in again. "Oh, Christ, it's freezing."

Joey smirked. "The kitchen and the bathroom are worse."

"You seem awfully amused," she grumbled, "considering your apartment is all on that side of the house."

"Well, I'm planning on being here."

She was inexpressibly relieved she didn't have to ask him to stay. "I don't want you to feel like you have to babysit me." She leaned to grab a pair of thick socks out of her laundry basket and pulled them under the covers. "If you want to go back to your place for a while, I promise I won't take any chances."

Joey continued to stir his coffee. "Glad to hear that. But everything I need is here." He mixed a mug of coffee for Eliza and brought it to her, along with a fruit-and-nut bar from a Tupperware box he must have brought down from his place the night before.

She took a bite and tasted apricots and pecans. Maybe a hint of ginger. "These are really good. Did you make them?"

Joey hesitated minutely, then shook his head. He selected something with seeds for himself. "Nope. My moms send me a care package every couple of weeks. I take the boxes back whenever I stop by for a visit."

Eliza took that in while she chewed. When she'd swallowed, she clarified, "You have two moms?"

Joey watched her expressionlessly. "Yep."

"Where do they live? Around here?"

"No, they're down in the city."

Eliza found herself staring into the murky depths of her coffee, unsure what to say. The silence became strained and she knew Joey was assuming the worst—that she was homophobic.

The truth was, his revelation made her feel depressed and jealous.

Embarrassed at her reaction, she raised her gaze to find Joey staring out the window, his jaw clenched. "Joey?"

He turned his head, expression stony. "Something wrong with the coffee?"

Eliza sighed and adjusted the comforter around her shoulders. She tilted her head, trying to find the right words.

"It's just... two moms, Joey. I try not to make comparisons, but I barely have one mom these days."

He blinked, the lines of his face softening.

She struggled out of the covers, put her mug down, and went to perch on the arm of Joey's chair. She touched his shoulder tentatively. "You have two moms. Who send you care packages. That is so lovely, and it makes me *so* jealous. And sad, I guess." Her eyes were blatantly watering.

Joey sighed and pulled her into his lap, wrapping her in a tight hug. He pressed his cheek to her hair and laughed. "There I was, thinking this was all about me. I've never hurt anyone's feelings before by telling them my parents are a lesbian couple."

Eliza rested her head on his shoulder. "You didn't hurt my feelings. I just had an ill-timed moment of self-pity. I'm sorry I upset you."

She felt him shake his head. "I wasn't upset. I was being stoic and protective."

"Oh, my mistake." Eliza picked up the Tupperware and moved some waxed paper around, perusing the selection.

Joey turned her in his lap so he could look, too. "Those are good." He pointed at some bite-sized balls. "They have dried cherries in them. They're full of antioxidants, according to mom Cindy."

She picked one up and sniffed it. "Do they have chocolate in them? Because chocolate would make me feel a lot better right now."

He leaned in to get a closer look, pressing their cheeks together. "It might be carob."

She drew back. "That's not funny. Don't joke about carob."

Joey laughed. "Carob's *good*. It's high in fiber, has lots of vitamins and minerals. Plus, it doesn't trigger migraines."

Eliza knew he was intentionally winding her up, but she

couldn't let it go. "Joey, tell me your mothers aren't carob fans. Or at least tell me they appreciate chocolate, too."

Joey was laughing so hard he was on the verge of tears. She shook his shoulder. "This is important!"

He winked at her and popped the ball in his mouth. "Mmm."

"Well?"

"Well, what?" he asked, chewing loudly.

"Is it *chocolate*?"

He smiled and put one of the balls to Eliza's lips. "It's chocolate."

She narrowed her eyes at him, trying to decide if it was a trick.

"I promise, it's chocolate."

Eliza ate the snack ball from his fingers, catching an intoxicating taste of Joey himself before rich, dark chocolate melted across her tongue. She groaned in pleasure. "Damn. That is very, very good."

CHAPTER 20

*T*oo soon, Eliza got up to start her day. Joey stayed where he was, nursing his coffee and enjoying her routine. She had animated conversations with the cats, talked to herself while planning her outfit, and cussed a blue streak the entire time she was in the bathroom. Joey sympathized—he'd been in warmer meat lockers.

He gave a passing thought to how beautiful her acceptance of his family was, but most of his thoughts revolved around her ass and how achingly perfect it was to have her in his lap. She overwhelmed his senses—her smell, the texture of her hair, and the way her eyes got big when she was aggravated with him.

He got out the files he wanted to study, but dammed if he could tear his eyes away from her.

With the fire going strong, it was warm enough to sit on the couch. Eliza was ensconced there with her laptop, transferring notes from her legal pad to a computer document while she sipped coffee and huddled under a purple and teal afghan. Luke had left, looking like he was on a mission, but the other two cats were lazing in the blanket's folds, taunting

Joey with proprietary looks—like they knew they were exactly where he wanted to be.

"What's your plan for today?" he asked when Eliza eventually put her laptop aside for a minute to forage through the Tupperware for more goodies.

"The guy is coming to look at the heat sometime between nine and noon, and one of the contractors said he would swing by this afternoon. I thought I would double check that the lights are working in the basement and there's a clear path to the boiler. Then I want to finish clearing the room upstairs."

Joey squared-off the stack of papers he'd ostensibly been studying and slipped them back into their folder. "I'll stick with you while you do those things. You need to call the sheriff, too."

Eliza groaned. "Ugh. I would rather clean out the Room of Repression upstairs."

Joey sympathized. "It's your call. I think you'll be safer if you report this and show them the history of harassment, but if you don't want to, I'll make sure you're as safe as you can be."

Eliza gave him a weak smile. "Thanks." She checked the time on her phone. "I guess there's no reason to put it off."

∼

*J*oey braved the cold in the kitchen to wash the dishes while Eliza made her call, giving her privacy. His headache had eased during the night, although the bruises at his temple were still tender. He had more mobility in his foot this morning. Sleeping with Eliza was apparently good for what ailed him.

Imagine the benefits of sex.

When he went back to the living room, Eliza was gathering clothes to upgrade her outfit from working-on-the-couch to meeting-with-cops.

"They're sending someone out?"

"Yeah." Eliza had jeans and a fuzzy dark-green sweater draped over one arm and was hesitating between two button-down shirts—one a white dress shirt, the other a lighter green plaid flannel. "I guess it's a slow day so far—they'll be here in fifteen minutes."

Joey walked to the window and studied the frost-covered landscape. There was ice in the low areas of the yard where last night's rain had frozen. "Once people get on the roads, they're going to be plenty busy."

Eliza followed his gaze. She put the dress shirt back, opting for flannel.

~

*I*t was hard for Joey to let Eliza deal with the deputies on her own, but it wasn't his story to tell and he didn't want to butt in and have local law enforcement underestimate how vulnerable Eliza and her mom were.

Instead, he made a tray of toast, tea, and a couple of fruit-and-nut bars from his moms for Minnie while Eliza talked to the deputies in the living room. The Effinham family had a lot of clout locally, but the deputies who'd taken the call seemed more interested in doing their job than playing politics. Deputy Sandoval was a serious woman in her thirties who probably took no shit from anyone. Deputy Smith was older and sort of anemic, but he had watchful eyes.

Joey sat and talked with Minnie while she ate her breakfast. She knew Doug had grabbed Eliza the night before and was clearly worried and angry, but Joey gauged her reaction to be within normal limits. She engaged with him about which blue yarn she should use for a custom chair slipcover she was starting. After that, Joey told her about his research project.

"That sounds like a lot of responsibility," she said, when he mentioned wanting to eventually head up the new division. "You'll want to live close to the office."

"I'll need a better internet connection at the very least."

Minnie frowned. "I don't think Eliza and I should live here anymore either. Maybe you can talk to her about that?"

Joey tried not to let his vast relief show. "You should tell her how you feel, Mrs. Philips. But whatever you ladies need, I'm here."

A few minutes later, Eliza came to the doorway. She was pale and had her arms wrapped protectively around her body. "Can I talk to you for a minute, Joey?"

He nodded and followed her to the living room, where she collapsed into her velvet wingback chair and pulled another afghan—this one red and silver—over her lap. Joey threw another log on the fire, then sat near her. "How did it go?"

"Okay, I guess. I told them what happened and gave them my file on Doug. They're going to go talk to him right now. That's why I wanted you here. I'm afraid…"

Joey waited for her to finish her thought.

"I don't know. I guess I'm afraid there'll be a big commotion, or I'll have to confront Doug. I'm afraid they'll come back and tell me they don't believe me and they're not going to do anything."

Joey went and crouched at her feet. "I've got a good feeling about the deputies who came out. I doubt they'll take his word over yours. And nothing's going to get to you while I'm around."

Eliza smiled weakly, tears in her eyes. "Thank you." She wiped at her cheeks in frustration. "I felt so kick-ass last night. I hate that I'm falling apart this morning. And we both know you can't be here all the time."

There wasn't anything Joey could say to that.

~

*D*eputy Sandoval knocked at the apartment door a few minutes later and Joey let her in. He'd introduced himself as the upstairs neighbor and a friend when she and her partner had arrived. They must have run his name through the computer since then and discovered he worked in personal security.

"Ms. Philips is lucky to have you around," Deputy Sandoval said, following him back to the living room.

With an apologetic glance at Eliza, Joey corrected the deputy. "She doesn't, though. Have me around, I mean. I'm on a medical leave for a couple more days, then I'm going back to work. I'm usually gone four or five nights in a row."

The deputy sat in a straight-backed chair that Joey had pulled up beside the fireplace. "Hmm." She paused to consider her next words, which wasn't a great sign. "Here's the situation, Ms. Philips. We can arrest Mr. Landis and charge him with assault and sexual harassment. That will tie him up for a day or so, but he'll probably be back here pretty quick. You can file for a restraining order, but in practical terms, it's going to be hard for us to enforce it out here."

Eliza looked grim but not surprised. "That's what Joey said."

They both glanced at him and he shrugged. "Common sense."

"What do you suggest, deputy?" Eliza asked.

"We're happy to take him in. I just don't want you to get your hopes up. This isn't going to permanently solve your problem with Mr. Landis. The sheriff said he would talk with the judge and Ray Effinham about getting him into a different living situation, but that's going to take time."

Eliza nodded. "I want him charged. I just... I need some space to think."

Deputy Sandoval slapped her thighs and stood. "Let's see what we can do, then. Taking the bruising into consideration, we may be able to hang on to him for a little longer."

Joey froze. Bruises? Eliza hadn't told him. And with the house near freezing, she hadn't shown much skin since then. Why wouldn't she tell him? He could have... Well, he would have wanted to know.

Eliza accompanied Deputy Sandoval toward the apartment's front door. The deputy was promising to inform her when Doug made bail.

Not *if*. When.

Joey followed at a distance, rigid with anger. Doug was very lucky he was about to be arrested, because otherwise Joey would be sorely tempted to go over there and leave some bruises of his own.

Eliza closed the door behind the deputy, locked it, and leaned against the wall with her arms folded.

An uncomfortable uncertainty had settled in Joey's gut. Had he misread things between them since last night? Did she want some distance right now? He leaned against the wall opposite her and shoved his hands in his pockets rather than reaching out to touch her. "Do you want to watch? Through the peephole?"

Eliza shook her head, so he bent to look himself. It wasn't long before the deputies emerged with Doug between them. He was handcuffed. Somebody had found a sweatshirt for him, but otherwise he was wearing only a t-shirt, stretchy basketball shorts, and flip-flops. He was going to freeze his nuts off.

One could hope, anyway.

Joey had expected screaming and ranting. Accusations against Eliza. Maybe against Joey too, although Doug likely didn't remember getting dragged back into his apartment or Joey searching it. Instead, Doug shuffled along quietly, shoulders hunched, shaking his head periodically as though to clear it. Joey would have said he was a broken man, except when his gaze crossed Eliza's door there was pure, resolute hatred in his eyes.

~

*W*hen the color had returned to Eliza's face and they'd installed Minnie in the living room in front of the fire, they checked the boiler, then went to finish clearing out the secret room.

It felt like there was excitement or anticipation in the air upstairs. The sort of energy you sensed in a crowd gathering around a fight or accident. *Tacky.* He projected disapproval at the house.

Maybe the excitement ebbed a little.

"Oh, I meant to tell you—I figured out why they called this the Egyptian room," Eliza told him as she pulled a new garbage bag out of the box. She'd changed into work clothes, topped with a fuzzy teal sweater-vest and an oversized sweatshirt she'd zipped to her chin. She'd been staying close to Joey, but her body language was still protective. He wanted to hold her, but she needed to make the first move. "Do you want to see?"

"Lay it on me."

She tugged at a section of red floral wallpaper trim hanging loose near the ceiling above the window. The paper peeled away in a long strip, revealing another border underneath depicting a river scene of herons strutting through turquoise waters and vibrant green foliage.

Joey joined her and studied the newly exposed paper. "This green may have been produced with arsenic if it's original to the house. I saw a documentary about deadly Victorian interiors."

Eliza dropped the floral wallpaper and studied her gloved hands. "Oh, that's terrific. What are the signs of arsenic poisoning?"

Nausea, abdominal pains, headaches, insomnia, hallucinations, delirium, anxiety, numbness...

"You haven't spent enough time in this room for it to be a problem," he said.

"What about the rest of the house?" Eliza's voice was tinged with panic. "What if there's more arsenic wallpaper under the paint and shit?"

"That's a legitimate concern." Given how tenuous he suspected Eliza's finances and support network were, he wanted to tell her not to worry—but he couldn't. There was a very good chance the house was emitting toxic gasses and poisonous dust.

"Shit. *Shit.*" Eliza turned her back to him, body rigid under her layers of warm clothes.

Joey moved in front of her to look at her face. She was blinking back tears, eyes fixed on the floor, holding her hands away from her body. He crouched and pulled her gloves off from the wrist, turning them inside out. He put them in a trash bag and got her a new pair from his bucket of supplies.

She pulled them on but otherwise didn't move.

"You can walk away from this. You should walk away from this. Right now."

Eliza cleared her throat. "I know. I do know that. I just…"

"What?" Joey hesitated, then put a finger under her chin, raising her gaze to his.

"I can't panic. If we're leaving, I have to do it methodically. If I panic, my mother will break." Eliza wiped her eyes on her sleeve. "A few more days won't make much of a difference. I can take that much time to make a plan and do things right."

She picked up the trash bag containing her potentially contaminated gloves and bundled the red flower border into it like she was picking up a steaming fresh pile of dog shit. Her face was pale, her jaw set.

"What does that plan look like? What's first on the list?"

She tied the trash bag shut, got another from the roll, and disappeared back into the hidden room. "I need to finish cleaning things out up here."

He followed her, leaning in the doorway. "Why? The best thing to do would be to leave everything in place and shut the door."

She sighed but didn't stop loading one of the few remaining piles of magazines into her bag. "I just have to. It's important to me. To... follow through. Finish what I started. Plus," she waved a hand around, "cleaning helps me think."

Joey could relate to that. He habitually inventoried and organized his gear when he needed to think. "What can I do?"

"You said you would take a load of stuff to the dump. Can you do that?"

"Sure." He didn't want to leave the Philips ladies alone in the house, even with Doug gone, but it was broad daylight and the dump wasn't far. He could get there and back in under an hour. He went and shoved the window open to get some fresh air moving through the space. "I'll start loading the truck."

After six trips hauling bags downstairs, he brought coffee and water to Eliza and they took a break, standing in the hidden room beneath thin blue light filtering through the tarp above. Eliza wore a bandana over her hair again to keep some of the dust and cobwebs off, and he decided he liked the retro look on her. Although there probably weren't many looks he wouldn't like on her. He wrapped a lock of hair that had escaped her bun around his finger and gently tugged until she smiled. She'd relaxed considerably since she'd started cleaning. He was glad he hadn't fought her on that.

"You're about done in here?"

"One more bag, I think," she said, downing half a bottle of water. It was cold with the window open and nothing but thin plastic overhead, but Eliza looked a little feverish to Joey's eye. Not unduly so, given how much work she was doing, but he made a mental note: *reassess color and respiration later*.

She tucked her water bottle into the pocket of her sweatshirt. "It would be crazy to actually clean these rooms, right?"

"Um, yep."

She nodded. "Just checking."

Joey was about to make her promise she wouldn't stay and clean while he was gone, when her phone rang somewhere deep inside one of her pockets. She stripped off her gloves to answer it. He gathered the plumber wasn't coming.

"Are you sure?" Eliza bit her lower lip and gazed up at the hole in the roof. "Okay. I understand. Please call me if anything changes."

She hung up and perched gingerly on the edge of the club chair. Other than moving it away from the rotting hole in the floor, they'd both been avoiding what Joey had dubbed the Throne of Wank. Eliza seemed to be overcoming all kinds of reservations about this part of the house today, though. Concrete problems like assault could give a person that kind of perspective.

"He's not coming." She poked at a puckered crack in the chair's leather armrest. "His first appointment was a burst pipe at a daycare center and he feels like he can't leave until he gets them up and running."

Joey leaned against the doorframe and finished his coffee. "Listen, I know you don't want to move out in a rush, but if the heat fails completely, we could take your mom to a hotel, right? She might enjoy getting away for a couple of nights."

Eliza sighed, flipping her phone around and around in her hand. "Sure."

He guessed she was calculating what kind of accommodations she could afford.

"I have a lot of points on my mileage card I can use on hotels. Let me take care of this, okay?" He didn't know if any local places would take his points, but it wouldn't put a big dent in his finances to pay for Eliza and her mom to stay somewhere nice for a couple of days.

"Oh, really?" Eliza looked a little dumbfounded.

"Well, you know, with all the travel…"

She shook her head, sighing wistfully. "Yeah, all that travel."

Joey shifted uncomfortably. His globetrotting must feel like a slap in the face to Eliza, who was trapped here caring for her mother. "Ah, anyway…"

She smiled apologetically. "Sorry. Just feeling mopey. If we go to a hotel and there's a balance, you'll tell me, right?"

"Sure." *Eventually*. "If you insist."

CHAPTER 21

*H*is arms, pinned behind him, screamed with pain. The voice inside his head was screaming, too. Not words. Just screaming. He shrugged a shoulder up to one ear trying to block the noise, but it didn't help. Nothing helped. Except his pills. Sometimes booze.

Sometimes she went away if he watched enough really dirty porn.

Stupid bitch, always nagging him about the babies.

Fuck that shit. All he wanted was some fucking peace and quiet.

The sheriff's cruiser turned out onto the highway and the voice cut off. Just like that. He shook his head, then tilted it this way and that, just to be sure. *Gone.*

He belched and relaxed against the cruiser's door.

CHAPTER 22

When Joey finished his water, he grabbed the last two bags and told Eliza he was heading to the dump. "It should only take me about an hour, but don't panic if I'm gone longer—the roads might be a mess."

"Okay." Eliza put her phone back in her pocket and picked up her gloves from the side table. "Thanks."

She watched Joey maneuver the bags of debris out the door. *Thanks?* How inadequate. All of her problems seemed far more manageable with a prospective hotel room safety net available. It was like Joey was carrying part of Eliza's weight of responsibility away, along with the moldy wood pulp and splintered paneling.

She braced her hands on the chair arms to stand and get back to work. The right side arm separated from the rest of the chair under her weight and the seat tilted toward the floor, dumping her on her butt amid chair wreckage. "Argh." Disentangling herself to stand, she found a leather-bound book under her right hand.

It must have been under the seat cushion. Eliza picked it up and turned it over. The words "cash book" were embossed on the book's cover in red and she was bitterly disappointed for a moment. Who hid away in a secret room with heaps of pornography and balanced the petty cash account? When she opened to the first page, though, she found not income and expenditures but columns of magazine titles and issue numbers in tiny, precise handwriting.

This, Eliza thought, could definitely be the work of the same person who'd packed this tiny room full of books and papers.

Her butt was starting to absorb the cold of the floor, but she flipped through the first few pages, trying to make sense of the lists. The titles were either general lifestyle or women's interest: *Vogue, Life, Vanity Fair, Smart Set, The Popular Magazine, Good Housekeeping, Woman's Home Companion*. The lists seemed to track which issues were keepers and which ones upset somebody named Ida. At a glance, Eliza inferred that Ida liked articles focusing on babies and homemaking—*do not lose*—and was distressed by travel articles and reports of family tragedies, marked either *storage* or *burn*. The lists began with 1908 magazines and carried uninterrupted through 1910, when the list maker began including journal type entries.

The first read: *Wednesday 20 April 1910, I continue to provide Ida with her magazines and paper craft supplies out of Mother's money, but she turns more and more often to her dolls, despite whatever admiration I might express toward her artistic efforts.*

"Oh, gosh." Eliza shivered, leaning back against part of the chair. "Dolls."

She paged quickly through the next quarter of the journal. Fewer magazine issues seemed to be making the cut, the majority apparently consigned to the burn pile. (As hard as that was to believe, considering how many had been stuffed into this hidden room.) The journal's author recorded Ida's increasing preoccupation with her "babies" and expressed frustration at his inability to engage her on any other topic. There was a brief notation in July of 1911 indicating that the writer had canceled most of Ida's subscriptions and was spending the money on "masculine" publications instead: *We are thoroughly habituated to receiving the monthlies here at the cottage—now at least they will be more to my liking.*

"Good for you, buddy." Eliza was starting to feel unexpected sympathy for this man who, she'd surmised, was stuck for years here at the cottage caring for a disturbed sister. "If you want porn, you should get porn." After all, she had Adventure Tenant, which wasn't porn, but *was* extremely self-indulgent.

After July 1911, the journal entries became sporadic. The diarist updated the book every few months with some notes on what Ida was eating and ways he'd successfully engaged her in something other than cuddling her dolls. In February of 1913 he noted attempting to celebrate Ida's twenty-second birthday—*festooned the Egyptian room in paper chains and flowers but to little effect—my dear sister only spoke to insist that it was her doll's birthday.* For his own twentieth birthday six weeks later, the writer apparently visited a local widow and shared delights with her—*such as befit the young and vigorous*—rather than staying home and playing dolls. *Understandable.*

Eliza eyes were beginning to burn from the effort of reading in poor light and her butt was frozen. She was getting a sniffle, probably from toxic mold spores. It was hard to put the journal down, though. *A couple more pages, then I'll get back to work.* She read through a summer's worth of entries extolling the virtues of local widows who provided the diarist with both handyman work and companionship of the carnal variety, and was about to close the book when she came across a sentence isolated on its own page, away from the florid descriptions of afternoon debauchery: *Thursday 2 October 1913, The door to the Egyptian room remains stuck and Ida cannot be calmed but by drug—she believes that Mother has stolen her babies.*

Eliza froze. A cold chill gripped her chest. The Egyptian room had been experiencing mysterious door-sticking since 1913? That was troubling. More troubling was the fact that Ida blamed a mother who was otherwise absent from the siblings' lives. In the light of day, Eliza had more or less convinced herself that the sense she'd had of a presence occupying these rooms the night before was a product of her imagination. But, well, maybe not?

Fingers brushed Eliza's cheek and she startled, dropping the journal.

"Hey." Joey was crouched in front of her, looking deeply concerned.

Eliza pressed a hand to her chest. "You scared the crap out of me." Her heart was pounding, adrenaline sour on her tongue.

"Sorry. I called your name a few times. You were staring into space. Are you okay?"

She flexed her fingers and rubbed her chilled hands over her face. "I was reading."

Joey frowned, eyes raking over her face and body. Then he picked up the journal, smoothed some wrinkled pages, and shut it to look at the cover. "What's this?"

"It's Porno Guy's diary. It was hiding in the chair. "

"Huh." Joey tucked the journal in his pocket and took her hands, pulling her to her feet. "Must be fascinating."

She followed him out of the hidden room, into the Egyptian room. "It is. He had a sister or something—Ida—who was really bonkers..."

Joey took her hand and tugged her along. "Tell me about it downstairs where it's warmer. You're cold as ice."

No joke. Eliza's feet felt like they belonged to somebody else. "I'm hungry, too," she said.

Joey gave her a funny look over his shoulder. "I'm not surprised. I was gone for two hours. There are power lines down all over the place. The roads are a mess."

~

*D*ownstairs, Joey sent Eliza to take a shower while he heated soup. With a mild but persistent tremor in her hands, she stripped off her clothes and put them straight into a plastic bag. They smelled terrible. Like a grave. She climbed into the shower and turned both knobs on full. After an initial blast of cold, the water warmed to tepid. Her legs and feet were so cold that they burned as it ran down them. How had two hours slipped away like that? She scrubbed her face, then let water pour over her stinging eyes, trying to rinse away as much mold contamination as possible. That room was disgusting. She was ill at ease in there. How had she spent two hours on the floor in there reading? It made no sense. The journal wasn't that compelling.

Was it?

Eliza dressed in the clean clothes she'd brought into the bathroom with her, then went to the living room to add more layers. Another pair of socks, at least. And maybe a vest underneath her sweatshirt.

She found Minnie and Joey sipping mugs of soup and discussing Minnie's current knitting project. She'd completed the top half of a teal chair cover and was trying it out on the straight-backed chair by the fireplace. When Joey said he couldn't believe how fast she worked, she waved off his praise. "It's just a rectangle."

"But there's a design." He set down his mug and crouched next to Minnie to get a better look. "How do you do that?"

Minnie showed him the back of the project where lengths of yarn in various shades of pink dangled in spools. Then she explained in general terms how to work in color. Eliza nearly intervened before Joey asked what the image was supposed to be, but she needed a good laugh. She still felt a little dead inside.

"What's it going to be?" he asked, right on cue.

Eliza's mom smiled beatifically. "It's the female reproductive system! It's a gift for the director of a Planned Parenthood clinic in Des Moines. These are the ovaries," she said, pointing, "and I've just started working on the uterus here." Minnie plucked a ball of fuzzy magenta yarn from the bag at her feet and tapped it on Joey's cheek. "This is going to be the endometrial lining. Don't you love how soft it is?"

Joey stared at Minnie, poleaxed. "That's… really something." After a moment's reflection, he added, "You should meet my mothers."

She tapped him one more time with the endometrial lining. "I would love to meet your mothers."

~

While they waited for the contractor, Joey worked on his research project, stepping out a few times to make short phone calls. The more time he put into the plan he was developing, the more excited he got. Eliza regretted monopolizing his time with her various crises.

And she felt… left out?

Well, it gave her some sort of pang to watch somebody else plan a new, exciting career move while she was stuck in stasis, never having enough extra time or energy or money to change tracks. Grant writing was fine, but Eliza often felt like she was enabling other people to do exciting things when, selfishly, *she* wanted to be doing exciting things.

Instead of researching her new grant project, she got up and wandered over to the window. Just enough light remained in the sky to see how battered and bare the trees around the house were. More clouds had rolled in—another storm front. They sat so low in the sky that they seemed ready to press the cottage and surrounding forest into the earth without warning. Eliza shuddered, still not entirely recovered from the deep chill that had seeped into her upstairs. *I want out. Away from this house. I want people and light. I want to look out my window and see advertisements, work trucks, pizza delivery cars. Proof of life.*

Perversely, she turned away from the window and got the journal from the mantle where Joey had left it. She should have been reluctant to even touch the book again. It was probably saturated with toxic mold and arsenic, in addition to being creepy. But she needed to know more about Ida and her brother. And whether Mother made any more appearances.

She took the journal to her reading chair and curled up, paging through until she found the entry about Mother stealing the babies. It was no less freaky the second time through, but the entries immediately after made no mention of further domestic weirdness. Instead, the writer had apparently redoubled his jack-of-all-trades activities, recording his encounters in a way that was half invoice, half little black book: *Mrs. Caldwell, repair of three straight-backed chairs, glue, dowels, sandpaper, varnish, fine bottom and pert breasts.*

"You Renaissance man," Eliza muttered, closing the journal. She felt a little better, knowing that life had gone on for the writer after the thing with the Egyptian room. There were a lot of pages left to read, but she should probably stop while she was ahead. She put the journal back on the mantle and stretched. Minnie and Joey were totally absorbed in their own projects. Night had fallen, although it was not quite five o'clock. She hadn't heard from the contractor.

Taking a page out of Joey's book, she stepped into the hall to call the guy.

Daisy followed her and sniffed briefly at the hall closet before racing back into the living room where it was warm.

The contractor answered after two rings. "This is Frank. Hold on a sec."

Eliza leaned against the closet door and listened while Frank paid for two cheeseburgers, fries, and a soda. Her stomach contracted at the idea of delicious, greasy restaurant food. *Fuck you, Frank.*

When he came on the line again, Frank expressed some reluctance to drive out her way on icy roads to bid on a project that likely wasn't going to get off the ground. "I know the property you're talking about, and it's a money pit. The family's not going to pay to renovate it."

"Please," Eliza begged, "I'm not expecting a renovation, but there's a huge hole in the roof and another in my bedroom wall. Can you at least come look at the roof? You can see all the damage from inside the house."

Frank didn't reply right away—he seemed to be chewing. Eliza was torn between hating him and wanting to offer him an obscene amount of money to bring her a burger. She heard paper being balled up, then Frank said, "Fine. Bowling league's canceled tonight. I'll be there in half an hour."

When they'd disconnected, Eliza sat on the floor with the closet door at her back and fantasized about French fries for a few minutes. In the living room, Joey and her mother were taking a break and chatting, debating the aesthetic merits of a thick endometrial lining versus a thin one. Their voices were decipherable but removed. As though a bubble of still-ness separated Eliza from them.

She let her head fall back against the door and closed her eyes. *That Joey.* He was a keeper. Minnie was certainly taken with him. And Eliza felt like a real person again with him around. He made her care about things she'd put on the back burner for the last few years—her appearance, her career. Her clinically dead social life.

She wished, momentarily, for her sketchbook. A sequence was unfolding in her head wherein Joey—no, Adventure Tenant—hung around the house by day wearing gaudy, reproductively-themed sweaters knitted by her mother. By night, he ditched the sweaters and saved heiresses—no, grandmothers and puppies—dressed like a special-ops fashion plate, then came home to Eliza bearing gifts of fast food and cute shoes…

She was well into her fantasy when suddenly Joey was shaking her violently by the shoulders. "Eliza! Come on, honey. Wake up. You need to move." His voice held a frantic undertone that drew her out of her stupor. She tried to open her eyes, but only succeeded in twitching her lashes. She was reluctant to let the dream go anyway.

The next thing she knew, Joey was slapping her face. Not hard, but insistently. Her cheek was so cold that there was no sting—just the impact of his hand against flesh that might have been somebody else's. Eliza managed to open her eyes, but Joey didn't seem satisfied with her progress. He gathered her in his arms and carried her down the hall, out of the apartment, to his truck.

"Where're we going?" she mumbled when he put her in the passenger seat, climbed in, and started the engine.

"Nowhere." Joey adjusted the vents until tepid air was blowing onto her feet and face. "I'm trying to warm you up without freaking your mom out. Why the hell were you just sitting on the hall floor?"

He sounded pissed. But scared, too. The fear, at least, was

infectious. Eliza's heart rate jumped and her awareness sharpened. She started shaking. The air coming out of the vents was warm now, but it wasn't a match for the cold shuddering through her body in massive tremors. "I don't know." What *had* she been thinking? "I was thinking about French fries, then I got tired and closed my eyes…"

"*French fries*? Are you kidding me?" Joey's eyes narrowed in outrage.

Eliza just blinked at him. The French-fry fantasy hadn't been intentional.

Joey sighed and rubbed a hand over his mouth. "You scared the crap out of me, honey. You were so cold and still, I thought you were dead for a second."

"I'm sorry. I don't know what happened."

Joey nodded, acknowledging her apology, but his mind seemed to be elsewhere. He stared out the windshield at the bleak, cold forest surrounding the cottage and drummed his fingers on the steering wheel. When Eliza stopped shaking, he turned and gave her an appraising once-over. "How would you feel about a nice night or two in a hotel?"

She was agreeing before she'd even fully parsed Joey's question. "Hotel. Yes. Let's go to a hotel."

CHAPTER 23

They sat in the truck for another few minutes while Eliza held her hands in front of the vents and shivered under a jacket Joey had wrapped around her shoulders. When her phone rang, her fingers were too numb to answer it, so he took it out of her hand and accepted the call.

He wasn't surprised to discover it was Frank the Contractor, who wasn't coming after all. "The roads are a disaster. I'm sitting here looking at a three-car accident on Old Mill Road—happened right in front of me. I'm gonna turn around and go home. Plus, look, I was thinking... Ms. Philips should really call a roofer, you know?"

Joey extracted a halfhearted promise from Frank that he would come out when the roads were better, but they both knew it was a polite lie. He was starting to think Chaste Tree Cottage had been blacklisted by the local construction and repair people.

It didn't matter. Eliza had agreed to stay at a hotel. Once he got her and her mom away from the cottage, he would be one step closer to convincing them to never go back.

He pulled out his own phone and called a couple of hotels

in town, eventually reserving two rooms at a place rumored to take pets if you got the right manager.

Then, with extreme reluctance, he took Eliza back into the house to pack. They were already losing daylight—which seemed neither humorous nor sexy at the moment. Joey was willing to risk driving on the icy roads to get them all away from this place, but he might have to draw a line at doing it in the dark.

~

*C*onvincing Minnie to go to the hotel was an eye-opening exercise in patience. Joey had wondered, from time to time, if she might not actually be in better shape than Eliza realized. He was all about being proactive, but it seemed like Eliza might be depriving her mother of some healthy independence by keeping to their strict routine and anticipating every problem.

Joey had never taken part in trying to convince Minnie to do something she didn't want to do, though. Her anxiety grew exponentially as Eliza talked, explaining that they needed to stay in a hotel until the plumber could repair the furnace because it was going to get dangerously cold overnight. Minnie latched on to bits of information that made sense to her and ignored everything she found distressing. At first, she adamantly refused to join them, believing that Eliza and Joey meant to spend a couple nights at the hotel together for a romantic get-away. "It's very nice of you to think of me, Eliza Jane, but I'm not going to be a third wheel. You kids just enjoy yourselves."

After several iterations of that conversation, Eliza sighed, slipped her arm through Joey's, and snuggled up to him. "Thanks, mom. We're really looking forward to it. The thing is…"

Eliza made more headway when she stopped trying to tell her mom she and Joey were just friends and instead emphasized that they already had two separate hotel rooms booked. Completely separate. "It's a special deal, mom. If you don't come, the second room will just go to waste."

Minnie clearly hated waste. She frowned, debating, but then shook her head. "It will be a bother, packing up all of my materials. And I really have a lot of work to do."

"We'll help you pack," Eliza insisted.

"I have plenty of room in my truck," Joey added.

"Plus, mom, you're really going to be too cold here. You won't be able to work if your fingers are frozen, right?"

That last point tipped the balance; after nearly forty minutes of haggling, Minnie grudgingly agreed to go to the hotel for a couple of nights.

Exasperated, she went to her bedroom to pack an overnight bag. When Eliza moved to follow, Joey caught her by the arm and gave her a quick once-over. "You look exhausted. Can I help you pack?"

She sighed. "Can you dump that laundry basket into a bag and put it in your truck?" she asked, pointing. "That's all I need, besides my laptop bag and the stuff on my nightstand."

Joey agreed. When Eliza tried to step away, he held her close for another second. "You know, I am willing to share a hotel room if we have to. For your mom's peace of mind."

Eliza smiled as she disentangled herself. "Don't I wish." Then, her hand lingering on Joey's arm, she looked back over her shoulder at him and added, "We'll see."

Joey's body tightened with a throb of lust. That sounded promising.

*J*oey had his own things packed and loaded in his truck in less than five minutes. When he checked back in with the Philips ladies though, it sounded like they were still only at the beginning of a very long negotiation and decision-making process. He leaned against the wall just outside Minnie's door and listened to Eliza work methodically through every detail of the process.

Did Minnie want to take her slipcover project?

Yes.

Which skeins of yarn would she need?

Well, she hadn't settled on how she was going to portray the birth canal yet, so maybe one more salmon pink skein, plus the gold and silver metallic yarn, just in case.

Reading material? Slippers? Did she have enough medication in her pill organizer to last a few days, or should they add more?

It was abnormally cold in the hallway, and Joey sensed just a hint of that grasping need from upstairs tingeing the dank air. He wanted to urge Eliza to hurry, but he knew that would be counterproductive. She was doing the best she could, and she was undeniably the world's foremost authority on Minnie.

Directing a menacing mental *watch yourself* at the hallway, Joey went back upstairs and got a spare duffle for Eliza's clothes. Time not being an issue, he folded her pants and shirts as he went, tucking her more intimate items into the bag's corners without looking too carefully. He couldn't help but note his own reaction to Eliza's undies and bras though. They were pretty basic and definitely not new, but that absolutely did not matter to his dick. He wanted her. In her basic undies, out of her basic undies... Didn't matter. More interesting was the surge of tenderness and affection he felt, packing her things. That was a new experience for him. One that didn't do anything to calm the protective impulse he was experiencing.

Slow your roll. Nobody here is going to appreciate caveman behavior. He focused on straightening Eliza's bedding to make sure he hadn't missed anything. When he picked up her pillow to smooth the blankets underneath, a notebook thudded to the floor. It landed facedown, open, with a good third of the pages folded back on themselves.

"Damn." Joey picked it up and tried to press the pages flat. He mostly averted his eyes. He would never read somebody's personal writing without an invitation. Surprisingly, though, the pages were filled with drawings. Comic strips. Before he could check himself, Joey was totally absorbed. He sat on the edge of Eliza's bed and went back a few pages till he came to the beginning of an episode.

The main character was a riot. *Adventure Tenant?* Joey snorted.

Although… "Hold up." He took a closer look at Adventure Tenant's face and, yep, there was a scar on the guy's jawline— the same one Joey had worn since he'd zigged when he should have zagged while subduing a knife-wielding stalker early in his career. He ran his thumb over the faint line. That had been simultaneously the best and worst day of his career. The stalker never should have gotten that close to their principal, but Joey had looked badass subduing him when the tabloid photos came out. He'd earned a nice bonus, too.

"Alright, A.T., let's see what you've got."

Joey followed along as Adventure Tenant received intel from a local, then commandeered a zodiac full of Vikings to provide him with transport up a river gorge. *Points for style.* Although not for subtlety—A.T. should be executing his mission under cover of darkness, with less colorful personnel. And the plaid shirt wasn't a good choice for moving unnoticed through a Nordic winter environment.

Still, Joey found himself nodding and *hooah*-ing as cartoon him climbed a cliff face, infiltrated a small village, and stole what looked like carrots from a workshop.

Carrots? He scanned ahead a couple of scenes. *Ah.* They were actually iron spikes, which A.T. used to slay Viking vampires five panels later and free a woman from captivity. The female in question—a modern socialite type who was woefully underdressed for local conditions—expressed a PG-13 amount of gratitude toward her rescuer, definitely angling for more, in Joey's opinion. A.T. declined any further compensatory sex acts in an exceedingly professional manner. Which… why worry about ethical boundaries if you were already breaking the rules of time and space? But Joey was just as grateful not to see his avatar having sex with a random woman. Particularly not a woman invented by Eliza.

He closed the book and slid it back under Eliza's pillow, which was probably where it had been stashed. Hidden? Joey thought the comics were great, but who knew how she felt about having people see them. He would have to confess to snooping when he got her alone again.

Eliza and Minnie were still negotiating in the other room. Joey looked around, wondering what else he could do to help facilitate their departure. Eliza had mentioned her laptop bag… Her laptop was already inside, but the power cord still trailed along the floor to a power strip that probably over-taxed the single ungrounded outlet in the room. He unplugged the cord and coiled it neatly, tucking it inside one of the bag's outer pockets. Then he added the stack of file folders from Eliza's work area, just in case.

A glance out the window showed that the sun was nearly down. The house wasn't getting any warmer. Or less creepy. Joey took the duffle with Eliza's clothes to his truck, then checked in with the Philips ladies again. It appeared that packing the craft supplies had been the easy part. A couple bags of yarn sat by the door, ready to go. Eliza was currently talking her mom through choosing clothes and toiletries, and that wasn't going nearly so smoothly.

"Mom, you probably don't need that many sweaters, but if you want to bring them, it's fine."

"No, I have to choose two." Minnie had three piles of riotously colorful sweaters laid out on her bed and was studying them with a critical gaze.

"Really, mom. This bag is big enough for them all," Eliza said, shaking out a huge, zippered plastic shopping bag. "Let's just pack them and move on. We should try not to get to the hotel too late. I think check-in is only until seven o'clock."

Her mom threw her hands up in the air. "I'll just stay here. It's your special get-away. I don't know why you want me to come." She settled herself resolutely in her work chair and picked up a different knitting project—this one a long purple cord with gold flecks that widened at one end.

Eliza pressed her palms together, probably praying for strength, and started back at the beginning, explaining why they had to leave and what arrangements had been made.

Her mother listened grudgingly while her needles flew, rapidly turning the wide end of her cord into a sort of net sack.

Joey stood in Minnie's doorway as the sky turned from orange to mottled pink to violet to fathomless indigo, silently recalculating the cost/benefit ratio of making the trip into town. The temperature was plummeting and an icy mist had rolled in. His weather app was showing an image he'd never seen before, but he was guessing it meant freezing rain. Either that or clouds shitting diamonds. The thermostat in the foyer had read *Tips for Winterizing!* on his last trip through, which was a pretty straightforward warning as far as Joey was concerned.

The hall behind him throbbed with cold and an increasingly grasping emptiness. Joey let it press against him until his back felt lifeless. He didn't know if he was actually keeping something evil at bay or just mounting a vigil over Eliza's stultifying act of patience, but standing there was sapping his will to live.

Finally, he had to move. "Eliza."

She turned to look at him, face drawn in fatigue.

"I'm going to go salt the steps. Stay in here with the door closed until I come back, okay?"

She nodded, her eyes drifting shut for a moment. Then she shook herself awake again and sat forward, readying herself for another round with Minnie. "I'm sure we'll be here."

CHAPTER 24

It was a relief to step out into fresh night air. Joey found a thin layer of ice already glazing the random tchotchkes on the porch. Ceramic garden gnomes, copper vases, and enameled chamber pots all glinted faintly in the weak light provided by the single forty-five-watt bulb next to the front door. A wind chime made of shiny disks clacked dully in the breeze, some of its various parts frozen together. It sounded like somebody rattling finger bones.

He ran the beam of his Maglite over the steps, then tested them. They were dangerously slick. He doubted Minnie and Eliza would make it as far as the porch tonight, but they needed a safe means of egress from the cottage, regardless.

He'd seen a bag of salt in the basement. He told himself he wasn't freaked out by the prospect of going down there to get it—he was a grown-ass man, it wasn't even the dinner hour yet, and the electricity was on.

Truthfully, though, he had some concerns. The house…

No.

The *doors in the house* had a history of closing and sticking, and Joey did not need to spend the evening locked in the basement. He jogged upstairs and grabbed two of his door wedges, then stopped in to tell Eliza where he was going to be.

Just in case.

Minnie was wearing a flannel nightgown over the velour jogging ensemble she'd had on earlier and was staring belligerently at Eliza, who was confiscating large numbers of artificial roses from Minnie's suitcase.

Joey leaned forward to get a better look. The petals of the roses were red and had "Durex" printed on them. "Are those...?"

Eliza sighed. "They're condom roses. They're not coming with us."

"Uh, right." That was a shame.

And yet, considering their provenance, not.

"Well. Carry on."

Joey locked Eliza's apartment door behind him and turned on both the foyer chandelier and the eighties-era track lighting on the wall across from the laundry room door. The thermostat chirped at him as he walked by.

"That's new." Joey stopped to look at the display and found a flashing battery icon in the lower right corner. Looked like the recent power outages had depleted the device's backup reserves. The scrolling message was at least marginally relevant in this case: *Please ensure your equipment is functioning properly.* "My equipment always functions properly. Check your own equipment."

He wedged the basement door open and tugged to make sure it wasn't going anywhere. The door didn't budge, although it flexed under the force of Joey's tugs. In general, Joey preferred a good, solid door. But he was lately coming to appreciate cheap, light-weight doors. This one would hardly hurt at all if it slammed shut on him, and he could kick his way through if he got stuck on the wrong side.

He flipped on the basement light and double-timed it down the stairs. He wasn't *that* spooked, but no sense in being the guy who lingered in a questionable environment waiting to be whacked on the back of the head or dragged into a crypt.

The bag of salt was right where he remembered. Fifty pounds, minus maybe a couple of handfuls. Joey twisted the open corner shut, hefted the bag to his shoulder, and took the stairs two at a time. In and out in less than thirty seconds.

His breath was visible in the foyer light when he paused to shut the basement door, slightly winded.

He salted the porch, then the steps, using liberal amounts since the house was a disaster anyway. Who was going to notice if it degraded the paint or masonry?

Plus, wasn't salt good for keeping evil spirits at bay? He'd seen something about that on a television show. Not that he thought television shows were a good source of security intel. He just didn't have anything else to go on.

As he carried the salt bag back up the steps, a freezing rain began to fall and he abandoned the idea of going to a hotel for the night. The ground was frozen. It was full dark. Nobody in their right minds would be on the road, so if he risked the drive and they went into a ditch, they would freeze to death before help arrived.

"Looks like you've got us for one more night," he said to the thermostat as he propped the salt bag against the wall beneath it.

Replace Air Filter, it replied.

～

*B*ack in Minnie's room, Eliza was sitting in the recliner with her head in her hands and Bo in her lap. Her mother was in the closet, looking for something.

"I'm sorry," Eliza mouthed.

Joey beckoned her over and led her into the living room.

"I'll be back in a minute, mom," Eliza called over her shoulder.

Joey moved a chair closer to the fireplace. "Sit here. You still look cold."

"I am cold." Eliza watched glassily as he crouched and got the fire going again. "I take it were not leaving tonight, after all."

He shook his head. "The roads are too dangerous. There's already ice on the ground and it's starting to rain again. I called the hotel. They'll try and keep rooms for us for tomorrow."

Eliza glanced toward the hallway, her face pale with apprehension as well as fatigue.

Joey took her hands in his and tried to chafe some blood back into them, redirecting her attention away from the hall. "The heat isn't working at all now. Can you talk your mom into sleeping in the living room with us?"

She nodded absently. "Probably. It'll be easier than talking her into going to the hotel." She sniffed and pulled a hand away so she could wipe her nose on a ratty tissue from her sweater pocket.

"How are you feeling?" Eliza wasn't focusing on anything. Instead, her gaze drifted around the room in a seemingly random pattern.

"I'm not sure. I think my brain is frozen. And I'm just really, really *sad*," she croaked. "And *tired*."

"Aw, honey." Joey lifted Eliza out of her chair and sat, settling her in his lap. He wrapped a handy blanket tight around her and pulled her close.

He expected a flood of tears. Maybe some clinging.

Instead, Eliza growled in frustration, shook off the blanket, and rose to pace in front of the fire. "I am *not* going to lose my mind over this house."

"No way." *Not without putting up one hell of a fight, at least.*

Eliza glared at him, having clearly picked up the subtext.

Joey folded the blanket and draped it over the back of the chair. "Let's move your mom in here and get some sleep."

Eliza heaved a sigh. She was flicking the fingers of her right hand nervously in a way that was reminiscent of Minnie's mannerisms when she was fighting anxiety.

Joey went to her and took her hands in his. She held on tight and stepped into his space, pressing her forehead to his chest. "I don't know what's wrong with me," she whispered. "It's like I'm trapped in a bubble or something. Nothing seems real."

He pulled her closer. After a moment of hesitation, she settled against him, cheek pressed over his heart. Joey ran his fingers through her hair until some of her tension bled away.

Then, he cupped her chin, turning her face toward his. Her gaze was warm again, showing signs of life. And, if Joey wasn't mistaken, interest in further basic human contact. He bowed his head and kissed her.

They'd been flirting for a while now, but they hadn't crossed the line of serious intent.

Joey was crossing that line.

It wasn't a deep kiss, and he didn't linger, but it was definitely a serious kiss. Drawing back, he checked Eliza's expression to make sure they were on the same page. She looked dazed again, but the good kind of dazed—the aroused kind of dazed. Joey smiled.

She smiled in return. "I feel much better now. You're very good at that."

"Flatterer." His whole body swelled with pleasure at her praise.

Eliza rose on her tiptoes, still smiling, and brushed her

lips over Joey's. She gave him a small nip, the faintest brush of her tongue. He groaned and pulled their hips tightly together. Every cell in his body was shouting *finally*!

Then Minnie's voice rang out from her room. "I found it!"

Eliza sagged in his arms, laughing. Joey buried his face in her hair, savoring her scent.

"What was she looking for?" he asked.

"Her anatomy book."

CHAPTER 25

Minnie settled down nicely once Eliza told her they weren't going to the hotel. She was, in fact, positively cheerful when she learned they were besieged by ice and freezing rain. Eliza tried not to be annoyed.

It helped that she was still enjoying an endorphin high from kissing Joey. That man could *kiss*.

And those hands!

If there were any justice in the universe, she and Joey would be trapped together in a cozy chalet right now—not in a freezing, creepy hovel.

Also, Minnie would be safely elsewhere.

Since life wasn't an Adventure Tenant comic, they made toasted cheese sandwiches and soup for dinner, and dined all together in front of the fireplace. Minnie perused her big anatomy book while she ate, marking a number of pages with sticky notes.

"Do you have a new commission?" Eliza asked. As the endorphins faded, she found she wanted conversation to ward off the unease she felt, sitting with her back to the hall-way. The living room door was closed, which helped, but if she didn't get out of her own mind she might seriously freak out.

Her mother shook her head. "I'm planning a gift for someone."

"Should I be worried?" Eliza teased. Sort of teased. You never knew with her mom.

Minnie smiled into her book, pressing a neon green rectangle of paper over a glistening forearm muscle, then flipped back to a three-quarters profile diagram of the human skull. She made a note in pencil that Eliza couldn't read. "Nothing to worry about, sweet girl."

Joey caught Eliza's gaze. He smiled, apparently unperturbed by Minnie's research materials. *That's promising.* Their eyes stayed locked for a long moment, until the plate of sandwich halves glided into Eliza's field of vision.

"Do you want the last one, honey?"

Eliza jumped at the sudden appearance of congealed cheese and greasy bread. "No, thanks, mom. I'm good."

His eyes never leaving Eliza's, Joey took the sandwich half and ate it in three bites in a comically exaggerated ravishing. Despite her unease, Eliza cracked up. She even felt some faint flutters of lust.

❧

*A*t bedtime, Minnie refused to sleep in the living room. Even Joey couldn't sweet-talk her into it.

"You're very kind to be concerned," she told him, "but I want to be in my own bed. I'll be warm enough. I get some heat from the fireplace, and I have lots of quilts and afghans."

That, at least, was true. Minnie had about eight handcrafted layers on her bed. And they could certainly keep the fire going. Eliza caught Joey's eye and shrugged. "I'll get her settled."

Minnie set her jaw. "I don't need you to hover, Eliza Jane. I can put myself to bed."

Since when? she thought, then regretted it.

Her mother rarely asked for help with anything—it was Eliza who hovered and fussed, making sure everything got done in an orderly fashion so there wouldn't be problems later.

Left to her own devices, Minnie might forget her pills occasionally or get off schedule with her meals, but she would manage in the short term. Maybe she would even benefit from having a little more space to make her own decisions and her own mistakes.

"I know, mom. Sorry. Just tell me if I can help with anything."

Mollified, Minnie excused herself for the evening. "I'll be just fine."

Eliza listened closely until the faint creak of mattress springs indicated her mom was safely in bed. She usually kept track of Minnie's routine in order to head off any emerging issues. Tonight she wanted to be sure her mother didn't suffer a mysterious collapse in front of the hall closet. Which made for an interesting change, at least.

When it was quiet on the other side of the wall, Joey added a couple of logs to the fire. Eliza found her pajamas and robe, intending to go change in the bathroom. Instead, she perched on the edge of the chair near the fire, reluctant to face the cold hallway.

Reluctant, also, to have a closed door between herself and other people.

Joey looked up from arranging the logs with a poker. He seemed to read her thoughts. "Do you want me to wait outside the bathroom door while you change?"

She wanted that—very much. But what adult woman had

someone stand guard outside her bathroom door because she was scared of a stupid hall closet?

"C'mon." He stood and offered her his hand. "I keep watch outside people's bathrooms all the time. I don't like to brag, but I'm very good at it."

Impossibly, Eliza found herself laughing again. "I'm sure you are." She allowed Joey to lead her to her crappy bathroom like he was escorting her into a state dinner.

With him at her side, she felt safe and nearly impervious to the cold. The frost feathering the closet door barely bothered her at all.

$\sim$

While Joey got ready for bed and had one last look around the house, Eliza crawled into bed with the journal. She was sort of addicted to the thing, even though she was pretty sure it was going to freak her out again eventually. "Widows, chairs, loose porch step, blah, blah…" She paged through to the end of October 1913, and found a new entry about Ida: *27 October, Have cut a new entry to the Egyptian room from the hall. Many days of work ahead to fit a door but worth the effort to end Ida's frantic despair over her dolls. Am concerned that she will not now leave the Egyptian room but anything is better than her crying.*

"Interesting."

"What's interesting?" Joey had come back to the living room and was turning off lights and banking the fire.

"I found a journal entry where he says he cut an entrance to the Egyptian room from the hall so Ida could get to her dolls. Did you notice anything like that up there?"

Joey pulled back the covers, patted Eliza's hip so she would scoot over, and slid in beside her. "Part of the wall inside the hidden room looked a little newer, maybe. Hard to tell with all the moisture damage. Are you going to read more?"

"I want to skim a few more pages, if you don't mind." Eliza still felt compelled to find out what happened to the writer and Ida, and there wasn't going to be a better time to read ahead than with Joey pressed against her side and layers of blankets shielding them from the cold.

Joey turned his face toward the door, dropping instantly into a doze. Eliza opened the journal again but couldn't help stealing a glance at the man next to her. He was gorgeous in repose—strong, handsome, vulnerable. Careworn but resilient.

"You're staring," he murmured, grinning sleepily.

"Sorry." Eliza smiled to herself and began reading again.

The writer chronicled months of struggling to get Ida to leave the Egyptian room. His tone varied from tender compassion, to aggravation, to hate, to rage, to despair, to remorse. Remorse usually followed extended visits to the local merry widows. He always found Ida hungry and unkempt when he got home. Eliza couldn't find it in herself to blame him for needing to get away. Ida should have had full-time professional care.

Eventually, the writer converted part of the Egyptian room into a small study from which he could keep an eye on his sister while enjoying a whiskey and some properly masculine reading. He described his construction efforts as inexpert but seemed pleased with the results. If he'd had a sizable fortune at his disposal, would the writer have turned the cottage into another Winchester Mystery House?

It seemed history had another plan in mind for him. By mid-1916, the writer was starting to wonder what would happen to Ida if he were conscripted to fight in the conflict in Europe. He recorded the salient points of a correspondence campaign with distant relatives who uniformly refused to have Ida in their homes or come out to Dos Alamos to care for her. Nobody, it seemed, wanted anything to do with a branch of the family they described as tragic, corrupt, or even cursed. The writer had some very unflattering things to say about them in return. Nevertheless, he persisted, focusing his efforts on an aunt in Ohio who apparently still felt guilty about something that had happened in 1906.

Just as Eliza was about to put the journal away for the night, she turned another page and found a letter on thin paper stuck next to an entry noting that the journal writer had registered for the draft and was dreading the upcoming conscription lottery on the fifth of June 1917. The letter was addressed to "My Dearest Edwin," and Eliza grinned. It seemed she had a name for the journal writer after all these pages.

My Dearest Edwin,

I have just discovered your correspondence with Aunt Irene and am shattered to know that our sister Ida is in such a terrible state. I feel so very fortunate to have little memory of Pearl and Willie— that is, Mother and Father—and no recollection whatsoever of their last days. I have just begun attending secretarial school but will endeavor to come out to Dos Alamos to see what can be done for Ida if you are called away. I shall need you to wire me money for the train, however, as Aunt Irene is very tight with her pennies and will assuredly not assist me. Know that I regret not having written sooner—I have no excuse besides acceding to Aunt Irene's fervent desire to pretend that I have no connection to events in California and have never lived anywhere but Ohio.

Yours,

Hattie

On the facing page, Edwin wrote: *14 June 1917, Have been called up and am ready to leave except cannot make Ida understand where I am going or why. Have resorted to sedatives in her tea. With any luck, Hattie will arrive in time for me to explain Ida's routines. I have little hope that a young girl—practically a stranger—will be able to manage her, but perhaps a young girl will have better luck than I in finding assistance.*

"Oh." How awful for Edwin, to have to leave both his sisters in such a precarious situation.

Joey turned onto his side and put an arm over Eliza's waist. "What's wrong?"

"Porno Guy got drafted. The first World War."

"That sucks." Joey scented Eliza's hair, then pulled her closer. "War sucks."

Eliza set the journal aside and turned off her lamp, leaving the room dark except for the glow of slow-burning logs in the fireplace. She slid back down under the covers and turned to face Joey, resting her hand on his waist in return. "Did you go to war?"

"Mmm-hmm. Little bit."

Eliza didn't know what to say—especially since Joey was more asleep than awake. "I'm sorry."

"S'okay. I signed up. Wanted to be a good guy. Help people."

She brought her hand up to cup his cheek, brushing her thumb gently over his tanned skin and laugh lines. "You couldn't *not* be a good guy."

He shook his head. "Didn't feel too good most days. Bored. Scared. Tired. Dirty. Not good."

"Oh."

He pulled their hips together and rubbed Eliza's back, then let his hand rest on her thigh, fingers curled possessively around the back of her leg. "Don't worry about it. Go to sleep."

Joey fell back asleep from one moment to the next. Eliza listened to his slow breathing and became aware of her own exhaustion. She was tired on every level—physically, mentally, emotionally. Having Joey near made everything she needed to do the next day seem feasible, but a little part of her worried that him being here at her side was too good to be true. Joey was a nomad. A habitual adventurer. He'd lived out of a go-bag as long as she'd known him, and for years before that. She believed that he meant it when he said he would stay with her. Help her. But what if he just couldn't?

She drifted off listening to the night sounds of the house and the storm buffeting the walls, aware that cold was pressing in all around them.

CHAPTER 26

*E*liza woke disoriented the next morning from a horribly vivid dream in which Easy had been trying to stab her in the foot with her shears.

She felt unaccountably betrayed, having always sort of thought they were buds.

Reaching under her pillow, she pulled out her notebook and pen. Some of the page corners were creased—maybe not the best hiding place.

Not that she had anything to hide. And Joey probably wouldn't recognize himself as Adventure Tenant anyway.

Making sure he was still asleep, she turned to a new page and started drawing—Adventure Tenant, not Easy.

She couldn't handle anymore abuse.

This morning there were no eager women, arch villains, or stark landscapes. Instead, Eliza indulged herself by drawing her hero cooking a hearty breakfast in a rustic cabin. She gave him a floofy black-and-white dog and a soft flannel shirt rolled to the elbows that showed off his wide shoulders and sexy forearms. No conflict, no mission. Just a happy guy relaxing with his pup.

She roughed out six panels, then went back and filled in some shading and details. Between the calming ritual of drawing and having Joey sleeping at her back, her uneasiness gradually faded. It was probably getting late, but she didn't want to check her phone and find out. She'd woken up alone far too many times in her adult life. She deserved this. And besides, how long could it take to get her mom and three cats into the truck?

Ha.

When Eliza found herself inventing punny titles for the cookbooks on Adventure Tenant's kitchen counter, she decided she probably needed to get on with her day. She put her notebook and pen inside her laptop case so they would stay together in the move, then turned on her back to stretch.

The combination of Joey's warmth and the morning light was soporific, and before she knew it her eyes had closed, and she was half dreaming about having a picnic breakfast with Joey and her mom at the edge of the orchard. In her dream there was an endless supply of waffles and orange juice laid out on a cheery cotton tablecloth. Bees buzzed around garden beds planted with lavender and roses. The cats napped on the old wall. She knew there were children around somewhere—maybe back in the house. Lots of children...

A sharp cracking noise intruded on Eliza's dream, jolting her awake. She sat up and looked around blearily, then pulled on the sweatshirt she'd left at the foot of the bed. The yard outside was brilliant with ice and frost, the sky a pale, winter blue with no clouds to obscure the sun. Incongruously, the scent of lavender and roses from her dream seemed to linger in the air.

There was another pop and a crack as a large branch crashed to the ground beneath a cluster of trees near the storage shed. She'd read an article over the summer about how local trees, stressed by years of drought, might be damaged by winter conditions. There'd been mention of falling limbs.

Eliza turned to Joey, expecting the noise to have woken him.

He hadn't moved a muscle. She picked up her phone from the edge of the mattress where it was charging and checked the time. Nine o'clock. And nobody was stirring?

That was wrong.

The cats, at least, should have been standing on her chest, demanding breakfast. Instead, they were curled around each other on the couch in a sleepy pile.

Eliza cupped Joey's face and rubbed her thumb over his cheekbone, then over his lips. He sighed but didn't wake. She shook his shoulder. "*Joey*. Time to wake up." When he didn't respond, she got on her knees and threaded her fingers through his hair at the temple. After a moment, he winced.

"Oh, crap. I'm sorry," she said. "I forgot you had a bruise there."

Joey blinked slowly, his gaze wandering around the room until his eyes met hers. He gave her a wide smile then closed his eyes again.

"No no. Time to wake up, Joey. It's late."

He sat up slowly like it was the hardest thing he'd ever done and peeled his eyes open, squinting at his watch as if it were alien technology. This sleepy, vulnerable look was adorable, and Eliza made a mental note to draw Adventure Tenant waking up gilded in sunlight very, very soon. But right now, she needed him in Action Man mode.

Maybe if she gave him a task, his training would kick in. "Joey, can you build up the fire? It's freezing in here."

He turned and took in the scene outside the window from under heavy lids. "Jesus, it's solid ice out there." His voice was deep and rough with sleep.

Eliza shifted on her knees and he turned to her with a calculating expression, like he was planning a tactical approach. She froze under his scrutiny. Still looking half-dazed, he took her chin in his hand and kissed her—a brief reminder of the night before. Except, there was something more possessive about this kiss. Less civilized. Definitely less toothpaste-y—but not in an entirely unappealing way.

Unfortunately, before Eliza could reciprocate, Joey patted her hip, slid out of bed, and went to rouse the fire.

The man was inarguably talented at rousing.

Why couldn't they be together in a nice villa somewhere?

$\sim$

*E*liza quickly used the bathroom, then sidled past the hall closet to check on her mother, ignoring the glint of what might have been ice on the floor in front of it. She should just open the damn closet and see what was happening inside. There was probably a perfectly rational explanation for everything—the sticking door, the moisture, the… well, it wasn't definitely ice. Not for sure. But she didn't need anything that was in there, and checking would give her fears more substance, even if she found nothing amiss.

Like Joey, Minnie was difficult to wake. Fortunately, the little space heater was still going, so the room was tolerable. Eliza sat on the edge of the bed and talked loudly about sexual double standards until her mother finally sat up and glared in annoyance.

Relieved, Eliza handed her a glass of water to keep her focused. "I'll make you some tea, okay? We can have break-fast in the living room when Joey has the fire going again."

Minnie nodded, but her lids were fluttering closed.

If I have to do the Sleeping Beauty thing, I should at least get to live in a castle.

~

*E*liza almost cried in gratitude when she found Joey up, dressed, and tidying the living room. She did shed a tear when he handed her a mug of coffee. If ever a morning called for caffeine...

"What's wrong?" Joey reached out and wiped the wetness from her cheek.

"Sorry. I don't know. Everything seems so hard this morning. I just want to go back to bed."

He grimaced. "I think we've all slept enough."

She shuddered, nearly spilling her coffee. This was why she hadn't opened the closet door—confronting her suspicions made them real. Talking about them gave them power. "I'm trying not to think about it too much."

Joey put both their mugs on the mantle and took her hands in his, rubbing them gently until her fingers unclenched. "Try to relax." He pressed a kiss to the inside of her wrist. "I'm sorry I was a zombie earlier. I'm awake now, though. We're going to get on the road, get to the hotel. It's going to be fine."

Eliza stepped closer, resting her forehead on Joey's chest. She loved his touch, his scent. It was like coming home, although she'd never had a home that called to her heart as much as Joey did. Rising to her toes, she brushed her lips over his. Joey smiled and kissed her back, pulling her tight against him with a hand at her waist. She tasted his mouth, then kissed the strong line of his neck, nipping at the tender flesh of his throat. She wanted to mark him. That had never happened before, either.

She needed to check on Minnie, though. Reluctantly, she

pulled away. Joey's pupils were wide, his eyes raking over her face, throat, and breasts. *Dammit.* "We really need to get to that hotel." Her voice was wrecked with desire.

Joey's grip on her waist tightened. "Lady, I will move heaven and earth to make that happen. Go get your mom. I'll throw together some breakfast."

~

*E*liza found Minnie sound asleep again. Her water glass was lying empty on the floor, its contents a dark stain on the braided rug under her bed. Eliza picked up the glass but ignored the spill. It took ten minutes to badger her mom into sitting up. The confidence and comfort she'd felt in Joey's arms bled away. How was it that every obstacle suddenly felt insurmountable without him? Just a week ago she wouldn't have felt this mild panic and disorientation at having to deal with something by herself—that was just how she rolled. Was this a normal part of partnering up? Or was she just feeling extra vulnerable because of the circumstances?

When Minnie was finally on her feet and mostly dressed, Eliza went back to the living room to see if Joey needed help with breakfast. He smiled briefly at her when she walked in, but other than that stayed resolutely focused on the omelet he was cooking over the fire.

Eliza's unease ratcheted up instead of dissipating. Something was off.

"Everything okay?"

He nodded curtly. "Breakfast is almost ready. Is your mom up?"

"Yeah…" Eliza cast around for a better conversational gambit. Joey was wearing the emotionless professional expression that she had so perversely enjoyed perfecting when she was first developing Adventure Tenant's character, but she wasn't enjoying it now. It made her feel alone.

Biting her lip, she turned to get the plates they'd been using from a little side table near the door. Before she could step away, Joey stood and caught her wrist. "Listen…" he began.

Cold punched through her stomach. Did he regret kissing her? Were they breaking up already? They weren't even really together. Abruptly, she was on the verge of tears again.

Joey spoke gently, no doubt seeing from the expression on her face that he needed to tread carefully. "I got a text from a guy in town this morning. He's got an apartment that's going to be free next week and I told him I want it." He paused, squeezing her hand. "I'm going to be taking most of my stuff into town today."

Despite everything, Eliza was stunned. She felt nauseous. "You're moving out?"

Joey reached out hesitantly to caress her cheek with his thumb. "It doesn't make any sense to stay here, honey. You know that."

She nodded numbly, feeling the framework of support and partnership they'd been assembling over the last couple of days fall apart. Abruptly, she was standing at the edge of a precipice, alone, in a stiff wind.

Her feelings must have been written all over her face, because Joey started babbling reassurances. "I'm not abandoning you and your mom, okay? You shouldn't be living here either, but whatever you decide to do, you can count on me. And the new place is big. You and Minnie would be welcome there until you find another place to live. Or," he hesitated, then hurtled them both over a relationship cliff, "you could move in with me. Split the rent, if you want…"

Eliza's mind was reeling. He'd announced a unilateral decision to move into a new place, and in the same breath proposed that they live together. They'd never even been on a date. "You're moving out," she repeated.

"Yes."

"Today."

He let go of her hand to run his fingers nervously over the stubble on his chin. "I'm going to take everything except my furniture with me today. I'll come back for the big stuff next week when I have the keys to the apartment. I reserved a room at the hotel until then. And one for you and Minnie, too."

Tears welled in Eliza's eyes—tears of anger, she told herself. Not hurt. Not confusion. She sniffed them away. "We can't afford a week at a hotel."

She turned to leave, but Joey caught her hand again and drew her back to him. "Eliza, I would be happy to cover your hotel room. I don't… I don't know how else to handle this, but I cannot leave you out here at this house. It's not safe, and frankly, this place is starting to scare the hell out of me."

Eliza shuddered. The house was scaring the hell out of her, too. And Joey was right—it wasn't reasonable to stay here.

Still, it wasn't in the plans—or her budget—to move out. Not this month, much less today. She would be at Joey's mercy for weeks if she accepted his offer. Could she really do that?

On her own, it would be exciting.

Maybe even romantic.

But being responsible for Minnie changed the picture completely. Her mom didn't cope well with surprises or disruption. Moving was already going to be a nightmare, even with lots of lead time to acclimate her to her new home.

Taking her to a hotel today and a new—possibly temporary—apartment next week was a guarantee that Eliza would be dealing with a full-blown mental breakdown for weeks, if not months. Her income would be decimated, and lord knew Minnie's production of gynecological-themed craft items would suffer.

Eliza knew Joey was doing the only reasonable thing he could, and being incredibly decent about it, but she felt abandoned. He was moving on, with or without her.

How nice for him that he could just put his own needs first.

"I'll have to think about it," she said, pulling her hand away. "Let's just work on getting my mother to the hotel for now, okay?"

Joey looked for a moment like he wanted to protest—maybe explain himself more. Instead, he acquiesced, his face relaxing into an impersonal pleasantness he probably deployed on the job with difficult clients. "Understood. When we've eaten, I'll start packing my truck."

CHAPTER 27

*M*innie, perhaps sensing tension in the air, refused to leave her bedroom for breakfast. Eliza made her a tray and delivered it—less graciously than she might have wished. Her mother bristled and got quiet in a way that suggested she would be obstructive and belligerent for the rest of the day.

"Perfect," Eliza muttered on her way back to the living room. A wave of cold licked at her right side as she stepped past the hall closet, but she was too aggravated to cower before a malignant feeling. "Fuck off," she snarled, kicking the closet door. Belatedly, she worried that something might retaliate, but the only result was that she hurt her toes and felt like an idiot.

Joey had cleaned up the rest of the breakfast stuff and left to begin packing while Eliza was delivering Minnie's tray. She surveyed the room, feeling empty and numb. Minnie's clothes, books, and craft supplies were packed into two medium-sized suitcases, and a large plastic shopping bag containing her entire sweater collection and a pair of Doc Martin's she'd insisted she might need.

Eliza found her own things folded neatly into a large black duffle, her pink pepper spray canister on top, nestled in the orange sweater-vest Joey hated. She dragged the bags that were already packed and her box of paperwork and notebooks into the foyer, then started gathering miscellaneous things they might want if they stayed away for more than a night or two, ugly-crying the whole while.

It smelled weird in the living room now. Like burning food and sour laundry. Eliza found herself checking the fireplace repeatedly. Had Joey tossed leftovers in the flames? Or maybe a pair of dirty socks?

She found nothing in the hearth besides the glowing logs that were being allowed to burn down to nothing. The room was already cold outside the fire's immediate radius. Eliza blew her nose and tossed the tissue in the embers, watching it flare up and disintegrate in a heartbeat.

Just like her connection with Joey.

She sniffed and wiped her nose again. Maybe the smell was in her sinuses. Maybe she had black mold growing in her nasal cavities. "Jesus, Lizzy, you're losing your fucking mind." Her voice seemed to echo around the room. Rough. Broken.

She barely recognized herself. What was happening?

Despite the cold, she needed fresh air. She opened the window next to her bed, fumbling to turn off the alarm she'd forgotten about, and let the chill wind battering the trees outside wash over her. It froze the sweat dampening her hairline and the tear tracks on her cheeks. The cold stole her breath until she drew herself up and forced air in and out of her lungs, her fingers clenching the window frame.

She had to get it together.

She had to get out of the living room so she could think.

Dazed, she walked on unsteady feet to the kitchen and collapsed in the nearest chair, resting her forehead on the battered Formica tabletop until, gradually, her mind cleared.

Something was very wrong here. They had to move out—with or without a suitable destination. She would not run away screaming though, and she would not have an emotional breakdown. The one thing she could still give her mother was a calm, orderly departure.

Joey had pulled the garbage bag off the window, presumably to use it for packing. Or maybe for garbage. Eliza got herself a glass of water and tested her voice to make sure she could fake normal, then called Minnie's general practitioner and psychiatrist to make appointments for later in the week. There was zero chance her mom wouldn't need professional care by the time this was all over.

That accomplished, she steeled herself to retrieve their moving boxes from the basement. Pigheaded resolve would only get her so far though. Joey had already packed most of their food from the pantry into plastic grocery bags that he'd lined up on the counter like little soldiers. Eliza rifled through them until she came up with half a mega-sized Toblerone that she was sure she'd bought sometime in the last calendar year and took a huge bite, sighing as the chocolate melted on her tongue. She swallowed and felt the sugar hit her brain. "Okay. I can do this."

≈

*D*espite being armed with nearly half a pound of Toblerone, Eliza hesitated at the top of the basement stairs, waiting for the hanging light bulb to explode or a swirling mist to wrap around her feet. Everything seemed perfectly normal, though. No hostile energies, no inexplicable cold.

"Okay then." Girding herself, she jogged down the stairs. The boxes she'd saved from when they'd moved in were still flattened, tied together with twine, and stacked neatly against the far wall. A few leftover rolls of packing tape sat on the floor next to them, which was excellent planning on her part, thank you very much. Eliza tucked the rest of the chocolate in her sweatshirt pocket, threaded the tape rolls over her wrist, and picked up the bundle of boxes. It was heavy, but she thought she could just barely manage to haul the whole load up the stairs in one go.

Which was fortunate, since she couldn't face multiple trips to the basement plus further exposure to the living room.

Upstairs, the cats eyed Eliza distrustfully while she folded the boxes back into shape and taped the seams. "You should be worried," she told them. "I have no idea where we're going, and who knows if they'll allow cats wherever we end up."

Maybe Joey's moms would take them temporarily? Eliza's heart squeezed at the thought of fostering them out, though. The cats were the most well-adjusted members of their little family—what would they do without them?

Determined not to cry again, she savagely yanked the next strip of packing tape off the dispenser, slicing her finger on the serrated cutting edge. It took a moment for the pain to register. When it did she gasped, squeezing her eyes tight against tears. *No crying.* Instead, she chanted *motherfucker* under her breath until she had enough control to find a paper towel and staunch the bleeding. She found a Band-Aid in her nightstand, applied it, and almost threw the bloody paper towel into the fireplace. The memory of tossing her splinter into the bushes and immediately being attacked by a feral wind stopped her though. Instead, she folded the paper and stuck it in her pocket, then got back to work.

She packed the living room as quickly as possible, taking only her bedding, Minnie's quilts and afghans, a few irreplaceable knickknacks, and a framed photo of her dad. She dragged everything to the foyer, which was gloomy, dirty, and cold from Joey going in and out.

The thermostat, glowing green in the middle of its dingy wall, was plaintively scrolling a request that someone guide it through scheduling. "Of all the things I don't have time for," Eliza sighed, feeling irrationally guilty.

⁓

*S*he probably should have been concerned when she found her mother sound asleep again. Sleeping wasn't how Minnie dealt with stress.

Or, she thought, *you could use this weird narcolepsy shit to your advantage.* Packing her mom's clothes and craft supplies would go much faster if she didn't have to answer questions or deflect Minnie's micro-managing. Thankfully, most of the craft materials were already in plastic boxes. Eliza carried those out to the foyer two at a time, then emptied Minnie's closet by taking armfuls of clothing to the living room and boxing them there. She was hot and sweaty before she'd packed half of the items. Whenever she was in the living room, she had to fight the urge to crawl onto her bare mattress and cry herself to sleep.

"These are not your feelings," Eliza told herself. "You are calm and rational. You love Joey, but you don't need him." She paused, one of her mother's tie-dyed tunic shirts clutched in her hands. She loved Joey? Eliza tested that statement, turning it around in her mind. It seemed true enough. Frustratingly, she wasn't too sure about the not needing him part.

She taped the clothes boxes shut and moved them to the foyer with cathartic kicks and shoves, surprised to find that half the stuff she'd left there was gone. She'd planned to rent a truck and come back later for the things they didn't need immediately, but Joey seemed determined to move them out today.

So much for "whatever you decide to do," she thought. She was being railroaded into staying at the hotel, and then probably at Joey's new place. She couldn't decide if she was more enraged or touched.

Finally, there was nothing left to do but get Minnie up and coax her out to the truck. Stalling, Eliza made a quick trip through the rest of the apartment to make sure they weren't forgetting anything essential. In the living room, she pulled a few of her favorite books off the built-in shelves. She'd sort of been planning on spending any free time at the hotel seducing Joey into adventurous sex acts, but was that a good idea? With her feelings careening all over the place, the sex would probably be more desperate than adventurous.

Not a good look on anybody.

Eliza opened a novel she'd read a dozen times to one of the good parts and sank down onto the couch to read. Just a couple of pages. Her feet were tired and cold, and her hand was throbbing where she'd cut it. She just needed a minute to herself. Before she knew it, her eyes were closing and a deep sleep beckoned. Eliza tried to stay conscious by tracking the faint noises of Joey's movements. There was a particular crispness to his footsteps outside—boots breaking through the layer of icy mud covering the parking area. The wind picked up and popping noises echoed through the forest a little ways off. Nothing to worry about, though.

Eliza was drifting back into the picnic dream when an explosive crash tore through the house, jolting her to her feet. Disoriented, she stumbled toward the hall. *"Mom?"*

A heartbeat later, Minnie screamed.

CHAPTER 28

*M*innie's room was a scene of icy wreckage. Eliza could barely process what she was seeing. One of the bare, skeletal trees standing close to the house had toppled, sending a massive branch through the window. Shrapnel fragments of filthy, frozen wood lay everywhere.

Minnie was trapped on her bed beneath a massive, clawing hand of branches and twigs. "Mom, I'm here. It's okay." Hopefully it was okay. If her mom was able to scream continually like that, she couldn't be seriously hurt, right?

Eliza started toward the bed, breaking small branches and throwing them aside to clear a path. Somewhere under the wreckage, the window alarm they'd installed was beeping haltingly. Glass crunched under her feet and she was glad she'd worn real shoes to do the packing. Her panda slippers had cleaned up pretty well in the wash, but they weren't shard-proof.

The room was already icy cold, invaded by incongruous outdoor scents—dirt, plants, non-stagnant water.

When Eliza got to her mom and took her hands, she

found them freezing. Minnie had stopped screaming in favor of hyperventilating. She didn't acknowledge Eliza—just stared at the tree on her bed in terrified disbelief. Her damp flannel nightie clung to her body like a cold shroud.

"Mom. Look at me. *Mom!*"

Minnie finally glanced at her, eyes wide with shock. "You have to get out of the bed," Eliza urged. "Can you move?"

It was hard to tell where Minnie's legs were under the covers. Was she pinned? Eliza shoved at the bigger branches, but they didn't budge. For a moment, she wavered on the verge of frantic desperation. Her mom needed her—really needed her—and she was powerless to help. What had she been thinking, moving her mom out to the middle of nowhere where they only had each other? *I promise to find her a support network*, she thought. *Just give me the strength to move this fucking tree.*

As if summoned, Joey appeared at her shoulder. "Get back," he ordered.

Eliza startled, her heart pounding impossibly faster for a moment.

Oh. Right. She wasn't entirely alone in this, was she? Joey might have blindsided her with his decision to move out, but he'd promised to be there for them, and here he was.

"Her legs might be pinned. I can't tell, and she won't talk to me." Eliza's voice shook. Actually, she was shaking all over.

Joey bodily moved her out of the way. "Let me see."

He approached Minnie with silent efficiency, snapping all but the largest limbs with the strength of his hands and arms, moving lithely over and around the furniture and debris, surefooted and deliberate. His face was expressionless, his eyes emotionless.

Adventure Tenant was here in the flesh. She wanted Joey.

One branch of a forked limb was wedged between Minnie's bed and the exterior wall, the other branch pinning her legs. Joey got some thick pieces of firewood from the living room to place around Minnie's legs, protecting them from further compression. Then he climbed between her and the wall and considered the branch from that angle. "If I can't move this with brute strength, I'll have to cut it away. That will be... disruptive."

Disruptive? That was putting it mildly. Her mother would blow a gasket. "Can I help?"

"No."

Joey braced himself, put his shoulder to the forked part of the branch and heaved. It shifted a few inches. He adjusted his grip and tried again, the tendons in his neck standing out with the effort. Glass crunched under his boots. On his third try, he moved the branch enough that Minnie could pull her legs from underneath. She drew her knees to her chest. Being freed brought her back to herself to a degree. She looked around at the damage, then up at Joey. "Thank you," she whispered.

He smiled at her, brushing pieces of dirty bark off his gloves and tucking them into his back pocket. "You're very welcome, Mrs. Philips. Are you ready to get out of here?"

She raised her arms in childlike agreement. Joey found a stable stance and gathered her up. He was careful to keep her nightgown pulled down her legs, but Eliza saw deep red marks on her mother's shins that would no doubt turn into spectacular bruises. She quickly kicked a few things out of the way to widen the path to the bedroom door, then stepped aside so they could pass.

As soon as they were in the hallway, Minnie insisted Joey put her down. He complied, but kept an arm around her. She looked sorrowfully back at her room. "Eliza Jane, will you please save my quilts? And the afghans?"

"Sure, mom. You go warm up."

Eliza pulled the items she knew her mother valued most

out from under the tree and stuffed them in a garbage bag. Everything was dirty, wet, and probably needed mending. She unplugged the space heater, which was still glowing cheerfully beneath a clump of mistletoe, grabbed her mother's sewing machine, and left, closing the bedroom door behind her. There were still some things in there her mom might want, but Eliza's priorities were rapidly narrowing.

In the living room, Joey had seated Minnie close to the fire and wrapped the ratty cat blanket from the couch around her shoulders.

"Oh, shit. All of the clothes are in the truck already, aren't they?"

He rose from working on the fire and leaned the poker against the marble surround. "Yeah, but I put the things for tonight in the cab. I'll get her a change of clothes now."

When Joey came back, he delivered a warm, eclectic ensemble that somehow included Minnie's favorite sweater and her Doc Martins. Eliza knew those hadn't been in the overnight bags—he'd had to dig through the miscellany to find them.

He stepped into the hallway so Eliza could help her mother dress, but hovered protectively by the door, putting himself between them and the hall closet. If Minnie hadn't been there, Eliza would have told him that the living room didn't seem to be particularly safe at this point, either. Instead, she focused on moving her mom along.

Minnie had some scratches on her arms and face in addition to the bruises coming out on her legs, but was otherwise uninjured. Eliza gave silent thanks as she settled on a footstool within arm's reach to help. She took Minnie's wet items as she removed them and handed her dry clothes in exchange. Her mom moved gingerly, thinking about every action before she undertook it. Eliza tried not to let her growing anxiety show. Freaking her mom out wouldn't make the process go any faster. Instead, she thought about her next steps. Was there a protocol for dealing with trees crashing through walls? Was it an emergency? Or more of a major homeowner's crisis? Were they officially homeless, even though most of the house was still standing?

Minnie finally sat down again, dressed but dazed. Eliza caught herself turning to stare at the fire. Before she knew it, she had her chin in her hand and her eyelids were drooping. She was so warm, and her mom was fine. They didn't really need to rush anywhere. Maybe they should make some toast. She could practically taste the hot, buttery goodness...

"*Eliza.*"

She startled. Joey was crouched in front of her, scrutinizing her with his professional face on. She frowned. He needed to relax. She reached out and cupped his cheek. Joey sighed and took her hand in his, bringing it to his lips. *That's more like it.*

Then he ruined the moment by pressing her phone and house keys into her hand and outlining their course of action. "The truck is packed and ready to go. I have the engine running and the heat on. I brought your cat carriers in from the shed."

Oh, right, those. She looked over at the carriers, then scanned the rest of the room. It was bare and cold. Through the window, she glimpsed the root ball of the tree that had crashed through Minnie's room. Toast was not a good idea. "Crap. We have to get out of here."

"That's the plan." Joey took her by the elbow and urged her to her feet. "If the hotel won't let the cats stay, there are people in town I can call. Somebody will take them until we figure things out."

She nodded.

"While I take your mother to the truck, you need to get the cats in the carriers and call whoever your contact is with the Effinham estate. I'll cut the electricity when we leave. Got it?"

Eliza nodded some more. Apparently, Joey didn't find her non-verbal responses very reassuring. "Eliza," he said, forcing her to make eye contact. "Tell me what your job is."

God, the man had beautiful eyes. "Pack the cats, call Ray Effinham." What were the chances it would be that straight-forward?

He gave her hands a squeeze.

Minnie stood and began unbuttoning her sweater. "I'm going back to bed."

CHAPTER 29

*M*innie's bout of denial was enough to jolt Eliza out of her own reality-adjacent state. She stopped the strip show and got her mom to leave the living room with Joey. Minnie's tone of voice became increasingly belligerent as she and Joey neared the front door, but Eliza trusted Joey to handle it.

She wouldn't feel that way about anybody else in the world, apart from Minnie's psychiatrist.

Since the cats were currently pacing the room, agitated and suspicious, Eliza started with calling Ray Effinham. Maybe the cats would forget something was up while she talked to him.

Ray didn't answer, so she left a voicemail. "Mr. Effinham, a tree fell through the back bedroom here at the cottage. The house is unlivable, so my mother and I are moving out today. If you're thinking of hassling me over not giving you ninety days' notice, let me remind you that a certified arborist recommended removing three trees near the house over a year ago, and this was one of them." She hesitated, then added, "Have a nice day."

Have a nice day? Who cared what kind of a day Ray was having? She was standing in the wreckage of a house that he and his family damn well should have taken an interest in maintaining. She was done with them. She went and got the carriers.

∼

*S*he should have grabbed Luke first. He was the leader of the cat pack. Once she'd crated him, Bo and Daisy would have wandered around, directionless and confused, until Eliza scooped them up as well.

She wasn't on top of her game, though. It had been a long week. When Bo wandered over to sniff one of the carriers, she shoved him in and shut the door without thinking. By the time she realized her mistake, Bo was crying, Daisy was cowering under the sofa, and Luke had disappeared. Which should have been impossible, since she'd shut the door to the hallway, but... cats, right?

Eliza underestimated how upset Daisy was and got lacerated when she reached under the sofa to pull her out. "Goddamnit, cat. I'm trying to save you from this house." She wrestled Daisy into the second carrier, leaving smears of blood on the floor and furniture. Daisy joined Bo in mewling pitifully, and if Eliza hadn't been on empty, emotionally speaking, she would have found it heartbreaking.

"Poor kitties," she crooned, shushing them through the metal grate doors. Her sympathy didn't soothe them at all, so she covered their crates with the cat blanket and went to look for Luke.

Five minutes later, there was no sign of him, and Joey was standing in the doorway looking frazzled. "We have to go. I've got your mom in the truck, but if we don't leave now, she's going to escape again."

"I can't find Luke." Eliza had gone from annoyed to concerned to damn near frantic. Where the hell was he? There weren't that many places to hide in the living room

Joey scanned the space, probably thinking the same thing. "We'll come back for him later. I promise. We'll have to pick your car up anyway. He'll be fine for a day, right? He's your tough guy."

She sniffed. "Yeah." Her heart broke a little. "I'll leave food out. He'll be fine."

Joey kissed her, quick but not stinting. Obviously, he didn't intend to take a step back from their developing physical relationship. Then he picked up the loaded carriers and headed for his truck.

Eliza followed, clutching her purse and laptop bag.

～

*O*utside, Minnie was climbing carefully out of the truck. "I think I left the stove on," she told them. "I'll be right back."

Eliza and Joey exchanged a look. He was as close to losing his temper as she'd ever seen him.

"I'll check the stove, mom. I need you to hold Bo on your lap, though. Please? He's really upset."

Bo was Minnie's favorite. After an agonizing moment of indecision, she allowed Joey to help her back into the cab and Eliza settled Bo's crate on her lap. "I'll be right back," she told them, and jogged back toward the house.

One of the porch steps was still in the shade and she slipped, her knee connecting hard with the step above. She wrenched two nails on her right hand trying to grab the railing and save herself. Her glasses slid down her nose. *I know this isn't a great idea*, she thought, breathing through the pain, *but I need to find my cat.*

"Eliza!" Joey called. "Are you okay?"

He started heading her way, but she waved him off. "I'm fine! Stay with my mother!"

Limping slightly, her right hand clenched in a fist, Eliza rushed through the house calling for Luke in the happiest, most fun-filled voice she could manage.

She probably sounded like she was inviting him to a funeral.

He wasn't in the basement, the laundry room, or Doug's unlocked apartment. The piles of dolls were a real trip, though.

Elisa's phone buzzed with a text from Joey: *Everything okay?*

Two minutes, she replied, and kept on looking.

Luke wasn't in the vacant upstairs rooms, and Joey's apartment was locked. Eliza checked her kitchen, bathroom, and bedroom—nothing. Her phone buzzed again, but she ignored it. She was headed back to the truck in a second, anyway.

In absolute desperation, she tried the hall closet, pulling her sleeve over her hand so she didn't have to touch the knob with bare skin.

The knob turned, but the door wouldn't open.

Her phone buzzed again.

"Come on, you fucker," she groaned, hauling on the knob. She braced one foot against the wall and tugged harder, her fingers throbbing. "I've opened you thousands of times, and now you're stuck?" There wasn't any visible ice or frost. The wood didn't look swollen.

"Luke?" She knelt and put her ear to the door—against her better judgment, since she'd almost died of hypothermia the last time she was down there. "Luke?"

Mother stole my babies...

"Shit." Eliza stumbled away from the closet, abruptly nauseous with fear and revulsion at the alien words resonating in her head. The odor of sweat and sour milk suddenly filled the hallway. Was she losing her mind? Furious, she yelled and gave the door a good kick, causing her knee to twinge and throb. When she tried the knob again, it wouldn't even turn.

There was no logical way Luke could have gotten into the closet, but she felt in her bones that he couldn't be anywhere else.

"I'm coming back for you, okay buddy?"

The house was silent.

❧

*J*oey was pissed when Eliza climbed into the truck and settled Daisy's crate on her own lap. Minnie was staring fixedly through the windshield, tears running down her cheeks and collecting under her chin.

Well, no wonder he was livid—nobody wanted to be abandoned with somebody else's crying mother. There had to be rules about that.

Nay, commandments.

"I'm sorry," Eliza told him as they bumped their way out onto the road. She would tell him about the closet and the voice later.

Joey sighed. "Luke's going to be fine. We'll go back as soon as we can. We'll put out tuna. Does he like tuna?"

She scoffed moistly. "Of course he likes tuna."

"Good. Fine. So, that's the plan. Tuna."

They didn't talk at all while Joey negotiated the one-lane road through the forest. The truck slipped sideways a few times, but Joey kept his cool and maneuvered through the skids like the road was a closed track and he was demonstrating for potential sponsors.

Eliza let him do his thing and stared out the window. She stopped seeing ice about a mile from the cottage, but the landscape beyond that limit was still almost unrecognizable. The river was higher than she had ever seen it, and everywhere she looked trees had been brutalized by the storm— stripped of leaves, their branches torn away. Everything was bleached of color. It was like driving through a black-and-white photograph. Or maybe a movie about the Great Depression, what with all the silent crying going on in the middle seat and the sad whimpers from the cats.

When the road got better, Joey relaxed and glanced over at Eliza. "We need some help. I called in reinforcements."

She twisted in her seat to look at him, aghast. "What did you do? Did you call social services?" Her heart was in her throat.

"What? No! I called my friend Marco. I asked him to bring my moms up here, since their car isn't good on ice. They'll meet us at the hotel in about an hour."

"Oh." Eliza slumped in relief. The cat carrier wobbled on her lap and Daisy yowled. "Shh, shh—sorry baby," she whispered against the metal grill.

Minnie patted the top of Bo's carrier and echoed Eliza: "Sorry, baby. Sorry, baby."

Eliza saw Joey's jaw clench. He glanced her way again. "Are you okay with them helping out?"

She laughed weakly. "I have no idea how they can help, but I'm happy they're coming. You told them we're, um, having a rough time with all the changes?"

"Yeah," Joey confirmed. "They understand. My mom, Sharon, was a cop. She's good in a crisis. I mean, they both are, but, you know…"

"She must be pretty unflappable," Eliza guessed.

Which was good, because she herself felt utterly flapped.

CHAPTER 30

"*A*ll set?" Smith asked when Loretta climbed into the department's ancient community service SUV and slammed the passenger door shut.

"No answer," she told him, putting on her seatbelt. She'd wanted to warn Ms. Philips that they were bringing Doug Landis back to pack a bag, but her number kept going straight to voicemail. Not surprising, given the wind damage that had occurred throughout the county overnight, but not convenient.

Smith frowned. Looking in the rearview mirror, he addressed Landis. "You have twenty minutes once we get there, got it? Happy to do a favor for the Effinhams, but I'm not risking our necks on these roads in the dark."

Landis sneered. His family might be grateful to the sheriff for this escorted trip back to the cottage, but Landis himself was not a happy camper.

Smith found the local classical music station, which was broadcasting a German opera, and hit the road. Loretta rubbed at her forehead, trying to ease the tension headache taking hold. There were days when she loved her job.

This was not one of them.

She could feel Landis staring at the back of her neck, and it was making her skin crawl. Just his breathing was extraordinarily grotesque. They might need the old SUV's extra weight and traction to get out to the Alder Street property safely, but she really wished it had a grill. She hated having that creep in her blind spot. She kept finding her hand hovering over her sidearm.

The classical station switched to a perky minuet. Instead of lifting Loretta's mood, it sort of freaked her out, given the situation. There was a brief station reminder that temperatures were expected to remain unseasonably low, and the semi-annual fundraising drive was starting soon, then a dreary requiem started playing, which was worse.

Looking out at the landscape of bare trees and a filthy gray sky didn't help. This part of the county felt awfully fucking remote, considering they were smack in the middle of the Northern California wine country. The roads were bad. Cell reception was bad.

People were on well water and septic tanks out here, for god's sake—like they weren't three miles away from a Hilton.

There were some odd folks around, too. Not necessarily dangerous, like Landis. Or like those gun nuts with the massive grow operation on county land that they'd busted a few months back. But odd.

Behind her, their cargo exhaled wetly and Loretta shivered, hunching deeper into the fleece collar of her uniform coat. The first thing she was doing when she got home was taking a hot shower. With the fruity body wash from her sister. Then she would make something comforting for dinner. She was debating the merits of chili mac versus chicken alfredo when the SUV hit black ice. She didn't panic right away, because Smith was a decent driver and he'd already successfully negotiated a few slick spots back on the main road.

Plus, they weren't going that fast.

When the skid turned into a spin, it occurred to her that there was a lot more shade on the ground here where the trees overhung the road. More shade meant more ice.

"Shit," Smith said.

It was the first time Loretta had heard him swear. Ever.

As they slipped off the shoulder and started rolling down a moderately steep embankment toward a tree, she hoped it wouldn't be the last.

CHAPTER 31

*J*oey checked his phone once they were parked in front of the registration entrance at the hotel, finding five texts from Marco and his moms letting him know they were on their way and making good time.

Marco: *En route. ETA 1335.*

Mama Sharon: *Confirmed reservation in your hotel.*

Mama Cindy: *I forgot the hemp bars!*

Mama Cindy: *But they had carob in them so it's ok. Nobody will miss them. I remembered the cookies.*

Mama Sharon: *Do your ladies play pinochle?*

Joey smiled to himself and zipped his phone back into his jacket pocket.

Eliza was leaning forward to peer at him around her mother. "Good news?"

"Yep. The rest of the team will be here in half an hour. They forgot the carob bars, which is fine, and my mom Sharon wants to know if you guys play pinochle."

"Uh…" Eliza looked doubtful.

Minnie sniffed and produced a cloth handkerchief from

her sleeve. She wiped her nose and tucked the handkerchief away. "I play pinochle. And I like carob."

Joey thought he saw Eliza mouth the words *thank fuck*.

Out loud, she said, "This should be fun then, Mom, right?"

~

*T*he hotel manager was reluctant to accept the cats, but once he heard their tale of woe and got a good look at Minnie's tear-stained face and shell-shocked expression, he relented.

The rooms were simple, but warm and comfortable. There were no apparent water leaks, the lights worked, and the doors had adequate locks. Joey set up a litter box in the closet (which perversely had more floor space than anywhere else in the room) while Eliza unpacked toiletries in the bathroom and put stuff in the dresser.

"Your mom looks better," he whispered into her ear when they found themselves crossing paths in the small corridor outside the bathroom. He also took advantage of the situation to pull her close and kiss her.

Eliza melted into him, returning the kiss with interest. Then she wrapped her arms around his waist and rested her cheek against his chest. "It's kind of freaking me out, actually, how much better she is since we got away from the cottage."

Joey frowned. He hadn't considered things from that angle. "Now that you mention it, it is kind of freaky. Do you think we should take her to the doctor?"

He followed Eliza's gaze to the bedroom where Minnie was laying out a new outfit, in between gently removing Daisy and Bo from the curtains.

Eliza shook her head. "I really think she's fine now. I mean, well enough that adding the stress of a doctor visit would be counterproductive."

Joey was happy to defer to Eliza's judgment. None of Minnie's injuries were worrisome, and she was no longer showing any signs of shock.

"Are you still mad at me for moving out?" he asked, his forehead pressed to hers.

She shrugged. "No. It was just hard to hear, on top of everything else going on. I understand. And I'm really glad for you that you have a new place."

"I meant it, about you moving in with me. On whatever terms. I'd really like to have you there."

She sighed and shifted to rest her cheek against his chest. "I can't give you an answer right now. There are too many things I need to figure out. But…"

Joey waited.

"I do wish I could just say yes."

He rubbed her back. "Me, too."

His phone buzzed in his pocket, a text from Mama Sharon: *we're here!*

~

"*N*ice place." Marco's gaze roamed over the pumpkins and hay bales decorating the hotel's porch. "Cozy. I should bring Beth here sometime."

"You could have brought her today," Joey said, giving his friend a handshake and backslap greeting.

"She's got a big afternoon of shopping planned with her sister. But she sends her love."

Joey's moms were at the back of Marco's SUV, unloading an ungodly number of boxes and bags. Cindy had three duffels at her feet, and Sharon was transferring plastic Tupperware boxes of food into her arms.

"It's like you were expecting me to invite you on a last minute get-away," Joey observed, grabbing two of the duffels. "How did you get out the door so fast with so much stuff?"

Sharon scoffed. "It's Tuesday. You know Cindy preps all her snacks on Mondays. We just had to put everything in the car."

"And Sharon has a go-bag ready for each of us at all times." Cindy grinned at her wife, chin stabilizing the top Tupperware.

"Ready for anything," Sharon confirmed. "We just had to throw a couple extra outfits and some boardgames in a tote."

~

*T*heir four rooms were clustered together at the end of a hallway. Marco said he would be available to drive the ladies anywhere they wanted to go, but mostly he was interested in kicking back and watching TV in his own room. "Tell me when there's a plan for dinner," he said, and excused himself. "ESPN is calling my name."

Joey helped his moms unpack, enjoying their banter and the loving looks and touches they exchanged. They were so generous and kind with each other. Authentic. He'd needed this after spending weeks working security for a couple whose marriage was unraveling into a bitter, toxic cesspit.

As they got settled, he told his moms what had been happening out at the cottage. Spoken aloud, it sounded like a tall tale. Creeping water leaks? Aberrant patches of frost? Doors that shut and locked themselves? Resident sexual assailants who collected and mutilated dolls? The most banal event was having a tree fall through Minnie's bedroom wall.

Not surprisingly, his moms chose to focus on that. Sharon shook her head. "What a shock. That poor woman."

"You've got us for as long as you need us, honey," Cindy

added. "We can even stay and help you move in to your new place next week."

"I'm glad you're getting out of that shithole." Sharon reached over and gently tweaked Joey's ear. "I don't know what you were thinking."

Joey had just snuck a chocolate apricot cookie out of one of the boxes and shoved it in his mouth, so he didn't bother trying to explain the inexplicable.

CHAPTER 32

*B*y the time Eliza took her mom over to meet Sharon and Cindy, Minnie was as lucid and rational as ever. The three moms hit it off like a house on fire (to use Joey's words), jumping immediately into a card game and snack-tasting extravaganza. Eliza stuck around for a while after Joey left to check in with Marco, but eventually realized that not only was her mother fine, she might even have more fun without her daughter hovering.

I should take advantage of this. Eliza excused herself, bemused at how enthusiastically the moms shooed her away. As she was shutting the hotel room door behind her, she heard Sharon say something about the minibar.

"Okay then." What to do now? Maybe a nice soak in the hotel tub? It had been ages since she'd had a hot bath. Actually, it had been quite a while since she'd had a hot shower, either. Showers at the cottage were tepid at best, freezing at worst.

She should really talk to Joey, though. They needed to clear the air, and she wanted to find out when they could go back to look for Luke.

Plus, she really needed to tell him about the closet and the voice.

Acid rose in Eliza's throat. Now that she was here at the hotel, she was starting to doubt her own memory. Would Joey find it credible that Luke was trapped in a hostile closet and Ida's spirit was speaking directly into Eliza's brain? Or would he think she was insane? He could be excused for that, since insanity obviously ran in her family.

Despite that kiss earlier, she worried he would tell her he didn't want her after all.

Eliza was hovering outside Marco's door, debating whether to knock, when Joey stepped out looking like a man on a mission.

She startled, then felt embarrassed at being caught lurking. "Are you going somewhere?"

"That depends." Joey seemed as relaxed as ever. No sign that he was planning a difficult conversation. "Can you leave your mom for a little while?"

Eliza nodded. "She's having such a good time. Joey, I can't thank you enough. Especially since I'm pretty sure this hotel doesn't take credit card miles as payment." She hated letting Joey go to so much trouble and expense for them, but to see her mom laughing with friends... It made her want to cry. For joy, but also in shame at how badly she'd let Minnie down by taking her to live at the cottage. She'd always thought that putting her mom in a residential facility would be the ultimate betrayal—that it was her duty to do everything possible to keep them together.

But maybe the energy she'd put into maintaining the cottage so they could get a rent credit would have been better invested in finding a nice facility and working her ass off to afford it.

Joey took her face in his hands and kissed her. "Hey.

Whatever you're thinking, I promise it's not as bad as it seems."

"You've just done so much for us, and now your moms coming up here…"

He shrugged and smiled wryly. "My moms were happy to ride to the rescue. It's kind of their thing, since Sharon retired."

Eliza could believe that. Joey's moms clearly had a need to nurture. Still… well, Joey obviously had plans. Maybe she should save her personal crisis for later. "So, where are we going?"

Joey swung a key fob around on his finger. "It looks like the weather's going to turn to crap again tonight and stay that way for a few days. I thought we'd pick up some cans of tuna and look for Luke."

~

They interrupted the moms long enough to tell them she and Joey were running a couple of errands.

"Have a good time, sweetie," Minnie said distractedly, barely glancing away from the cards in her hands.

Cindy waved them off as well. "We're fine. Bring back dinner, okay?"

Eliza exchanged a glance with Joey, then shrugged and turned toward the door. That was more than fine by her. Before she could step away though, Minnie caught her arm. "Take this with you," she said, pulling a yarn object out of the tote bag she used as a purse.

Eliza took the purple lump in her cupped hands and almost dropped it, surprised by its heft. "What the heck is this, mom?"

Minnie pushed some of the yarn aside to reveal a white

cue ball nestled in a knit pouch. "It's a slungshot, dear. In case you run into trouble."

"A what? A slingshot?"

"No, a slingshot throws things. With this, you swing the weighted end around by the cord and *smack*! No more problem."

What? Eliza felt deeply off balance again. "We're basically going to the grocery store, Mom." Not the whole truth, but she didn't want Minnie to worry. Her mom was already reshuffling the deck though, getting ready to deal the next hand.

Sharon, on the other hand, was clearly trying very hard not to laugh. "Why don't we call that a macramé project, okay? Because carrying a slungshot is a felony in California."

Eliza felt her cheeks flush in mortification. She and her mom were making a *great* impression on Joey's parents, clearly. "I, um…"

Joey stepped forward and took the slungshot, tucking it in his coat pocket. "Don't worry. We'll leave this macramé project in the car."

Sharon waved them off and picked up her cards.

❧

*J*oey led her to Marco's SUV. "It has seat warmers and satellite radio. Plus, you might decide to unload your boxes and move back in if we take my truck."

"Har-dee-har. I would not," Eliza insisted.

"We've both already moved in there once against our better judgment."

She pulled her sleeves over her hands and burrowed further into her sweater. "Okay. You have a point."

They stopped in at a local mom-and-pop market and

bought out their supply of canned fish, then started for the cottage.

The feeling of dread Eliza had been nursing only grew as they passed through the storm-battered landscape. Everything was cold and desolate, the acres of grape vines outside of Dos Alamos both frost-bitten and half-drowned. They saw few cars on the main highway, most people wisely opting to stay home.

Joey was attentive to the road conditions, but he kept glancing at Eliza from behind his shades.

"Something on your mind?" She wasn't sure she wanted to know—she couldn't handle any more insights about the cottage. She still hadn't told him about the closet and the voice, but clearly they were on the same page vis-à-vis the overall wrongness of the house. Voicing her suspicions seemed redundant.

Joey flexed his fingers on the wheel. "Just thinking about your mom. Sharon and Cindy offered to stay as long as we need them... Do you think your mom will keep enjoying their company? Or is it going to be too much eventually?"

Eliza sighed. "I don't know. I thought I was the expert on her, but I've really screwed things up."

"Honey, you're definitely the expert on Minnie. And you love her so much. You haven't screwed up."

She laughed. "Oh, Joey. Love is nowhere near enough to keep my mom going. If you knew..." Eliza closed her eyes and took a couple of deep breaths. Talking about her mom's mental health problems made her feel physically ill.

"You can tell me." Joey reached over and squeezed her hand. "If you want to. Or not."

Did she want to? There would be no going back from this conversation. Still, better to know now if her mom's problems were going to be a deal-breaker for him. She realized she held his hand in a death grip and tried to relax.

Taking a deep breath, she said, "My mom has schizophrenia."

Joey made a sound of sympathetic encouragement and threaded his fingers through hers.

To her surprise, Eliza started talking again, telling him everything. "She was fragile after my dad died. But, I mean, basically things were normal. I thought we were doing okay. Things started falling apart after I went to college. The first year was okay. Then, during the second year, she started really letting things go. The house was dirty. She stopped getting her hair cut."

They passed a tow truck pulling a minivan out of the ditch at the side of the road, and Joey dropped her hand for a moment to slow and then pass in the empty oncoming lane. She met him halfway when he reached for her again, needing his touch.

He caressed her knuckles. "You don't have to tell me everything right now. We have lots of time."

She shook her head. "No, I want to. Just… stop me if you don't want to hear it."

"Of course I want to hear it."

"Okay." She cleared her throat. "So, when I went home during spring break, right before graduation, mom was skeletal. Filthy. She had all these wounds that were infected." Eliza took a steadying breath. "I tried talking to her about it. I wanted to understand. And she kept saying it was all to be expected, under the circumstances. Not to worry about her."

"So did you find out what was wrong?"

She laughed, brokenly. "Well, it turned out my mom thought she was dead. Like, literally dead. For almost three years. And she didn't tell me—or anyone—because she didn't want to be a bother. She just carried on, but she didn't see any point in eating or bathing or being careful not to hurt herself. Or getting help when she did hurt herself," she added, thinking of the putrefying wounds. "Finally, I told her she smelled really bad and offered to help her shower. And she snapped at me. She was like, *Of course I smell bad! How do you think you're supposed to smell when you're dead?*"

Tears were running down her cheeks. She wiped them away with her sleeve and tried to catch her breath.

"I'm getting the picture, honey." Behind his glasses, Joey looked shattered. "You don't have to tell me any more."

Eliza dug a tissue out of her pocket to wipe her nose. "That's it, really. She was admitted to a psychiatric hospital. She's better now. She's on medication and she has regular visits with her psychiatrist. She could probably live on her own. I just..."

Joey gave her hand a squeeze. "I get it. You don't want to take a chance."

"I feel like if I'd been around more, I would have seen the warning signs." They'd turned onto the forested back road. The trees surrounding them were dark with moisture except where large limbs had torn away in the storm, leaving bright, raw wounds on their trunks. "Except, I mean, who would suspect that their mother thinks she's dead?"

"Not a lot of people." Joey kissed her fingers, then put both hands on the wheel and let Eliza drift in her own thoughts for the rest of the drive. She was grateful for the peace and quiet. She was wrung out. Exhausted. And what if this was one of the last times they drove anywhere together? Joey didn't seem overly perturbed by the schizophrenia thing, but given time to think it over, he might still decide he didn't want to settle down with someone whose mother spent years believing she was a zombie.

CHAPTER 33

*E*liza was shocked by the air of abandonment that already seemed to have descended upon the cottage. Or had it been this grubby and dilapidated all along? Hard to believe she'd actually been living here until this morning.

Joey was staring intently at the house, looking even more disturbed than Eliza felt. "Do you remember how well you pulled the front door shut behind you?"

Oh. The front door was gaping open. "I don't know. I guess I closed it the way I always do. Maybe it's swollen again?"

Joey scanned the yard. "Stay here while I check inside."

Eliza suppressed a shiver. "Do you think something's wrong? Who would break in in this weather? There's no one around."

Joey glanced at her. "I don't have a theory, honey. Something just seems off. I want to be sure it's safe before you go in there, okay?"

She took a steadying breath. Joey's concern had her imagination begging to go into overdrive. "Sure."

"Keep the doors locked. I'll be back in a couple minutes."

Joey returned looking irritated. He tapped on Eliza's window, indicating that she should unlock the door. When she did, he opened it and leaned an arm on the car frame, pushing his shades up on his head. "Did you tear the place apart looking for Luke earlier? When you went back to turn off the stove?"

Eliza felt herself flush with embarrassment. "Um, yes? I mean, I left doors open."

Joey looked back over his shoulder at the house. Then he shook his head. "Well, I can't tell if somebody else ransacked the place or if you made a mess looking for your cat, so you'd better come in with me." He made room for her to climb out of the SUV.

"Okay. I'm sorry." She slipped past him, cradling the cans of fish in her arms.

"Don't worry about it," Joey told her, closing the door. "But stay close and pay attention to your surroundings, okay?"

Eliza tucked a few cans into her pockets so she would have at least one hand free. "Okay."

∽

*S*he followed Joey into the house, pausing just past the threshold. Joey shot her a questioning look. "What's wrong?"

"I guess this is how I left it. It just feels weird." The thermostat had cycled to a different set of messages again, alternating between *Disarmed by User*, and *Monitoring*! The foyer was cold and dark, muddy footprints covered the checkerboard tiles, and dead leaves had drifted in through the door while it hung open. Something up on the roof was tapping rhythmically in the wind, which was gaining strength.

Joey frowned and adjusted his grip on the Maglite flashlight he'd taken from a black duffle in the back of Marco's SUV. "If things weren't already so weird around here, I would trust my gut and get us the hell out, but…"

Eliza laughed nervously. "I know. I mean, we never came out and said it, but the house is haunted, right? Or am I crazy?"

Joey cast his gaze around the atrium above their heads. The chandelier was swaying almost imperceptibly. "If you're crazy, I'm crazy. That wasn't right, you falling asleep in the hallway."

"And the doors closing by themselves," Eliza added. "Don't forget that." She still hadn't mentioned the hall closet or how crazy she'd felt while she was alone in the living room.

Joey blew out a breath. "You know what? Let's tell each other ghost stories later. When we've got Luke and we're back at the hotel."

"Good thinking."

Joey had already cleared each room (his words) to make sure there weren't any human-sized intruders in the house, but they went through them again, starting with the attic and moving down through the vacant second-floor rooms and Joey's apartment. Every time they entered a new space, Eliza's heart raced and she got sweatier under her arms. She must have been doing a shitty job of hiding her apprehension because Joey stayed close, a hand on her shoulder, arm, the nape of her neck. They called for Luke, leaving open cans of fish on the second-floor landing and at the bottom of the stairs in the foyer.

They really needed to spend time together when there weren't noxious smells involved.

"Doug's apartment first, or yours?" Joey asked when they'd reached the ground floor again without any sign of the cat. "Or should we check the basement?"

Eliza shuddered. "The thing is, I tried to check the hall closet before we left, and the door was stuck. Can you look at it? I don't see how Luke could have gotten in there, but I just have this feeling..."

Joey grimaced. "It doesn't pay to ignore feelings around here."

They went into the apartment and he repeated all of Eliza's moves—pulling, bracing his foot against the wall, examining the way the door sat in its frame. "Fuck."

"That's what I said."

He gave her a strained smile. "Let me grab the crowbar out of the SUV. Do you want to come with? Or stay here and keep an eye on the fish?"

"I'll watch the fish." Maybe Luke would come out if it was just her in the house.

Eliza sat on the bottom stair in the foyer with Joey's Maglite clutched in both hands for a minute after he left. Maybe Luke had another family in the area that he considered his own. He might be nice and warm in some rich family's house a mile away. He was a handsome cat. He probably had options. In her heart, though, she knew he was trapped somewhere in the cottage.

She went back into her apartment and checked the living room again. Thick clouds covered the sky outside, and fat raindrops were starting to splat on the window glass. She shone the flashlight under the couch and chairs, checking in the built-in cupboards below the bookshelves. There was still some heat lingering in the stone of the fireplace. Eliza ran her hand along its façade, happy to warm her chilled fingers. Something on the mantle caught her eye. It looked like... she stepped closer.

It was the journal. "I was sure I'd packed you," Eliza said, taking it down. She had, hadn't she?

Setting the flashlight on the mantle to read by, Eliza

opened the book to where she'd left off in 1917, with Edwin heading off to war.

The next entry picked up in November of 1921: *I am home but things are hardly better here than they were in the bloody trenches of Europe. Hattie must have departed soon after I wired of my return. I suspect she was too ashamed to face me. Poor Ida is a wretch. A waif, well and truly enslaved to laudanum such that I see no hope of weaning her off it. Doctor Franks concurs. I wish I knew what happened here while I was away. Or perhaps I don't.*

"Oh, that's sad." Eliza felt betrayed by Hattie, much as Edwin must have. She'd seemed like such a nice girl. Couldn't she have done better?

On the other hand, she'd been awfully young. And alone. Younger than Eliza had been when she moved back in with Minnie.

Eliza paged quickly through more entries where Edwin sounded depressed and hopeless, apart from occasional bouts of interest in an orchard he was planting—no doubt the one behind the cottage. Ida's decline continued.

Aware that Joey should have been back already, Eliza was preparing to put the journal in her pocket when a page with frantic, tremulous handwriting caught her attention. The word "child" jumped out at her.

"What the hell?"

Eliza found the beginning of that entry: *17 May 1922, I woke to find a child sitting alone in the foyer babbling to herself. A note pinned to her sweater reveals that she is Ida's child. I don't want to believe it, but she looks just like our mother, Pearl, though perhaps fairer. The father—a coward who refuses to name himself —took her away at birth but returns her now that I am home. She is nearly two years old. I cannot keep a child here in this house with Ida, and I cannot leave Ida alone. I do not see a way forward.*

"Holy shit." Stunned, Eliza closed the journal and tucked it deep in her jacket pocket. A baby. Ida's baby. "Hattie, you really fucked up. Poor Ida." No wonder she'd been such a wreck when Edwin got back.

There was break in the wind and the rain. The Maglite rolled toward the edge of the mantle and Eliza lunged, barely grabbing it before it fell. She clutched the flashlight in shaking hands, the beam bouncing erratically over the walls and floor. An acrid odor of burning flowers rose from the dying embers in the hearth.

Eliza stumbled to the living room door, the sad desperation of the house overwhelming her. Also, she was really freaked out. The window alarm she'd deactivated started beeping behind her. She didn't look back.

She wanted Joey.

The alarm in the kitchen window activated, then the one in the bathroom.

Where was he?

In the hallway, movement to her right caught her attention. She turned and saw her bedroom door open of its own accord and swing inward, letting weak evening light creep down the hall. It illuminated faint tracks of drywall debris overlain with puddles of muddy water left behind when they'd evacuated Minnie's bedroom. The puddles nearest the closet door were ringed in delicate frost. The alarms in there were beeping, now, too.

Eliza was shifting her weight to run for the foyer when the door to Minnie's room swung inward as well. She turned the flashlight beam that way, stumbling backwards when it illuminated Doug standing just inside the ruined room by her mother's dresser. His tennis shoes and sweat pants were caked in mud. Blood covered half his face. He clutched one of Minnie's pillowcases, bulging with who knew what, in one hand. In the other hand, he carried an axe.

Eliza screamed.

Where the hell was Joey?

CHAPTER 34

$\mathcal{I}$t only took Joey a moment to find Marco's tools. He would have been back at Eliza's side in under a minute, if the sound of fast-moving water coming from north of the cottage hadn't caught his attention.

They shouldn't be able to hear the river that distinctly from the house.

Shouldering the tool bag, Joey shut the rear hatch of the SUV and started toward the porch. He should go straight in, tear the closet open, and get Eliza out of there. Luke, too, hopefully.

Except, if the river was flooding, they needed to consider alternative exit routes. And maybe they didn't have time to tear open the closet. Joey still had a bad feeling about the house, but he'd searched it from top to bottom—parts of it twice—and not found any threats. Not apart from the usual, anyway.

The wind gusted, slanting the rain that had begun to fall sideways. The storm was rolling in from the north, which meant there'd probably already been significant rainfall upriver. Joey set the tool bag on the porch and, after another moment's hesitation, turned away, jogging toward the sound of rushing water.

Even with the leaf canopy in tatters, it was dark under the trees and Joey had to pay careful attention to avoid fallen branches and patches of ice. The smell of wet was overwhelming. Wet dirt. Spongy, rotten wood. Turbid water. He slid to a stop just past where the narrow path he'd been following curved around a small rocky outcropping. The river was rushing through the woods, not at all where it was supposed to be. He judged that it was less than three hundred meters from the house, nearly kissing the stone wall that encircled the orchard. As he watched, the water line advanced from the far side of a large oak to the near, surging up its trunk and drowning a cluster of saplings growing among its roots.

"Crap." Joey took a second to survey the movement of the water across the landscape, then turned and headed for the cottage at a dead run. They needed to leave, with or without Luke.

～

*C*oming out of the trees, Joey blinked, wondering if his eyes were playing tricks on him. The house's peeling blue walls seemed luminescent against the dark, overcast sky. The upstairs windows glowed an orangey red.

He wiped his sleeve across his brow and ran harder now that he was covering open ground. It had to be an effect of the setting sun.

He leapt up the porch steps in two strides and grabbed the crowbar from Marco's tool bag, figuring it would be a waste of time they didn't have to try and talk Eliza into leaving without checking the closet.

He cussed when he found the front door shut again—

firmly this time. "Are you kidding me?" The knob grated in its socket, fighting him. Even when he'd forced it to a full turn, the door didn't budge. Joey was lifting the crowbar to break the door's half window when a small flurry of paint flakes whirled to the porch floor and the door popped open on its own.

Weird as fuck, Joey thought, but his instincts were screaming now. He shouldered his way in.

Something was indeed very wrong. If the thermostat flashing *Intruder!* wasn't enough of a clue, the headless doll slumped outside Eliza's apartment door definitely gave it away.

No.

Joey moved soundlessly across the foyer's tile floor. Eliza's apartment door was shut and locked. He dug his copy of her key out of his pocket and opened it as quietly as possible.

His hand was shaking.

Joey's hands never shook—not until after the action was over, anyway.

Get it together.

With his crowbar at the ready—and deeply regretting his decision to leave all his weapons in the hotel room safe—Joey entered the apartment.

There was debris all over the floor of the hallway, and he thought at first that Eliza might have found her own tool and tried to tear open the closet door. But that creepy, high-pitched giggle wasn't coming from Eliza.

There was a sound of smashing dishes in the kitchen, then a mug sailed into the hallway and shattered against the wall. Eliza screamed, "Get the fuck away from me, you freak!" and Joey positively identified the giggling as coming from one Doug Landis.

Who was supposed to be in jail.

There was a thud, followed by the shriek of tearing wood. Doug laughed again, breathless. "I almost got ya that time, huh? That one was pretty close."

Joey crouched and peered around the doorway, hopefully out of Doug's line of sight if he happened to look behind him. The creep was armed with a heavy axe that he dragged along the floor when he wasn't swinging it at the walls and cabinets. He didn't seem to have the upper body strength to use it effectively, but his unpredictability and bulk would make him plenty dangerous.

Eliza was backed into the corner by the pantry, fast running out of dishes to throw. If she retreated into the pantry itself, Doug would have a good chance of striking her, as inept as he was.

Doug shuffled around, looking for a new target to smash, momentarily quiet in concentration. The river sounded distinctly closer. They were running out of time.

Joey stepped into the kitchen. He wanted to catch Doug unawares and whack his swinging arm with the crowbar, then fully subdue him once he was disarmed. A piece of china crunched under his boot and Doug froze. Joey swung the crowbar, but in a lucky move, Doug blocked his swing with the axe handle as he pivoted to see what was happening behind him.

Doug was a mess. He had blood all over his face, his clothes were filthy and torn, and he looked one hundred percent crazier than the last time Joey had seen him, which was really saying something.

Joey shifted positions and brought the crowbar up for another try. As Doug moved to engage him, Eliza darted out of the corner with a feral scream and brained Doug on the back of the head with the flashlight Joey had left her. Stunned, Doug began crumpling to the floor. For good measure Eliza, still screaming, sprayed him in the face with her little pink canister of pepper spray.

Her scream dissolved into a coughing, hiccuping sob as the pepper spray fumes hit her, and then she was quiet, shaking with adrenaline.

"Well done, beautiful." Joey's eyes, nose, and throat stung, but he was grinning as he walked over to the kitchen window and threw it open so the pepper spray would dissipate.

Eliza turned to him, her eyes reddening and wide with disbelief. "Did that just happen?" Her voice was hoarse.

"It sure did."

"We need to call the sheriff."

Joey shook his head. "No, we need to get the hell out of here. The river's flooding."

CHAPTER 35

*E*liza watched as Joey dragged Doug's sorry ass out of the kitchen and down the hall toward the front door. Doug was screaming weakly. Mostly about his eyes, but also something about "those fucking bitch babies" and wanting his gun. Thank god Joey had turned that over to the deputies.

Looking around, Eliza tried to think what she should do. Her eyes kept tearing. Her nose stung, and she had a terrible taste in her mouth.

They were leaving.

The house was going to flood.

A can of Pringles caught her eye from the back of the cupboard she'd emptied while fending off Doug. How weird was that? She pulled the can out, flipped the lid off, and ate a chip. Surprisingly fresh. She ate another.

"Eliza! Get out here!"

Joey sounded mad. Eliza put the lid on the Pringles can, tucked it her empty jacket pocket, and went to find him. The shattered dishes in the hallway gave her pause, though.

"Oh. *Luke*." They hadn't found her cat yet.

Joey came rushing back in, looking like the situation was straining his professionalism. His eyes were probably watering because of the pepper spray, though. "Eliza, what are you doing? We have to go! There's water right at the foundation outside your bedroom."

Eliza shook her head. "We have to open the closet. We never found Luke." She was ready to beg, but she didn't have to.

Joey grabbed Doug's axe from the kitchen and walked unhesitatingly to the closet door. "Stand back."

"Um, where's Doug?"

Joey readied the axe for a swing. "I tied him to the porch railing with your mom's macramé thing. It won't hold him forever, but I can take a minute to break down this door."

"Oh."

"Anyway," Joey grinned widely at nobody in particular, "I'm the one who's armed now."

He looked a little maniacal. Arousal suffused Eliza's body. Maybe this was why things hadn't worked out with the guys she'd dated in college.

Joey took aim at the wall next to the closet door and landed three blows in rapid succession. He pulled some dry wall away with his hands, peered inside the hole he'd made, then took a few more swings.

Eliza kept looking back toward the foyer, expecting to see Doug coming for her again. She knew she should be more concerned about the river, but the destructive force of nature seemed inconsequential next to the prospect of having to fight off an axe attack again.

"Flashlight. Eliza, give me the flashlight."

She startled, then handed Joey the Maglite. The hole was big enough that he could stick his head through the wall now. He pointed the flashlight down inside the closet.

"I'll be damned."

"What? Is it Luke?"

Joey nodded. "He's in there. I think he's... asleep."

Eliza swallowed hard. She'd fallen asleep right by the closet and almost frozen to death. Luke was just a cat, and he was actually in the closet. "You have to get him out."

Joey was already pulling at the wallboard, testing for weak spots. "On it. Go check the water level." When Eliza moved toward the front door, he pulled her back. "No, look through the bathroom window. Or your bedroom window. I'm staying in between you and Doug."

"Okay. Just get Luke out." She ducked around Joey to her bedroom.

The door had swung mostly closed again. She pushed it open and was surprised to find the room bathed in warm evening light. Eliza couldn't recall this soft, pink-orange glow ever gracing the walls before. It made the room seem nice. Peaceful.

It was a treacherous sense of peace, though, because below the windows a torrent of muddy water and debris rushed past the house. The level seemed to rise before Eliza's eyes. She tried to remember how the property sloped. Would the river have reached the SUV already? What about the driveway?

Back in the hallway, Joey was attacking the wall with primal ferocity. Eliza left her bedroom door open behind her, letting the light filter into the hall. It caught the planes and edges of Joey's face, which was set in a mask of raw physical effort—her very own warrior.

Finally, he set the axe aside, kicked some debris out of the way, and knelt to reach into the closet, pulling Luke out by his scruff. The cat dangled limply from his grip. Did that mean he was still alive? If he'd frozen to death, surely he wouldn't be so pliant.

Eliza reached for Luke, but Joey shook his head. "Let me

put him in my coat. He needs the warmth." He was already heading toward the front door, axe in hand.

Eliza hurried after him. "But he's alive?"

Joey hesitated. "I think so." He didn't sound sure, and he turned back to Eliza to give her an apologetic smile. She saw his eyes widen.

"What?" She spun around and found the closet door open. A current of warm air that smelled of lavender, hot stonework, and fresh-mown grass flowed toward them down the hall. It wrapped around Eliza, lifting a strand of wet hair from her face. *Mother has my baby.*

Eliza recoiled, bumping into Joey. "Holy shit."

"You said it." Joey wrapped his free hand around Eliza's upper arm like he wanted to drag her away, but for a moment, the two of them just watched the closet door sway in the pink evening light.

"Fuck me," Eliza whispered, awed.

"Later," Joey said. "We have to get the hell out of here. Now."

∽

he thermostat was flickering in the foyer: *Arm. Stay. Arm. Away. Welcome!* Water lapped at the bottom porch step. The SUV was still on dry land, but not for long.

Doug was gone, Minnie's improvised weapon dangling loose from the porch railing. Joey tucked the slingshot in his pocket and scanned the yard. Then he took Eliza's hand and led her toward the SUV. The water by the house was above Eliza's ankles. It was freezing, and she regretted not wearing better shoes. Sneakers had seemed adequate when they'd left the hotel, but steel-toed boots and a hardhat would have been a smarter choice.

Actually, battle gear would have been good.

Joey left her standing about fifteen feet back from the vehicle. He circled it with the axe at the ready, and Eliza realized he was making sure Doug wasn't lurking on the other side. She tensed. When would that asshole stop being a problem?

She'd put the hood of her jacket up, holding it in place against the wind, but rain still pelted her face, obscuring her glasses. Black clouds laced with lightening were advancing on the cottage from the west. The cute solar lanterns Eliza had placed around the parking area months ago were glowing their little hearts out, embers against the night.

Joey sloshed back and escorted her to the passenger side of the SUV. "Get in."

She obeyed with alacrity. The floodwaters were licking the back tires of the SUV now, and two of her little lamps had been swept away.

Joey jogged around the front of the vehicle. He was nearly to his own door when he abruptly disappeared.

"Joey!" Eliza started to open her own door, then thought better of it and hit the locks instead—just until she knew what was going on. Climbing over the center console, she turned on the Maglite and shined it toward the ground.

Joey was on his knees in the water, struggling with a topless Doug, who had his bloody shirt wrapped around his head and was armed with… something short and metallic, plus what was possibly a brick.

Normally, Eliza wouldn't have worried about Joey in a confrontation with Doug, but he was hampered by trying to shield Luke. She unlocked the doors, scrambled out of the SUV, and took a swing at Doug's head with the flashlight. In her mind, she could hear her mother saying, "*smack! No more problem.*"

Unfortunately, Doug's shirt blunted the impact and he only redoubled his efforts to shove Joey down into the water.

Eliza stepped sideways to get a better angle with the Maglite and slipped, the knee she'd hit on the porch step giving out. The ground was turning into mud now that the floodwater was swirling over it. Too bad she hadn't managed to get the gravel redone. She caught herself on her hands and knees, briefly losing her grip on the flashlight. While she was reaching for it, Doug managed to backhand her across the face with his cold, muddy arm, nearly sending her glasses flying.

Eliza's face was mostly numb with cold, but she thought he'd split her lip. She seized the flashlight and brought it out of the water. The beam illuminated Joey shielding Luke with one arm and while trying to hit Doug somewhere vital with the garden gnome.

Doug had a chisel. He didn't have a good grip on it, but he'd managed to at least gouge Joey's forearm.

A surge of floodwater washed over all of them, carrying a branch into Joey's right side. His sleeve caught on it, and Doug took advantage of the distraction to body slam Joey, knocking him off balance.

Eliza screamed and whacked at Doug's shoulders and head with the flashlight again. When that had no effect, she kicked at him under the water, hoping to get him in the nuts.

Joey inhaled water and Eliza saw his eyes go wide. He finally gave up protecting Luke and swung a left-handed punch at Doug's ear. Then another. Doug roared and flailed wildly.

Suddenly, there was a confused flurry of movement and Doug rocketed back into Eliza, screaming in pain. She lost her balance and fell, a wave of floodwater slapping her in the face. Eliza clutched at her glasses and blinked the water out of her eyes. Luke clung to Doug's face, shredding the flesh of his cheek with powerful thrusts of his back legs.

The attack only lasted a moment, then Luke jumped onto the hood of the SUV and disappeared into the darkness.

Doug fell back on his ass and clutched his bleeding wounds.

Joey staggered to his feet, puked water, then lurched at Doug. "You sonofabitch," he gasped. He slammed Doug against the side of the SUV and secured his hands behind his back with the tail of Minnie's slungshot. "You fucking sonofabitch."

Then he turned wild eyes on Eliza. "Get in the truck."

Eliza stood, still clutching the flashlight. She might never set it down again. Her clothes were soaked to her body and the flood water was almost to her knees. She managed to hoist herself into the driver's seat, then clamber over the console to the passenger side. As Joey dragged Doug around to the back of the SUV and rolled him into the cargo area, she scanned the yard for any sign of Luke, but he'd disappeared.

She felt bereft.

Cold and bereft.

Joey splashed back to the driver's side and climbed in. Water lapped at the floorboard. He slammed his door shut and started the engine. Eliza didn't know how he'd kept the keys in his possession this whole time, but she was beyond grateful.

"Will we make it to the road?" she asked.

"Yes." Joey sounded like he would carry Marco's truck out on his back if he had to.

For a heart-stopping moment, the tires failed to get traction. Then the SUV lurched forward and Eliza sobbed in relief.

CHAPTER 36

*J*oey stopped the SUV at the top of the drive and turned on the scanner, flipping through channels until he caught someone reporting county road closures. Doug was still making weak noises of outrage in the back, but he quieted when Joey told him to shut the fuck up or he would leave him to drown.

As they sat there listening to an older man calmly read off the list of roadways blocked by flooding or fallen trees, Eliza shook and cried. Joey took her left hand in his and lifted it so he could warm it with his breath, then did the same for the other, placing gentle kisses near her torn nails.

"Luke will be fine," he told her. "He's in a tree somewhere, waiting this out. We'll have him back before you know it."

Violent slashes of rain rolled across the windshield and a branch bounced off the hood of the SUV. Eliza nodded, gripping Joey's hand tightly. "Sure." If anyone else had tried to make the same promise, she wouldn't have believed them. But Joey had already given Luke back to her once. She trusted him to do it again.

Joey called Marco, updated him, and told him the route

they would be taking back to the hotel. Then he cranked up the heat and pulled onto the road, leaving the cottage behind.

Eliza tucked her hands into her armpits and stayed very quiet while Joey navigated a different back road—this one heading away from the flooding. She'd never known fatigue like this, and couldn't envision going back to the hotel and helping her mother through even the most minor crisis. She had nothing left to give. What were the odds she could just take a hot shower and drop into bed?

They hadn't gone far when a figure walking toward them along the shoulder raised a hand in an authoritative signal to halt. Joey stopped well back and they both held their breath until the headlights revealed that it was Deputy Sandoval.

Joey put his window down and identified himself, yelling over the wind and rain. He unlocked the doors when the deputy got to the SUV and she slid into the back seat, dripping rainwater and emanating cold. She had a swollen gash on her forehead and bruising on the right side of her face.

"What happened?" Eliza asked as Joey aimed the SUV's vents toward the back seat.

Deputy Sandoval glanced at Doug, who seemed to be asleep in the cargo area. "We slid off the road. Hit a tree. Landis climbed out and took off while my partner and I were trying to extract ourselves. Smith stayed with our vehicle. I was hoping to flag down a ride so I could warn you that your favorite neighbor was out here on his own recognizance."

Eliza twitched. "We found out first hand."

The deputy grimaced. "You can tell me the full story somewhere warm and dry. Later. I assume you'll want to press charges again?"

"*Yes.*"

Sandoval smirked and tapped Doug on the shoulder. When she had his attention, such as it was, she mirandized him.

*T*hey arrived at the hotel at the same time as Marco, who was carrying five pizza boxes and had a shopping bag looped over his wrist.

Eliza could have kissed him.

"I should have gone with you. Sounds like a wild time," Marco said, handing the pizzas to Joey.

"It was a clusterfuck." Joey shook his head. "I think every decision I made was wrong."

"At least you took my ride instead of your truck—you needed the extra traction."

Joey shifted the pizza boxes to one arm so he could hit the elevator's up button. "Yeah… I'll get it detailed for you tomorrow."

Marco frowned. "Is it bad?"

Eliza dissolved into giggles, probably because she was so tired. They both looked at her and she laughed harder. "It's…" She snorted. "A little muddy."

Joey placed his free hand at the nape of her neck and guided her into the elevator. "Don't worry about it," he told Marco. "I soaked up most of the water with towels at the sheriff's station. It probably just needs a good vacuuming."

Eliza calmed under Joey's touch. The heady aroma of pizza in an enclosed space helped too.

Man, she really needed some sleep. Or something.

Deputy Sandoval had let her shower at the station when she'd finished documenting Eliza's Doug-inflicted injuries, and she'd leant her some clothes from her locker. So now Eliza had a sort of friend date in her future, if she wanted, to return the outfit. Or she could just drop the clothes off at the station with a note.

But she thought she'd suggest a coffee date. She needed

friends, and Deputy Sandoval was really kick-ass. Funny, too.

Joey had had a few text updates from his moms saying that Minnie was fine, absolutely fine, could really hold her liquor (joke!), and they were going to need to set up Netflix in the hotel so they could watch their favorite documentaries together.

Eliza collapsed at the small breakfast table in the moms' room and watched in numb relief as Minnie proved, indeed, to be absolutely fine. She ate pizza and grapes with a good appetite, finished at least her fair share of brownies, and excused herself to take her evening meds at the correct time. Then she came back, ready to party on.

Joey sat next to Eliza, his leg pressed to hers. He'd showered and changed into old, soft jeans and a green hoodie that did great things for his eyes.

Not that his eyes weren't spectacular at all times, of course.

He reminded her to eat her pizza when she found herself staring into the middle distance. When she'd finished what he apparently considered an adequate amount, he fed her grapes and bites of brownie off his fingertips. Plus, she could hardly forget that he'd helped prevent her from being axe-murdered by Doug a few hours earlier.

He really was the perfect man.

Unfortunately, Eliza needed to move. As tempting as it was to fall asleep against Joey's arm, her knee was stiff, her muscles ached, and her eyes were still a little dry and irritated from the pepper spray. She needed a hot bath, a Tylenol or three, and her pajamas.

For the first time in years, a nice, relaxing soak seemed within reach. She kept expecting her mom to run out of steam and get that confused, glassy look in her eyes, but she seemed solid.

"I'm going to go have a bath," she whispered to Joey.

"What are you doing after that?" His breath tickled her ear. His tone of voice sent heat rushing through her body.

"Maybe I'll drop by your room for a while?"

"I'll be there."

CHAPTER 37

*J*oey was pretending to work on his research project when Eliza knocked on his door an hour after she'd left to go have a bath. He'd excused himself shortly after she had, to the vast amusement of Marco and all the moms, who were sure he and Eliza were going to spend the rest of the night having wild sex.

Joey wished he felt that certain. They'd had a ridiculously crazy day, and while he felt closer to Eliza than ever, she might still be miffed at him for signing the lease on his new place without telling her about it.

He closed his laptop and got up to let her in.

She was adorable in her purple plaid sleep pants and gray hooded sweater. She had Marco's Maglite in one hand. Her hair was twisted up into a knot on top of her head, the tendrils at the nape of her neck damp. Her skin was pink—from her bath, he assumed, although with any luck she was having dirty thoughts, too.

"How are you doing?" He closed the door behind her and invited her to sit on the little couch under the window while he took the chair next to it.

"I'm fine," she said, sinking back into the cushions and kicking off her slippers. "Better than you, probably."

She stood the flashlight on the floor by her feet. She was wearing thick gray socks that matched her sweater.

She'd dressed up.

Joey grinned, unaccountably smitten all over again.

She was looking at him expectantly.

Right. "What do you mean?"

Eliza laughed and rolled her eyes. "Tough guy. I mean the big gash in your arm."

"Oh, right." He'd disinfected that after his shower and closed it with liquid stitches. He wasn't worried. "It's fine."

Eliza looked skeptical. "I hope so. And I'm sorry that Doug hurt you."

Joey leaned forward. "You have nothing to apologize for. Nothing. Understand?"

She looked away.

Joey got up and wedged himself next to her on the small couch. "I mean it—you didn't do anything wrong."

She sighed, rubbing her temples. Her glasses were kind of crooked. "I feel like I did everything wrong."

From her tone of voice, Joey suspected this wasn't just about them running into Doug at the cottage—as if she could have prevented that. He was the one who'd fucked that up somehow. The little shit must have been raiding the shed for sharp and pointy tools while Joey was clearing the house.

He brushed a strand of Eliza's hair out of her face. "What did you do wrong?"

"Well, for one thing, I moved my mom out to the middle of nowhere when clearly she needs friends. You know, we lived in town—in Dos Alamos—for a while after we left Mountain View. Then the rent went up on that apartment, and we hadn't connected with anybody by that point, so I didn't think moving to the cottage would make a difference."

She picked up the flashlight and clicked the button. It turned on, although the beam was weak.

Joey took it from her and examined the lens. It was pretty scratched. "Marco won't care about this. We buy these in bulk for the office. I have an extra I'll throw in his truck in the morning."

She took it back and turned it off. "I was actually going to ask if I can buy it from him. I'm very attached to this flashlight. I feel like it's a part of me now."

Joey smiled. "I'm sure he'll want you to have it. Especially if you explain your special bond."

Eliza nudged his arm in exasperation and set the Maglite back on the floor. "Anyway, I've just been thinking about the cottage. Trying to remember why moving there seemed like a good idea. I should have figured out a way for us to stay in town. Tried harder to help my mom build a social group."

"There must have been some advantages to living at the cottage. You seemed happy enough there when you showed me around that first day."

She laughed. "Well, I'd always wanted to live in a pretty house. Something with character and history, you know? And there was so much space. Nice walking trails. My mom is always really relaxed and happy when she's communing with nature."

"You certainly got character and history."

Eliza shivered and moved closer to him. "Yeah, well, I am *super* over that."

He laughed, wrapping his arms around her. She smelled amazing. "I hate to bring it up, but how would you feel about a converted loft with all new interior construction and earthquake retrofitting?"

She groaned but didn't pull away. He considered that a win. "It sounds amazing. I just don't know if I can..." She took a deep breath. "There's a lot of stuff I need to figure out right now."

"I know. It's an open offer. You can stay temporarily. Or we can call it open-ended. You can just visit if you want…"

Eliza laced their fingers together and was quiet. Joey savored her warm weight pressing against him. He'd saved the girl a few times in his life, but he'd never gotten to cuddle with her afterwards.

Not that he'd ever wanted a client—or anyone—the way he wanted Eliza.

When she spoke again, she surprised him. "I wanted to get an MFA."

"Really?"

"Sort of. I mean, my dream career would be to have a successful webcomic. I keep telling myself that I have no credibility as an artist, though, and I need to get a degree." She shifted, drawing her knees to her chest. "Now I think that's probably just an excuse to put off trying." She studied the way their hands looked together. "I'm going to use the money I saved for school to help my mom find a good place to live and start my webcomic anyway. I've been working on some new ideas. And I've been researching the publishing process—webpage design, social media. Advertising."

Joey squeezed Eliza's hand. "It sounds exciting."

She swallowed hard. "It's scary."

"It will work out fine."

Eliza met his eyes. "Do you really think so?"

"Yeah, I do. I like your comics."

It took her a moment to catch the implication of what he'd said, then she turned crimson beneath her freckles. "Shit. *Shit.* Did you look at my notebook?"

"Yep. Not on purpose. It fell out of your pillow case when I was packing your things." He kissed the frown off her lips.

255

"I like Adventure Tenant. He's a cool dude. Much cooler than me."

"Oh, no. Crap. I can explain..." Her mouth opened and closed a few times as she struggled for words. Her blush had traveled down her throat to the soft skin of her upper chest. Perhaps beyond. Joey moved "getting Eliza's sweater off" to the top of his to-do list.

"I'm waiting," he said, playing with the zipper pull sitting just above her breasts.

"What?"

He pulled downward. Just an inch. "For an explanation."

"Well..." Her voice was faint. Breathy.

"Obviously, you're obsessed with my ass. You can admit it." He pushed her sweater aside and kissed the mounds of her breasts, glancing up to make sure she was okay with this. Her eyes were dilated, her respiration and pulse rapid.

"I might be. A little."

"That's okay." He considered the tank top she wore under the sweater, then tugged its lace edge down so he could place kisses closer and closer to her nipples. "I'm obsessed with your ass, too. I wish I'd thought to write stories about it."

Eliza laughed. Her hand moved toward her zipper, then she changed course and ran her fingers up under Joey's sleeve instead, squeezing his biceps. "Not just your ass. I mean, the stories aren't just about your ass."

"Mmm-hmm. There are Vikings, too." He unzipped her sweater and pushed it off her shoulders. "And all that travel. To erotic... I mean, exotic places."

Eliza tugged at the hem of his shirt and he pulled it off.

She gasped. "Oh my god, oh my god." She touched the bandage on his forearm gently, the ran her hands over his chest and up to cradle his face in her palms. "I can't believe this is happening." She rose on her knees to kiss him.

Joey could hardly believe this was happening either, but

just to be sure she didn't lack for encouragement, he grabbed her ass and drew her closer.

When she'd tasted his mouth—thoroughly, exquisitely—she pressed her forehead to his and caught her breath. "I do want to travel. A little. If my mom is doing okay."

Joey kissed her mouth, careful to avoid the raw spot where Doug had apparently clocked her. "Only a little?"

After a moment, she sat back, dazed. Her eyes kept dropping to his chest. And his crotch.

He cleared his throat. "I'm waiting for an answer, and my eyes are up here."

She gasped, eyes meeting his. "Right. And I do love your eyes, but..." Her gaze dropped again. "There are a lot of distractions. What was the question?"

"You only want to travel a little?"

She half-smiled. "Well, maybe more than a little. Especially if I had someone to come with me sometimes?"

"I have a passport, and I know all the best places." He gave up playing and pulled her into his lap, settling her over his erection. "Plus, I know how to evacuate from most of them in under two minutes."

Eliza made a noise that was somewhere between a gulp and a laugh. Her eyes were bright with desire. He traced the pad of his thumb over her cheek. She leaned in and he kissed her again.

It was the first time they'd been close without the threat of the house hanging over their heads. Neither of them had cold extremities, and while it was possible Minnie might shout for Eliza at any moment, Joey thought she was probably asleep by now.

He took his time, tracing Eliza's lips, face, and neck with his lips and fingertips. He placed his palm flat on her chest and waited. Eliza moved it to her breast, sighing when he cupped her, shivering when he brushed the pad of his thumb over her nipple. She met him touch for touch until finally, when they were both gasping, she ground against him, pressing her whole body to his with serious intent.

Joey had meant to take things slow. Not push. Not rush. But before he knew it, he'd cupped Eliza's ass with both hands and was pulling her hard against his erection. Once. Twice. He groaned and they both froze, their pulses pounding against each other at every point of contact.

Eliza laughed shakily. "Are we getting carried away?"

Joey thrust against her involuntarily—a small but telling movement. "Definitely. But we can stop. Maybe we should stop."

She ground against him. "Uh-huh. You're probably right. Long day. Lots of crazy shit."

Joey buried his face in Eliza's hair and laughed. If he weren't wearing jeans, he would be asking nicely if he could slide into her right now. Those sleep pants felt like they would tear open with hardly any effort on his part at all. And he had plenty of condoms. Fresh ones. Pre-lubricated. He knew exactly where they were.

Joey realized he'd been unconsciously running his fingers along the center seam of Eliza's thin pants, dipping into her recesses with each pass. He was about to pull his hand away and apologize when her eyes fluttered shut and she moaned.

Holy god. She was shaking. And, fuck, was she about to come?

"You're so beautiful, Eliza," he whispered. "Can I make you come, honey?"

Eliza made a strangled sound. "*Please.*"

"Please make you come?" Joey clarified. Maybe a little sadistically.

She hit him on the shoulder. "Yes, please, make me come *for the love of god!*" At least she was laughing.

Joey caught her bottom lip with his teeth and bit it gently, then kissed her deeply while he rubbed her clit with one hand and pinched her nipple with the other. It wasn't long before Eliza twisted in his lap, froze, gasped, and shuddered against him as he gentled his touch and finally just held her close.

He was hard as a rock and about two seconds away from coming in his pants, but now was probably a good time to slow things down. Better late than never, right?

Although it didn't feel better.

While Eliza caught her breath, plastered in a boneless sprawl across his torso, Joey rubbed her back and played with her hair, brushing it out of her face and staring at her profile. How had they not done this before? They were excellent together. This was clearly what he'd been put on earth to do—touch Eliza everywhere and make her come.

Well, and hopefully slide into her and see how good that could be, too. "Eliza?"

"Hmm?"

"Will you please take your clothes off and get in my bed?"

She sat up and gave Joey a patently fake, wide-eyed stare. "Whyever would I do that?"

He smacked her butt, then stood and let her feet drop to the ground. "I'll show you. It'll be worth it—I promise."

CHAPTER 38

*I*t was three days before they could go back and look for Luke.

Three *incredible* days.

Minnie seemed to have really turned over a new leaf now that she was away from the cottage.

The nights, of course, were an order of magnitude more incredible than the days, what with all the sex.

Friday morning, Eliza and Joey had an early breakfast without the maternal cabal, then headed to the cottage in Joey's truck. Marco had stayed long enough to help move their belongings into storage, then he'd taken his freshly-detailed SUV and gone home.

Eliza guessed her own car was a total loss. If it hadn't been swept away, it would be filled with mud. She'd seen news footage from other houses in the area where water had risen three feet up the walls of people's living rooms.

Caving to her anxiety, she called Deputy Sandoval from the road to confirm that Doug was still in jail. The deputy assured her that, although the Effinham family was working a back-channel deal to have Doug remanded to a mental health facility, he was definitely locked up and would stay that way.

Somewhat surprisingly, Deputy Sandoval offered to meet them out at the house. Eliza accepted, then hung up and told Joey the fuzz was coming. "Do you think they consider the house a crime scene?"

"She may want to look around to satisfy her curiosity, but I doubt they're going to try to process any evidence. Nobody got hurt…"

Eliza made an offended noise.

"Anyway, it would be a waste of resources to comb through flood debris when they have our statements. That's about as good as it's going to get, under the circumstances."

Eliza had come to the same conclusion, but it would be satisfying to see somebody bag the axe as evidence and present it to a judge in court. The fact was, Joey *had* been hurt. And she had a tender spot on her hipbone where one of Doug's wild swings had glanced off the journal in her pocket. Not to mention a split lip that was taking some of the fun out of their sexy hijinks.

Eliza's consternation must have been obvious, because Joey reached over and squeezed her thigh in a way that was sure to redirect her attention in a hurry. Eliza squealed and slapped his hand away. "Not while you're driving, mister."

～

*E*liza had been dreading returning to the cottage. She hoped that, having spent three days spiritually detoxing at the hotel via family meals, card games, and plenty of good, clean sex, the cottage would have lost its hold on her. There was no telling, though. As Joey had pointed out, they'd both moved in against their better judgment in the past.

Her first sight of the house put paid to those fears, though. Nobody would be living at the cottage anymore.

The yard was a debris field. Branches and mud were piled to the top of the foundation on the north side of the house. The hydrangeas below the porch railing had been stripped away. The house itself seemed to have been lifted off its river-stone foundation and plopped down again several feet to the southwest. A portion of Doug's apartment listed precariously over empty space. A spray-painted red X covered the front door and a red sign bearing the word "UNSAFE" was affixed to a porch post.

"Holy shit." Joey brought his truck to a careful stop in a relatively clear spot.

"What?"

He pointed toward the tree line beyond the house. Doug's yellow Datsun was lodged half inside the tool shed. His recliner lay on its back in a drift of mud near the bumper, springs exposed, charcoal underlining fabric fluttering in the morning's crisp breeze. Dozens of dolls lounged cheerfully in the muck nearby, their fixed smiles and wide eyes trained on the sky.

Eliza shuddered. "That is not right."

"Not even remotely."

"Maybe Luke can find his own way into town. We'll leave him a trail of tuna fish cans starting from here."

Joey turned off the engine and opened his door. "You know you wouldn't do that. Let's go."

Sighing, Eliza got out and met him at the back of the truck, where they had a case of tuna cans to open.

After a minute of pulling lids open by their tabs, the smell of fish began to overpower the aroma of mud and rot. "We may be going home with a dozen cats. Even ones who aren't homeless."

"No," Joey said sternly. "You are not turning the new apartment into a cat shelter."

"But it would make Minnie so happy. She can crochet them all personalized beds. In uterine pink."

Joey choked on a laugh and shook his head. "Have mercy."

They'd borrowed a humane trap from an animal rescue group in town, which they set up in the truck bed with three cans of fish inside. They placed the rest of the cans along the tree line, carefully picking their way through the debris. Eliza was glad Joey had insisted on stopping to buy good rubber boots for her at the local surplus store—although every penny he spent on her made her keenly aware of her frail finances.

They found her Sentra under a section of gazebo, buried in mud up to its headlights. Eliza was too overwhelmed by recent events to feel the loss. It was just a car. Her furniture was just furniture. If they could find Luke, she would happily write off the rest.

Although, she was going to miss her writing chair and her favorite frying pan.

When they'd placed all the cans, Joey righted a rugged blue ice chest that neither of them had ever seen before and they sat together amid the destruction, waiting. After a minute, Eliza pulled off her gloves and reached into her pocket for the journal. It was significantly worse for the wear, the cover torn and dented where Doug's dull axe blade had made contact. About a third of the pages were stuck together, since it had gotten soaked while they'd struggled with Doug in the floodwaters.

She began gently separating pages around where she'd found the entry about Ida's baby.

"Why did you bring that back here?" Joey asked.

"I'm not sure. Closure? I want to find out how the story ended. And then never come back here again."

Joey kissed her temple. "Good idea. Let me know if I can help."

Eliza smiled, concentrating on her task. Some of the writing was illegible where the ink had run and she feared the fate of Edwin, Ida, and the baby might have to remain a mystery. Finally, though, she found the last entry she'd read before being attacked by Doug: *I cannot keep a child here in this house with Ida, and I cannot leave Ida alone. I do not see a way forward.*

Poor Edwin. What would Eliza do if she had to choose between caring for a child or her mother?

23 June 1922, I let my guard down, believing Ida had no interest in her daughter, and nearly paid a terrible price. She took Mary into the Egyptian room and barricaded the doors while I was occupied with begging yet another housekeeper not to quit. I could hear nothing from inside the room, and neither Ida nor Mary responded to my yelling or pounding or pleading. Finally, seeing no other recourse, I tore through the wall, finding them after nearly an hour of frantic effort, both senseless on the floor. Perhaps Ida managed to access the laudanum and dose them both—I do not know. I have boarded up all access to the Egyptian room, but Ida roams the rest of the house at all hours frightening Mary and myself, as well. Nights spent in the bloody, freezing trenches of France were hardly more desperate. There, at least, I was in the company of men. Here I have only a tiny, silent child at my side while the wretched living ghost of my poor sister circles us.

Eliza shivered.

Joey, who had begun reading over her shoulder at some point, drew her into his lap, holding her close. "You don't have to read this. Or we can wait till we're back at the hotel."

She shook her head. "There are only a few more entries, I think. I want to finish."

"Okay." Joey rested his cheek against hers. "Turn the page."

The next entry was a single sentence with no date: *God forgive me, I have been drugging Ida senseless this last week and still I cannot sleep for fear that she will do something to the child.*

Joey grunted.

The following pages were stuck together and blank as far as Eliza could tell. "Is that it?"

Joey took the journal from her, pulled a knife from one of his pockets, and patiently worked the pages open with the blade. One more entry appeared: *28 October 1922, Ida has been at peace for nearly three months now and yet Mary still refuses to speak other than to wail when I leave her sight. It is too cold now to spend our days in the orchard and we are neither of us easy in the cottage. I cannot bear to be in my study or the solarium, though the Egyptian room remains closed. I have left keys to the cottage with a land agent in hopes that it can be sold. Perhaps enough time has passed that nobody will mind anymore that Father murdered Mother beneath the maple tree. Regardless, Mary and I leave for San Francisco tomorrow.*

Joey smoothed the page containing the final entry and gently closed the journal, handing it to Eliza. She tucked it back in her jacket pocket and they sat unspeaking until the sound of a vehicle coming down the driveway broke the silence.

It was Deputy Sandoval, at the wheel of a forest-green, older-model Jeep Cherokee with an aftermarket suspension job that lifted it a good eighteen inches higher than factory specs. The deputy parked near Joey's truck and climbed out. She stared at Doug's car, chair, and dolls in disbelief for a moment before waving at Eliza and Joey and picking her way toward them. "Nice day for a cat hunt," she called out. She was wearing a Dos Alamos PD sweatshirt and jeans—probably not on duty.

It was a nice day, actually. The sky was blue again—as if nothing had ever happened—and the air was crisp but not uncomfortably cold. "Good to see you," Eliza called back as she and Joey walked over.

"Any luck?"

Eliza shook her head. "We haven't checked the house yet."

"Good. I love it when people follow instructions," Sandoval said, gesturing at the red sign forbidding entry or habitation. "I'm going to have a quick look." She plucked an open can of fish out of the bed of Joey's truck and walked toward the cottage.

Eliza watched her with her heart in her throat. "Be careful!" The house looked like the most whimsical deathtrap ever, with its sparkling clean gingerbread details and sunlight glinting aggressively from the windows. The weathervane fox drifted lazily back and forth in a gentle breeze. The storm had apparently freed it up.

Sandoval raised a hand in acknowledgment but didn't look back. She walked the perimeter of the house, then climbed the front steps, testing each plank before she put her full weight on it. When she got to the top, she froze, staring up in apparent amazement.

Joey and Eliza exchanged a glance and walked to the base of the steps.

"What is it?" Eliza called. "Is it Luke?"

Sandoval glanced over her shoulder at them. "No, not Luke. Sorry. It's just…"

Joey took Eliza's hand and they climbed the stairs to stand next to the deputy.

The foyer was awash in light, sunbeams dancing off the black-and-white floor tiles. Orange and red leaves spilled down the staircase from the second-story landing like a fairyland carpet runner. The roof in the center of the house was gone. The thermostat was lying on the floor at Eliza's feet, its display dark.

"What happened here?" Sandoval asked. "The Wizard of fuckin' Oz?"

It did sort of look like a tornado had excised part of the roof with surgical precision.

"I can't believe I'm seeing this." Joey's voice was, indeed, flat with disbelief.

Eliza let go of his hand, picked up the thermostat, and put it in her pocket with the journal. *You tried, little buddy.*

They went back down into the yard and circled the house until they could see the Egyptian room. The roof was gone behind the widow's walk railing, and brilliant sunlight shone through the window from the inside. It was actually kind of pretty, in a disturbing way.

"That is some creepy shit right there," said Sandoval. "It's like a giant kicked the top off an ant hill or something. You must have had some bad secrets hiding in the attic."

"Close." Eliza handed her the journal. "Although I think most of the bad stuff was in the Egyptian room—that one there," she said, pointing at the glowing window in question. She and Joey took turns outlining the highlights of the family tragedy recounted in the cash book.

"So, you think Edwin murdered his sister with opiates?"

Eliza looked at Joey, who shrugged. "It seems like it. Although, I have a hard time believing it was completely intentional. He must have been almost as out of his mind as she was by the end."

Sandoval considered the journal. "And the baby would have been Mary Effinham."

Joey put an arm around Eliza's waist and drew her close. "It seems likely."

"Well, she grew up okay. I guess Edwin did right by her."

∾

*W*hen the deputy had driven away, Joey took Eliza's hand and led her on a slow, careful exploration of the woods around the cottage. They found a lot of trash, plus somebody's garden gnome leering up at them from a nest of branches and shredded patio cushions.

The stone wall surrounding the orchard had taken heavy damage in places. That one maple that seemed to thrive on neglect was looking great—as though it had found the storm-and-flood experience invigorating. The fruit trees had taken a beating, but most would probably recover.

"Edwin would be happy to see his trees hanging in there," Eliza said.

Joey stepped around some soggy plywood debris and picked an apple that had somehow survived everything. After wiping it on his shirt, he quartered it, cored it, and offered a piece to Eliza, teasing her lips with the juicy flesh until she took a bite. It was delicious.

They picked their way through the orchard, tucking a few more apples into their pockets. "We should come back next summer and see how the stone fruits react to a diet of river silt," Eliza suggested. The property would be nice without the house sitting on it. Maybe the Effinhams would demolish the cottage and put the land up for sale...

A vicious wind whipped through the orchard without warning. Eliza looked up in surprise, and a cloud of particulate debris struck her face, grit lodging in her eyes.

"Oh, motherfucker," she hissed, hunching over. She shielded her eyes with her hands and tried blinking. The tiniest movement of her lids caused pain to lance through her corneas.

"Let me see." Joey crouched in front of her. He pushed her glasses up onto her head and gently wiped dirt and tears from her cheeks.

"It *hurts*."

"I have some eye wash in the truck. Let me walk you over there." He guided her out of the orchard with one hand at her waist and the other on her shoulder, opened the passenger-side door, and boosted Eliza into her seat. The wind buffeted their backs the whole way.

While Joey rummaged around in the truck-bed tool box, Eliza sat very still with her hands cupped over her eyes. The wind wasn't letting up. Every few seconds, something pinged off the windshield or the body of the truck—light debris lifted out of the drying mud or torn away from the surrounding vegetation.

Joey was taking forever.

"Is it there?" she called. "Maybe we should just drive back to town."

"Give me a minute." Joey had to raise his voice over the sound of gusts through the tree branches. "It's underneath a bunch of stuff."

There was a thump as something alive landed in the footwell next to Eliza's leg. "*Joey!*"

His footsteps fell hard on the ground as he rushed back to her. "What's wrong?"

A mud-caked animal jumped onto her lap. "Is it Luke?" she asked when she sensed Joey standing in front of her. "Please tell me it's Luke." The critter rubbing against Eliza's face and hands had matted fur and smelled like sewage and tuna.

"I... guess?" Joey stepped closer, then hesitated when the animal froze and hissed.

Eliza froze, too.

"Look, it's definitely a cat, and it's the right size and color —I think—to be Luke. Why don't you grab it by the scruff so we can shut the door and get it confined?"

"Great idea." Eliza explored the cat with her left hand

while keeping her right arm wrapped loosely around it. After a couple of blind pokes at the animal's ribs, she caressed her way up its spine until she was petting its head. The cat followed her motions, turning its head side to side so she could alternate scratching behind its ears. When it started purring, she knew it was Luke.

"It's him. Joey, it's him."

As she caressed Luke's bedraggled body, he gradually calmed, arranging himself on Eliza's thighs. She slowly pivoted in her seat until Joey could close the door.

When Joey climbed into the driver's seat and shut his own door, Eliza felt Luke turn to inspect him. Then he applied himself to sniffing Eliza's chin and swiping at her tears with his tongue.

"I have the eye wash and some towels if you want to try and wash some of the debris out," Joey offered. "You'll have to move your cat, though. He's not going to enjoy a saline shower."

Eliza laughed shakily. "Give me one of the towels. I'll wrap him up and hold him to the side."

Joey put scratchy cloth that smelled like metal and automotive grease under Eliza's hand. Luke dug his claws into her thigh when she draped the towel over him, but otherwise didn't resist being bundled up and tucked under her right arm.

Joey put a thicker towel across Eliza's legs and turned her face toward him, cupping her cheek in his hand. "This stuff is really cold—I'm sorry."

"Go for it. I think my eyes are actually on fire."

*A*fter five minutes—or maybe an hour—Eliza could see again, although her vision was a little blurry. Joey wiped the last of the cleaning solution off Eliza's face and leaned in to kiss her gently on the lips. "Your poor eyes."

She settled her glasses back on her nose. "They feel better."

"They're red as hell. We found your cat, though, huh?"

Eliza's eyes welled again. "Yeah, we did. Thank you."

She looked around the yard. The sun had disappeared behind a gauzy layer of clouds that was growing thicker by the moment. The cottage no longer glowed. It looked sad. Lonely. She turned to Joey. "I know the house is red-tagged, but is there anything you want to grab before we go?"

Before Joey could reply, a brutal gust of wind rocked the truck so hard that the shocks squealed. Eliza and Joey both grabbed the oh-shit handles as the cab tilted sideways. Luke slid along the dash where he'd been perched and jumped onto Eliza's chest with a yowl, scoring the exposed skin over her collar bone with his claws.

As soon as the cab leveled out, Joey reached around Eliza and Luke, grabbed her seatbelt, and fastened it. He had to raise his voice to be heard over the roar of the wind. "*No*. We are leaving *right now*."

A cyclone of debris swirled around the truck—slips of paper, leaves, cardboard, twigs. The occasional small branch. A piece of silky red fabric struggled sinuously across the windshield, then disappeared into the darkening sky.

Joey put the truck in gear, his face grim, and started maneuvering toward the driveway. Something hard glanced off the roof of the cab above Eliza's head and she ducked toward Joey, heart pounding.

He hit the brakes, throwing his right arm protectively across her chest, and they both peered up at the trees to see if any branches were about to come hurtling down. A flash of light slashed across Eliza's peripheral vision, followed by an explosion of thunder she felt in her bones.

She screamed, Luke dove for the footwell, and Joey, twisting to look back at the cottage, gasped, "Holy fuck!"

A wisp of dark smoke curled up from the center of the structure, and, as they watched, another bolt of lightning danced along the widow's walk above the hidden room. The fox weathervane glowed electric blue against the black sky as it cartwheeled away. Pieces of the roof started to peel off, disappearing into the darkness. The smoke column rising from the house thickened, and the faux tower tore off and spun to the ground, crushing Doug's Datsun.

"*Joey!*" Eliza clutched at his thigh. "Drive! Please!"

He hit the gas. The wheels spun for a terrible second in the mud, then got traction. They bounced violently up the drive, branches glancing off the windshield.

Joey barely checked for oncoming traffic before turning onto the road and gunning the engine.

CHAPTER 39

"*T*here's a place." Eliza pointed at where a gray minivan was pulling away from the curb in front of Joey's new apartment building.

"On it." He slid his truck into the spot and they climbed out.

Eliza stretched, admiring the Thanksgiving decorations in shop windows up and down the block. Halloween had come and gone while they were still at the hotel, and they'd largely ignored it, apart from demolishing a huge bag of fun-sized candies while binging Netflix shows with the moms. Ghosts didn't seem all that cute this year.

She gathered their bags of Indian take-out from the footwell and followed Joey's fine ass toward the lobby door. He had a rug wrapped in plastic slung it over his shoulder.

"Long day," he said, punching in the access code and holding the door for her. "You ready to dine in front of the fire on our new rug?"

It *had* been a long day. They'd spent most of the morning with Minnie, taken Luke back to the vet to have his stitches removed, and driven to the Ikea in Emeryville to pick up a few essentials.

"Just don't let me fall asleep on the floor." Eliza adjusted her grip on the bags and sidled past Joey, deliberately brushing against him. The food was deliciously fragrant and so hot it was melting the plastic. Joey was so hot she couldn't seem to keep her pants on. *Decisions, decisions.*

"Not when we have a perfectly good bed."

Eliza grinned and hit the elevator call button. They'd thoroughly tested their new bed's structural limits and determined it would likely stand up to a lifetime of hard use. But more data was always better. "I like your priorities. Way to keep your eye on the ball, son."

They rode up to the third floor—the penthouse, as they'd taken to calling it. The building's ground floor housed a Vietnamese coffee shop and an art gallery whose owner sold a lot of whimsical items by local artists, in addition to watercolors of vineyards and wildflower-dotted landscapes that appealed to tourists.

Actually, Eliza liked the watercolors, too, and was considering getting one for the apartment as soon as her budget allowed.

Maybe she would offer them a few of Minnie's craft projects in trade if her mom agreed. The gallery owner, Mr. Klein, had been in ecstasy over the prophylactic-themed scarf her mom was wearing when they visited. The interlocking condom pattern *was* striking—subtle but effective. Anyway, Minnie's craft production looked to be headed into overdrive. Deputy Sandoval had put them on to a co-op retirement community with a resident caregiver, who happened to be the deputy's aunt. It was located in an old summer camp about a mile outside of town, and the vibe was definitely more "hippy artist colony" than "active retirement." Eliza'd had some doubts. She'd wanted her mom to be in Dos

Alamos proper with easy access to shops, restaurants, and the library, but Minnie had taken one look at the place and declared that she was moving in forthwith.

Fortunately, somebody had been looking for a roommate.

The elevator dinged past the second floor and Joey got a speculative look on his face, as usual. That space was vacant, awaiting some renovations, and Eliza figured he was scheming to acquire it for the new location of Griffin Security. He'd worked his ass off to finalize his report before they'd moved out of the hotel, and it had been well received by his boss.

To celebrate, Eliza had drawn a full-page comic strip featuring a "sexy executive" version of Adventure Tenant who left a trail of swooning coworkers in his wake as he walked to his corner office in a shiny, towering, *very* phallic Griffin Security Building.

Joey had framed it and hung it on the wall in the new kitchen.

Getting the report off his plate meant Joey had been able to focus most of his attention on getting the new apartment set up and helping Eliza move Minnie into her new home. It had taken very little time to move their physical possessions, since everything they'd saved from Chaste Tree Cottage fit in Joey's truck. Minnie's place came furnished. He and Eliza had ordered what they needed online from the comfort of Joey's bed at the hotel, in between bouts of sex and setting up the website for Eliza's just-launched webcomic.

Just as Eliza was ready to sag against the elevator wall and close her eyes, the car stopped and the doors opened. Joey pushed the hold button and let Eliza step off before negotiating his way out with the rug.

It was weird, stepping out of a generic, office-style elevator straight into what was essentially the living room. Eliza was having a hard time getting used to that part of the new set-up, but she appreciated being able to stop the elevator at their floor and know nobody was coming in uninvited unless they found the stairs and forced their way through two fire doors. Plus, her knee still ached a little from her fall on the cottage's porch steps, and she thought Joey's foot still hurt, even though he categorically refused to acknowledge any of his injuries.

Eliza cranked up the heat on the loft's home automation module while Joey turned on the lights. Supposedly, you could set the temperature via phone app from anywhere in the world, but she wasn't ready to go there yet. It was enough that when you set the thing to seventy-three degrees, the loft heated or cooled to seventy-three degrees within minutes. It was a goddamned miracle, in fact.

Setting down the take-out on the sideboard by the elevator door, Eliza plugged in her phone to charge and set it in the key basket, next to the old thermostat from the cottage. She wasn't sure why she'd kept the thermostat, or why she'd installed a fresh battery. Loyalty? Nostalgia? Now that they were safely out of the cottage and it had been reduced to rubble, she could admit there'd been some good things about the place.

Like meeting Joey, for instance.

And, well, it was hard to deny there'd been a lot of fresh air.

Mostly, the old thermostat was inert. Tonight, the display said: *Welcome John! Feels like comfort.*

Eliza and Joey exchanged a glance. "Do you want to tell me who John is?" Eliza asked.

"No idea," Joey told her. "But I'm sure he's a great guy. And he's in luck, because it's going to be damn comfortable in here tonight."

"John needs to get his own comfy loft. This one is full up."

Eliza got plates and utensils from the kitchen and

unpacked their dinner on the coffee table in front of the fireplace while Joey removed the plastic from the new rug with practiced flicks of a knife. The rug tried to curl back on itself, but once they'd put the coffee table on it and plunked themselves down with their plates, it had no choice but to relax and lie flat.

Eliza sniffed. "Gotta love that new carpet smell."

"Like having a nose full of sheep?"

"Yep."

Fortunately, the spicy curry scent of their dinner quickly overpowered the wool and plastic odors of the rug. "I like it, though," she said, tracing part of the rug's geometric pattern with her fingertip. "I don't think you need anything else in here. Except maybe a few plants."

"We can get you some plants tomorrow. I don't have anything scheduled besides a run."

Eliza shook her head. "Don't get plants for me—it's your place."

Joey sighed. Eliza knew he was tired of having this conversation. They'd had some version of it every single day since watching the cottage disintegrate in a clear-sky storm that hadn't affected any other part of Dos Alamos.

She couldn't seem to stop bringing it up, though. Was she allowed to be this happy? Was it okay to accept this leg up? It all seemed too easy and perfect. But, on the other hand, wasn't that how a good relationship should feel? How far into couple-hood did you have to be to accept the gift of shelter? Eliza was chipping in on rent and utilities out of her grant-writing money and MFA savings, but she was agonizingly aware that this lifestyle—living in a beautiful loft in the center of town—would be entirely out of her reach if Joey weren't paying for the bulk of it. Visits to her webcomic were still in the double-digits, most of them probably accidents, so while she'd enjoyed getting that project underway, it was far from paying any bills.

"You're doing it again," Joey said, smoothing the lines of concentration between her brows with a fingertip and kissing the tip of her nose. "What happened to going with the flow?"

That had been her resolution the day before: *I'm going to go with the flow, take things hour by hour.* The day before that, she'd resolved to remember to breathe. "Sorry. I think I've only felt like a mooch a couple of times today, though."

"A vast improvement."

Eliza sighed, put her plate back on the table, and leaned forward to kiss Joey on his frustrated frown. The frown melted away and he wrapped a hand gently around her nape, deepening the kiss so he was tasting her. Reminding her that they shared a lot more than an address.

After a moment, he got rid of his own plate and pulled her into his lap, straddling him. Eliza took advantage of the proximity to run her hands over his warm, hard chest before wrapping her arms around his neck and kissing him again. Then she pushed him down onto his back on the carpet, pinning his hands next to his head. As usual, the vision of her small hands wrapped around Joey's wrists—and the long-suffering expression he wore as he tolerated her play—made her feel both silly and horny. She leaned forward to bite the tendon in his neck, then whispered in his ear, "I have some ideas about plants that aren't toxic to cats. Like, how would you feel about growing an indoor lawn?"

Joey laughed, caught off guard. "Whatever you want, babe. We can try growing jungle vines from the ceiling as far as I'm concerned."

"Hmm. Kinky. Will you want to beat your chest and call me Jane?"

Joey laughed again and flipped Eliza beneath him, gently

shoving Daisy out of the way when she came to investigate the happenings. Then he set about giving Eliza a very precise chain of faint hickeys down her throat to the swell of her breasts. "Mine," he growled. "Mine, mine, mine." She squirmed and squealed beneath him.

∾

*L*ater, completely sated, Eliza lay awake in bed—they'd finally made it there at some point—listening to Joey's easy breathing and the light traffic outside. She was too happy to sleep. She felt alive. Awake. Extremely satisfied by an evening of love-making that culminated in a hot shower for two in the loft's immaculate new master bathroom.

Their immaculate new bathroom. She had to admit she felt a little proprietary about its bright clean tiles, gratuitous towel-warmer, and skylight. It was a bathroom that could cause a girl to make bad relationship choices.

Joey was never going to be a bad relationship choice, though.

She smiled and burrowed further under the covers, pressing her leg and hip against his to take full advantage of his warmth. It was freezing outside, but just cool enough in the loft to sleep really well. The cats were curled in soft lumps across the foot of the bed, relaxed and content. Joey turned toward her in his sleep and she wrapped herself around him, finally dozing off with his heart beating against hers and his breath ghosting over her cheek.

ACKNOWLEDGMENTS

Thank you to my first readers and proofreaders: Zara, Liddi, Sylvie, Dayna, and Cheryl.

32846368R00178

Made in the USA
San Bernardino, CA
17 April 2019